AMERICAN BADASS ACCOLADES

"Poignant, funny, and edgy. In his debut novel *American Badass*, Jeff Chacon takes us on a wild trip to Las Vegas. Instead of fear and loathing, we get humor and heart."

—JONNA GJEVRE, author of *Requiem In La Paz*

"Think you know all about zombies? Think again. In Chacon's mind they are principled, loyal friends and fathers with more than brains on their minds. And they are funny—above all else they are hilariously funny. Part zombie, part comedy, part social commentary, American Badass says as much about the living as it does the reanimated."

—JACK MANESS, author of *Song Of The Jawhawk*

"Ron watson is my new hero. Sure, he's dead, but he's evolving (revolving?). He eats only people we'd want him to eat, has enough couth to duct tape his own body parts together, and is trying to patch up old relationships – sometimes with that duct tape. Strap in, bitches. This fresh, funny, irreverent z-ride goes to 11."

—FLOYD JONES, author of the
forthcoming novel *Blueberry*

"I don't have to read it, I was sitting next to Jeff at Carnaval Court when he came up with everything."

—ANTHONY REYNOSO, co-author of
e-male: *Of Mouse And Men*

"Brains."

—RON WATSON, Zombie

AMERICAN BADASS

AMERICAN BADASS

JEFF CHACON

WOODEN STAKE PRESS

Published in the United States by Wooden Stake Press, LLC
Denver, CO
www.woodenstakepress.com

ISBN 978-1-940936-04-8

Let me tell you 'bout the book that I've been readin', it's got all my favorite words . . .
—THE BLACK CROWES

I

It's always best to start at the beginning...especially when your death is the beginning.

II

Call me Zombie.

III

It is a truth universally acknowledged that a single zombie in possession of a good hunger must be in want of a human meal.

With apologies to Jane Austen, of course.

CHAPTER
-1-

Ron Watson was hungry again. And from across the vast expanse that is the Denver International Airport terminal, he could see the men with guns looking for him. Sure, Ron had just eaten Kenny Jones, and in fact still had some of Kenny's delicious flavor on his lips–he tasted a lot like a McDonald's McRib, Ron thought – but everybody knows that shuffling from men with guns takes a lot of energy and, thusly, food. So Ron was hungry, according to his stomach...which was alerting him to the hunger via a noise not unlike somebody lightly and slowly farting into a paper bag.

The ticket agent slowly looked down at Ron's stomach and back up again with a stare that said, *I don't wanna know*. She lifted up her cheerily made-up face and smirked at Ron. "Do you have any bags to check, sir?"

Later, after Ron graced the cover of *People* magazine for the third time, the ticket agent would be the president of the local Ron Zombie Fan Club and even get Ron's autograph at the 2nd Annual ZombieCon, but right now Ron was not famous and looked nothing like himself. In fact, he had done his best to look human: chalk from a high school football field in Longmont—near Kenny's house—hid the scars on his face, and apparently hid the the fact that he was dead. Nobody was asking any questions, except for the men with guns, who actually would have a lot of questions if they were to catch up to Ron, who was doing his best to not let that happen. He smelled like a dead cat and his hair was all matted up from not being washed in some time, but he was wearing a flannel shirt. Ron hoped the ticket agent would assume he was a flannel-shirt-wearing human from Boulder (and not a zombie) and let him get on the plane. His stolen driver's license said Longmont, but that was close to Boulder. And, really, if you smell bad and have dreadlocks and are wearing a flannel shirt, Boulder is a good guess.

"Any bags, Mister....Jones? To check?"

"No." Sure, most zombies can only moan and grunt, but getting a *no* out of moans and grunts is not difficult. Ron just sort of spat it out and let it sit there, hoping the ticket agent would buy that his version of *no* was human. He looked back at the entrance to the terminal; the men with guns were searching. For him, no doubt. They were not obvious men with guns, because in an airport that would be quite disruptive to the general order of things, but Ron knew who they were. He had seen them in Longmont. And Boulder. And Denver. In fact, the men with guns were all over Colorado. That's one of the reasons he was leaving the land he loved – the land of legal marijuana, tall mountains, healthy people, and men with guns – and going to Las Vegas, the exact opposite of Colorado. Las Vegas, the land of drunks, tourists, down-on-their-luck beggars, and dreamers. Ron was a dreamer–he dreamed of being human again. He knew Las Vegas well enough that he had a strong feeling that a zombie wandering around Sin City stood a better chance of fitting in amongst the dreamers, the drunks, the tourists, and the down-on-their luck beggars than he did amongst the fairly normal human beings of Colorado. Nobody seemed to hassle anybody in Las Vegas, so that's the kind of place he needed to be right now.

"You have a carry on?" the ticket agent asked.

Yeah, sure, Ron had a carry on. It contained everything that was important to his life. In other words, it was empty, except for a few items of clothing that he stole from Kenny Jones. Ron was a zombie...but he did have a (mostly empty) messenger bag with him. Because while Ron might have been dead, with no possessions whatsoever, he wasn't stupid. And he knew that if he tried to get on a plane anywhere post-9/11 with no checked bags and no carry on, the humans would yank him into some private room deep in the bowels of the airport and ask him what the hell was going on. Then they'd figure it all out, and he'd end up dead. Again. And he didn't really want to be dead again. He didn't want it all to end because he forgot to bring a bag on the airplane. That would be stupid, and Ron wasn't stupid. He was just dead. There was a difference.

"Carry on, Mister Jones?"

"Yes." He looked at the gate agent and wondered if she wore her cheery makeup every day or just when she was working. Maybe on her off days she dressed up goth. That would be cool.

"How many, Mister Jones? You're allowed two." She stared through him like he wasn't there, Ron thought. You and your fucking cheery face. You never dress up goth, I can tell.

"One." The words was semi-formed, as his mouth seemed to be capable of only one syllable at a time. Ron realized that the more he was around humans and the more he listened to their speech patterns, the more he was capable of speech himself.

"Very good, Mister Jones. Here's your boarding pass. Proceed through security to the train and to gate C41. Your flight to Las Vegas leaves at 11:30. They'll start the boarding process about 15 minutes prior. Enjoy your flight to Sin City! Have a cocktail for me!"

Fuck you, cheery human fuck, Ron wanted to say, but he knew better. She was just doing her job; she wasn't trying to make him miserable by reminding him he was a zombie. No, Ron was fully capable of doing that himself. Besides, in his previous life, the ticket agent–Cindy, by her nametag–would have been in Ron's bed at some point. She was just the kind of girl that he enjoyed. Brunette, tight little body, pleasant smile. Really, Ron enjoyed every type of girl, but brunettes were his favorite. And more often than not, he knew how to get them into his bed. A smile here, a compliment there, an innocent "accidental" meeting over here...next thing you knew they were waking up in his downtown Denver loft to a fresh pot of coffee and '80s music on the radio in the morning. But Ron knew that if he made a pass at Cindy, his semi-formed single words would be more of a hindrance than anything. *Me. Like. You. Want. Sex.* Caveman pickup lines from a zombie disguised as a human? That's going to work every time.

Ron shuffled off towards the security area at the middle of the terminal as the men with guns approached the Alaska Airline check-in desk twenty feet away. *Good fucking thing I didn't choose to go to Alaska,* Ron thought. *I'd be under arrest right now. Not only that, I'm sure I'd freeze in the winter and thaw out in the summer, still undead. Still wondering how the fuck I got here.*

But, really, in that slow zombie brain of his, Ron knew how he got here. The mutant virus got out, people ate people, there were zombies everywhere, blahblahblah...you know the story. It's as rote to American culture as "Mary Had A Little Lamb." But unlike the lamb, who followed Mary to school one day, the humans in this story bucked the fable system and fought back. And, being human and being American, they were ingenious about it and scrappy about it and eventually rid the country of zombies. What's more American than killing off a culture? And so, a year or so after the Great Zombie Extermination, everything was back to normal. Republicans and Democrats returned to saying anything to get elected, public school systems went back to being woefully underfunded, and zombies were just a memory...unless you were Ron

Watson. Last Zombie Standing. Or whatever. It might have been cool, Ron thought, if he didn't have to always fucking hide it from everybody. And if it didn't attract bullets.

Shuffling through the security line that snakes around the Denver International Airport floor like a rabid python looking for its next meal, Ron realized people were looking at him. He hoped they just assumed he had some kind of ailment or reduced capacity. If the humans thought he looked like a terrorist, or hell, anything out of the ordinary, they might study him further or point him out to the men with guns. Close examination was not in Ron's best interest at the moment. How long could football field chalk on a face last? He didn't want to find out. And talk about disruptive to the general order of things: since the Great Zombie Penetration, the Great Zombie Skirmish, and the Great Zombie Extermination, nobody had seen a zombie, according to the 24 hour news networks. Certainly, if a zombie had been seen since the President declared "Mission Accomplished" (MA) with a banner saying the same across the former Zombie HQ, it would have made the nightly news. And Ron didn't want to be the first zombie to be found Post-MA. A zombie discovery today, at Denver International Airport, would certainly turn into a Denver International Incident. And then Ron would never get to Las Vegas.

"Where are you going today?" The security guy was looking past him at the men with guns, who had made their way to the back of the security line, whilst also checking Ron's stolen ID and boarding pass. It was quite a multitasking feat.

"Brains."

"Where?"

"Um." Ron struggled for a moment, his slow zombie brain betraying him like it was the most popular girl in school and he was Plain Jane. Where the fuck was he going again?

"Vegas." There it is. And wow, a two syllable word. Things were looking up.

The security guy perked up, smiled, and looked directly at Ron. "I love Vegas. Where are you staying?" Oh, shit. Where *am* I staying, Ron wondered. How do I answer this? Shit. Mandalay Bay was too many syllables. MGM? The Wynn? Palazzo?

"Brains."

"Where?"

"Pa...ris." Yeah, Paris. Ron had stayed at Paris when he was human, and it was easier to say than *Palazwhateverthefuck* and smarter than *Brains*...although Ron thought that if he owned Las Vegas, he'd open a hotel just for zombies and call it Brains. Think of the buffet!

"I love that place. So elegant. Enjoy your flight, Mr. Jones. Win some money for me!"

Ron wanted to say *fuck you*, but security guy really wasn't responsible for his predicament and he didn't want the men with guns to get suspicious. Any more suspicious than they'd be if they heard him say *brains*, anyway. Fuck. He also thought he should conserve his words, since he didn't feel all that in control of himself at the moment, so he gave the security guy a head nod. Like teenagers do. It's amazing how much communication between people–or, in this case, zombies and people–occurs without words. Ron could get used to this. If he ever could get used to anything anymore, after the accident.

Ron Watson died during the Great Zombie Skirmish in a motorcycle accident on a gorgeous Colorado highway on a gorgeous Colorado day, while working for KILLZ (Kill, Impale, Lacerate, and Lay waste to Zombies), the start-up government organization responsible for wiping out the zombies, and was promptly resurrected as a not-so-gorgeous zombie. The irony was lost on Ron in his zombie moments and hit him like a three-quarter-ton truck in his lucid moments. And perhaps *resurrected* isn't the correct term; really, he returned in some lesser form. A motorcycle accident does that to a guy, especially when the accident's other participant is a three-quarter-ton truck. So Ron returned – we'll use that word–as a classic zombie, right out of a George A. Romero film: bloody wounds on his face from where the truck's grill hit him, dirty clothes, and a shuffle where a walk use to be. Initially, it was a great look, because he really fit in well with zombie culture. Which is to say when he and six other zombies were munching on a live human's brain, they all looked like zombies. In that way, it was much like a boy band at a boy band concert–everybody looked like they belonged there. Which, in zombie terms, is a good thing. You don't want to be mistaken for a human when you're hanging out with zombies.

Until the humans gained the upper hand in the Great Zombie Skirmish and turned it into the Great Zombie Extermination. When the humans started running up the score like Peyton Manning playing against the Jacksonville Jaguars, looking like you belonged with the bunco (the term coined by social media to mean *pack of zombies*) munching on an accountant's brain was a death knell. For most zombies. Once KILLZ was up and running, and every Tom, Dick and Bubba practiced shooting guns until they were sharpshooters and became homegrown men with guns, it was pretty much over. Bullets through the brain for every zombie... except Ron. Ron somehow survived the onslaught of beer-fueled redneck humans who formed militias and took back their country. The funny thing is, Ron was a redneck-at-heart human, before the accident. And he always thought being a redneck was a badge of honor. Then he tried to explain to the rednecks that he was one of them, as they were shooting all his zombie friends, and none of them listened. Of course, trying to explain that you are human whilst looking like a zombie at a boy band concert is counterproductive, truly. That's like trying to commit to not looking up porn on the Internet.

"Choose any line." Time to put his bag on the belt and go through security. Wait, security? Weren't people required to remove their shoes to get through security? Sure, people were, but what about zombies? Ron realized this was a stupid question. When trying to appear human, you had to act like a human. He just hoped his feet were in good shape. He had failed to steal any socks from Kenny Jones, because he was a guy zombie and everybody knows guys sometimes forget details like socks when they are shopping for clothes. He was going to expose his feet to the world once he removed his sneakers and put them up on the belt. And at this moment, he couldn't remember if his feet were affected by the motorcycle crash at all. Shit. Would the men with guns show up at security, see his feet, and recognize them as Zombie Feet? Was there such a thing as Zombie Feet? Ron looked around. No men with guns nearby right now. Fuck it, time to go for it, Zombie Feet or not, Ron thought. Nothing to fucking lose at this point, right? And if I'm successful, I get to disappear in Las Vegas. If I'm not, Denver International Incident. Ron smiled at his own joke; it was the first time that he could remember smiling as a zombie. Two syllable words and a sense of humor? It sure was feeling like this trip was a good idea.

CHAPTER

-2-

The security line in front of him came to a complete stop and a hush fell over the gathered throng. Ron had traveled enough as a human to know that a hush at an airport is never really a good thing. He looked around. Sure enough, the men with guns were approaching the body scanning machines to talk to the men with scanners. Ron wondered if the body scanning machines would detect that he was dead.

After a brief discussion, the men with guns stood next to the men with scanners at the entrance to the body scanners as the line started moving again, and Ron realized he had no time to contemplate if those were actually zombie scanning machines. He did, however, have time to contemplate if this whole thing was going to fall apart right here, like a zombie after a few months of not eating. No, he didn't have time for this contemplation either–the line was moving and there was a gap in front of him. A gap in a line at an airport, Ron figured, could only indicate trouble to men with guns. Seriously, who the fuck would not move with traffic whilst in a security line at a major airport? Dammit.

Ron shuffled forward while the men with guns and scanners looked intently at each passenger passing through the scanner. He could turn away and run...except all he could really do was shuffle, and he imagined he'd be gunned down faster than you can say victim has not been identified. He had seen how fast humans could shoot down zombies, both as a member of KILLZ and as a member of a bunco, and he didn't want to see it again right now. The fucking humans could shoot down zombies. They had embraced firepower and carnage like you'd expect from a culture obsessed with guns and violent movies. Fucking humans.

And there were fucking humans all around him right now, except for the ever widening line gap in front of him, and it was time for Ron to either take off his shoes or turn around and cause a scene. Or, really, taking off his shoes might cause a scene anyway – Zombie Feet and all that.

Fuck it, Ron thought, I don't really have an option. I'm either leaving this place in a Zombie Bag–a common item during the Zombie Extermination–or on an airplane. He reached down and removed his stolen sneakers. Fortunately, the shoelaces were gone and he didn't have to tie or untie anything. That would save some time through security, and made Ron feel slightly "hip." He imagined all the zombie kids were wearing shoes without laces these days. Once the shoes were off, he looked at his feet for a moment. Not bad, actually. All ten toes, minor lint between the toes, and nary a scratch on the surface. Nothing that a homeless person–or a hippie from Boulder–wouldn't be proud of. Really, Ron always took good care of his feet, because the brunettes liked that. He put his shoes up on the security belt and approached the men with guns and scanners.

"Where you headed?" a man with a gun asked. The gun wasn't visible, but Ron knew. He just fuckin' knew. The man had on those mirrored douchebag sunglasses and his voice sounded like that of a government robot worker, Ron thought. John Fuckin' Wayne for a paycheck. He's getting paid to come after me but he's only coming after me because he's getting paid. Otherwise he wouldn't give a fuck. Ron knew the type; they were the guys who had populated KILLZ when Ron was alive.

"Br -" Ron froze. No. Not brains. I'm not going to brains, you stupid brain! Fuck. Fuck. Fuck. Fuck.

The man with a gun dropped his hand towards his waist, where his gun probably was. He removed his sunglasses slowly, tilted his head a few degrees and squinted his eyes. "Where you headed, sir?" He looked like the demented host of a cheesy game show featuring B-list celebrities you've never heard of. The wrong answer here would not only not get you what's behind Door #3, it would also get you killed.

"Breyyyyyygas. Laaaas Vayyyyygas." If zombies could sweat, Ron realized, he'd be sweating like a teenager with a pocket full of freshly cooked meth talking to a cop. Jesus.

The man took a step forward and placed his nose an inch from Ron's cheek. "Vegas, huh?"

"Brr–yes." What the fuck is wrong with me? I know more words than brains!

The man walked around Ron slowly, looking at his face the whole time. "You from Boulder?" he asked while he walked.

"Broulder," Ron mumbled and nodded his stinky unwashed head. Maybe mumbling would save his ass. Nobody understood Ron's mumbles when he was alive, it would be fucking great if they didn't understand him now, thank you very much.

"You smell like it. Why don't you fuckers ever wash your hair? Is that some kind of hippy code or some bullshit?"

"Brainshit–yes."

"You nervous, boy?"

"Yes, br–sir."

"You know marijuana is legal now, right?"

Ron took a deep breath and smiled slyly at the man. "Br...right. Forgot."

The man took a step away from Ron, put his douchebag sunglasses back on, and smiled at Ron. "You hippies are so fuckin' weird."

A commotion broke out in the security line three lines to the right of Ron, and the man's walkie talkie started talking; "CODE BLUE! CODE BLUE!" The man with a gun looked at Ron and said, "You're lucky. Code Blue. That means some fucking punk just tried to go through security with his shoes on. I gotta take care of this and you can go, but know that before Amendment 64 I would have had your ass." He took his sunglasses off and looked Ron deep into his dark zombie eyes. "You understand, hippie?" Spit came out of his mouth and landed on Ron's face chalk. Fucking human.

"Yes. Sir."

The man put his douchebag sunglasses back on and ran towards the commotion, where three security guards were already beating the fuck out of a guy who looked to be about twenty-five years old and probably forgot to take off his shoes. Normally, Ron might have been curious about the details of the commotion, but this was not a normal time. He had to go before the men with guns and scanners finished assaulting the guy with the dangerous loafers and came back to him.

As Ron headed towards the body scanner, he wondered. Was he lucky? Or was the man with the gun lucky that Ron didn't eat him right then and there? All this stress was making him hungry, after all. Some people need a cigarette when they're stressed out, but zombies? They need food. And Ron had no idea where he was going to get his next meal.

The last person he ate was Kenny Jones, and Kenny Jones was a drug dealer based in Longmont, Colorado. Ron not only ate Kenny, he also took his stash of cash and his wallet. Funny how drug dealers leave cash and wallets out in the open. Then again, his drugs were out in the open, too. And Ron easily faked being a meth addict for Kenny. He had the look, so Kenny believed him when he said he needed to score. That part was true. Kenny, however, was sadly mistaken about what it exactly was that Ron needed to score. And now Ron was Kenny Jones, according to the cash and credit cards and ID in the wallet in his pocket. Kenny was a meth-addict hippy, so he looked like a zombie anyway...thusly, Ron had no trouble passing for Kenny. Even at an airport. So much for airport security, right?

As Ron approached the body scanner, he looked back. The men with guns–or Douchebags with Mirrored Glasses, as Ron was now calling them in his head–had multiplied, so there were now six of them. They were still making a mess of the no-shoe kid's face, which was bloodied so that it now resembled a zombie's face. Based on the distraction for the men with guns–sorry about your face, kid, but you're really helping me right now, Ron thought–Ron knew that once he was through the airport's security checkpoint he was probably home free. Ron walked through the body scanner without incident–apparently it didn't give a shit if you were alive or dead–and went to pick his empty carry-on off of the belt. To his surprise, the line gap in front of him had closed up and there was now a line to retrieve bags off of the belt.

Why? The man in front of Ron was taking his sweet time. More like his sour time, really. He was a businessman, if wearing a suit to the airport and carrying a laptop makes a man a businessman. Ron didn't like to stereotype, but he found that as a zombie it was often necessary, just to save time and get the lay of the land. Furthermore, an in-depth analysis of a person's character is often untenable when you spend most of your time hiding from the same humans you're trying to analyze, so you save time by stereotyping.

It was obvious that Mister Stereotypical Businessman hadn't checked a damn thing at the ticket counter. It was all here, in his two manatee-sized carry-ons, still on the belt. The man either a) didn't want to pay the checked bag fees, or b) didn't want to wait for his checked bags at whatever airport he was going to hog up next. And now everybody behind him in the security line was paying the price. Ron hoped this guy wasn't on Ron's plane, because it was obvious to Ron–and to everybody behind him–that Mister Businessman's carry-ons were in no way, shape or form going to fit in the overhead compartment. It'd be like squeezing one hundred zombies into a one-zombie bag. Ron chuckled to himself and silently wondered when his sense of humor had gotten so weird.

"Sure, Ed, I'll call you later." The businessman turned, and Ron could see that not only had he been ignoring his two Space Shuttle sized carry-ons on the belt, but Mister Businessman had also been talking on his phone. No wonder the line wasn't moving. Jeez. Some people just live on their own planet.

Ron wondered what Mister Businessman would taste like. He tried not to eat too many people, because he felt guilty about it. He still considered himself a human on many levels, after all, and more than anything he wanted to be human again. But sometimes, if Ron felt like somebody deserved it, he would partake, guilt notwithstanding. It kept his energy up. Maybe if he could find a time to have himself some businessman special, he could do more than shuffle. And maybe he could use three syllables in a word! Ron pondered the world of possibilities as he waited for his bag.

If he ate the businessman, he'd have to dispose of the parts AND the businessman's Mount Rushmore sized carry-ons. Which, it seems, the businessman was having trouble getting off of the security belt at the moment. While he was making another phone call. Yeah, Ron thought, some people deserved to be a meal. And if he could eat Mister Stereotypical Businessman it would make Ron happy...making the businessman a Happy Meal. Ron chuckled at his joke and wondered if could eat him without drawing attention to the man and/or his baggage.

"Hi honey. I'm at the airport in Denver. I should be boarding in a while. Some idiot tried to go through security with his shoes on. Anyway, send my love to the girls and tell them I'll see them tonight." Shit. There was no way Ron was going to eat the businessman now. The businessman had daughters. Motherfucker.

Ron Watson was a fucked-up zombie; he was a zombie with a conscience. A fucking conscience, he'd tell you, because he didn't necessarily like it. He'd eat anything that breathed, if his stomach had its way. But his heart had a different idea. And somehow his heart led his stomach around like a wife who's promised sex later tonight leads her husband around today, so he only ate people he felt deserved it. Not only that, but Ron also had a daughter. With a blonde. Which is why he liked brunettes. Things with the blonde didn't go so well after their daughter was born, so Ron and the blonde split up after a few years. And Ron started chasing brunettes...but the girl of his life was his daughter. Stella lived with her mom, but Ron was as good an absentee dad as he could be, because she was truly the one thing that made his heart sing. Sure, brunettes in his bed were fun and motorcycle riding was fun, but Stella had her hands around her daddy's heart so tight that nothing could separate them. Well, nothing but a motorcycle accident, anyway. And now Ron hoped that the horrible day when he died on Highway 93 in Colorado wasn't the end. In fact, he hoped that this, right here, was a beginning. Because the last time he talked to Stella she had moved with her mom to Las Vegas...where Ron was headed now, with a little help from Kenny Jones. And the Douchebags in Mirrored Glasses. And the Kid With No Shoes and No Face. If Ron actually made it to Vegas, maybe he could find his daughter. At the same time, maybe he could find his humanity.

Ron shuffled to Concourse C. Flight 72, direct to Las Vegas, leaving at 11:30 in the morning. He had lasted all this time in Wild West Colorado. He had made it through security at Denver International Airport. Somehow, he had gotten this far. Now? Now he was heading for Vegas. It felt right. If anything really feels right when you're a zombie.

CHAPTER
-3-

Ron was still hungry. The flight attendant on the plane was standing over him, offering him a choice–if airline snacks could every actually be a choice–between hard-as-rock pretzels, over-processed 'cheese' squares, and who-knows-whats-in-them cookies. All Ron could think was, what, no brains? One day, Ron would open his own airline–Air Zombie, or maybe Bloodwest Airlines–and simply offer passengers bites of other passengers.

"Sir? Pretzels, Cheese Nubbies or sandwich cookies?"

"No."

"No, what, sir?"

The flight attendant–a trim young man with fabulous effeminate style–seemed to have a stick up his ass about manners. So Ron decided he would have a stick up his ass–his undead ass, that is–about no manners.

"No fucking snacks."

"A simple *no thank you* would be nice, sir."

"No, fuck you, brains."

"Sir?"

"No...thank you." Ron remembered that he was a zombie and would not hold up well under any sort of close examination, so he decided to keep the attention off of himself. But his hunger was affecting his decision making, obviously. Hunger made him decisive...about not being hungry anymore. He would need to find somebody to eat and soon. But addressing this particular dilemma on a national flight on a national airline didn't seem like the best decision, because, again, it was post 9/11. If anybody on this plane saw any sort of violence or blood, Ron had the feeling he and the entire plane would be escorted by fighter jets to a secret base in New Mexico faster than you could say *conspiracy*. Which Ron couldn't say, actually. Not right now–too many syllables.

Ron was in seat 14C, an aisle seat; he could have sat by the window in row 13 but there was no fucking way he was sitting in row 13, even though it was available. He had had enough bad luck in his life and death to meet his bad luck quota, thank you very much. He had an aisle seat because his slow shuffle through the airport had almost made him late and by the time he got on the plane he realized that none of the motherfucking inconsiderate humans had saved him a window seat not in row 13. Surely, he would have preferred a window seat; then he could have looked down on the nation that, because he was hungry, looked a lot like lunch. All that food and no one to eat. Oh, well, he'd have to make do with the aisle. At least he was getting the hell out of Colorado–where every man and his cousin had a shotgun, an eye for zombies, and a Wild West attitude–and heading to Vegas, where nobody gave a fuck. Hopefully.

Back in the day, Ron would sleep on planes, every time, and he would bug the shit out of whoever was sitting next to him, because he tended to employ their shoulder as a fluffy pillow, no matter how fluffy it really was. Now? Sure, somebody was sitting next to him–a typically overweight American male in a typical American sports jersey, Ron noticed–but hell, everybody knows zombies don't sleep, so Sports Fan was in no danger of Ron nodding off and calling him "baby" whilst logging some Zs. Ron wished he was back in college, where falling asleep anywhere–even in class–was easy for him. But, alas...Ron picked the SkyMall catalog out of the seat back in front of him, thumbed through it, and wondered who the fuck would buy a booze belt or travel duct tape. Especially from a mall in the sky.

About halfway through the short flight, the blonde across the aisle in seat 13D smiled at him. She looked delicious. And sexy as hell. Wait–did Ron want to eat her or fuck her? How did this get so confusing? His stomach hunger seemed to be brawling with his lusty hunger. Boy, back when he was alive, there was no confusion whatsoever–Ron was horny all the time. And rarely–or never, really–did food get in the way of that. Sometimes food and sex even went together, like the time one of his girlfriends covered his torso with honey and licked it all off. All of a sudden, Ron missed being human even more than usual. Which is to say he missed it a lot.

"You going to Vegas?" The blonde turned to face him, as well as a blonde in an aisle seat on a tin can in the air can turn to face a zombie, and Ron noticed her breasts. Well, really, when your breasts are barely contained in a skimpy white tank top, of course they're going to get noticed. They're almost asking for the attention. Ron was surprised the blonde's tank top didn't have have 'Please Notice My Titties' written across it, because that really was the point of the entire tiny piece of fabric. Women in skimpy white tank tops were always selling something, Ron thought, and he was always buying what they were selling. He was the target market for titties. Ron Watson, the titty demographic. He was an easier sell for titties than a bored housewife watching Home Shopping Network at 3 am was for fake jewelry–for 3 easy payments plus shipping and handling, natch.

"Duh." Ron thought the answer was obvious. They were on a flight to Vegas, after all. Besides, duh is a one syllable word. Easy to say.

"Oh, huh-huh! You're funny!" The blonde laughed and Ron smirked. At least, it felt like a smirk. Sometimes, it was hard to tell if his brain signals for facial expressions were reaching his face. Really, Ron thought, I need to spend some time practicing my facial expressions in a mirror. Make sure they look alive. Make sure my face is still in one place. Ron had seen all the zombie movies; he understood that over time his face stood a good chance of falling off completely, even when it was covered in football field chalk. That, Ron, thought, would put a wet blanket on his plans. A bloody wet blanket. If people saw Ron without a face, they'd either arrest him or hire him for a Michael Jackson video. And Michael Jackson was dead, so that choice was out.

"Duh." Ron thought a little reincorporation was funny. And it was, yes, easy to say.

"Oh, huh-huh-huh! You're *very* funny! I'm Bambi."

Of course you are, thought Ron. You're Bambi, and I'm Thumper. Thumper the Zombie.

"I'm Ken."

"My ex-boyfriend was named Ken." Of course he was, Ron thought. Of course. Ken and Bambi. When the entire world was off-kilter, it was perfectly okay to mix non-anatomically-correct plastic dolls with beloved fairy tale animals. Too bad she wasn't named Barbie, Ron thought. That would be perfect. *Ex-boyfriend named Ken AND beautiful tits? Come on down, you're the next contestant on Be My Barbie Doll!* Maybe Ron could fuck her AND eat her. In a literal sense, of course. And in that order. He hoped, really, that he'd get a chance to eat her in a different literal sense while he was fucking her. So to speak. Ron always enjoyed getting his girlfriends off before he took his turn. It was flat out sexy and generally considerate. The female orgasm was as beautiful to Ron

as just about anything else on earth, and if Bambi gave him the opportunity, he'd be sure to go in search of that beauty.

"Ha ha." Ron's laughter was slower than Bambi's. He hoped it
reeked of sophistication and not of desperation. Or un-dead-ena-
tion. Ron knew he needed to eat soon; the jokes in his head were
making less and less sense.

"Buy me a drink?" Wait, what? A drink? Um, really? Me?
Zombie Ron? Buy you, Bambi McTitties, a drink? On an airplane
bound for Las Vegas? Seriously? Ron wondered if he had ever gotten so lucky, so fast, when he was actually alive. Maybe this Vegas
idea was better than he thought.

"Drink?"

"Yeah, drink. You buy me a drink."

Hey, wait a minute, Ron thought to himself. Bambi was sitting
by herself, on the aisle, on a plane from Denver, bound for Vegas.
What was wrong with this picture?

"You...alone?" Ron had to ask.

"Not for long, Ken. Tonight, I'm all yours. You look like you
could use some company."

Bingo. There it was. Ron had spent enough time as a living
person in Vegas to understand that *company* is the code word for
I'm a hooker, and you're going to pay to spend time with me. He had
run across this problem before, more than once. You're sitting in
a bar in Vegas, late at night, you're dressed well, you look like you
know what you're doing with your life, you're drinking a mixed
drink with appropriate citrus accompaniment, and all of a sudden BAM! The most gorgeous creature you've ever seen sits down
next to you and starts talking about how you need some company
tonight. And how she wants to go back to your room. Yeah, Ron,
when he was alive, was a hooker's target market, a hooker's demographic, and he knew the drill. And this was the drill, right here.

"Oh, no."

"No, what, sugar?" Bambi's tits had come across the aisle and found their way directly into Ron's eyesight. And were now rubbing up against his arm. And were now somehow in his hands. Man, they were nice. Even in his zombie hands.

"Um, excuse me, ma'am, you should sit in your own seat." The Sports Fan next to Ron obviously had shitty taste in women and shitty taste in adventure and was willing to share both. Ron, being the altruistic gentleman that he was–and because he didn't really feel like he was done with this particular adventure yet, even if she was a hooker–decided to help Sports Fan see the error of his ways. So he turned to his right, looked the young man in the eye, lifted his lips, put his teeth together, and hissed with all his zombie might. He wasn't sure he looked scary, but the kid let out a yelp, sunk down in his seat, grabbed his own copy of the SkyMall catalog from the seatback in front of him, and pretended like he never cared about the blonde sitting in the zombie's lap next to him. Ron turned back from the Sports Fan, because he did care about the blonde sitting in his lap. Temporarily, anyway. The attention was nice, even if this wasn't really going anywhere beyond titties. Which, honestly, is oftentimes enough of a reason to pay attention. Temporarily, anyway.

"No, what, sugar?" Bambi clearly wasn't worried about the Sports Fan in the middle seat, either.

"Brains."

"What?"

"Gotta...go."

"Go ahead, honey, the bathroom is back there." Bambi looked back towards the 737's bathroom, putting her plump breasts directly into Ron's face. "And it's available," she purred. "Perhaps I could...join you?"

"No, I...no interest." Ron couldn't figure out why he wasn't interested, either. He really was. He'd really like to fuck her and then eat her. But the fact was she was a hooker...Ron wondered if zombies actually had standards. Say, if a bunco of zombies broke into a mental institution, would they starve themselves because the brains weren't good enough? *Oh, shit, boys, we should really go look at the college and see if there are any brains there.* Ron laughed.

"Ha ha! You ARE funny!" Bambi's breasts seemed to be talking to Ron, and at the same time they were enveloping his face like a child's blanket. If a child's blanket was made out of skin and hot blonde, that is. Ron felt himself get an erection for the first time in his zombie life. Bambi noticed it too. "Oh, honey, you are funny...your funny bone proves that. Yummy." She laughed at her own joke, all the while giving Ron that *I'm gonna fuck you so hard tonight, for a small fee, plus shipping and handling* look.

"No money." Ron thought that might get his point across.

"What?"

"Not...paying for it."

"Oh." Bambi climbed off of Ron, to his dismay, and went back to her seat across the aisle. Ron was going to miss her tits. She sat down and grunted. "Is it obvious?" she asked without looking at him.

"Yes."

"Crap."

"Sorry."

"Dammit." She turned to look at him; her face had grown younger by ten years. "I don't really know how to do this."

"You do."

"I do?"

"Sure."

"I got you excited. I guess that's something. Then again, most guys get excited when the wind blows." She turned back to face the front of the plane and sighed a deep sigh, like somebody who's just been told they didn't make the varsity chess club.

Ron hated to see her self-esteem plummet like this. He always thought of himself as a sympathetic and polite creature, so he decided to help her out.

"I have no money," he lied. Of course he had money. He was on a plane to Vegas, wasn't he? And Kenny Jones had left a LOT of cash out in the open–a hearty portion of that cash was now in Kenny's wallet, which was now in Kenny's pants, which were now on Ron's body. So he was flush with cash. But he didn't want to tell Bambi that. As much as he had zombie wood right now and had made fast friends with her human breasts, he still wasn't going to pay for it. Fucking zombie conscience, always getting in the way of a good time. Ron's zombie conscience was a lot like Patty Gray's mother in junior high school. Ron and Patty would be dancing close enough in Patty's garage to feel each other up, and Mrs. Gray would always come out into the garage and separate them. *Two feet apart!* And Ron's human wood would slowly, painfully dissipate, and all the action he would get would be in his wet dreams.

"Oh, you poor thing." Here came Bambi's breasts again, silently announcing themselves as if they were entering a fancy dinner party. *Presenting, Mrs. and Mrs. Tit and Melon.* Ron laughed at his own stupid joke, realized he still had zombie wood, and thought to himself that he really wanted to fuck her. Really. But he knew that if he fucked her, he'd eat her, and she really didn't deserve to be eaten, as far as Ron could tell. Great, Ron thought, I really am a zombie with a conscience, even when I'm hungry AND horny. Right now, Ron wished he was one of those zombies with no conscience whatsoever. He'd be fucking and eating–or eating and fucking and eating–every woman on this plane. He'd make them scream, and then he'd make them scream again. It'd be a zombie orgy; blood and cum everywhere. Strangely enough, this did nothing for Ron. These people didn't deserve to die. Sure, they deserved to be fucked. Everybody could use a little more screwing, Ron thought. But he had always felt that way. *If everybody had sex twice a day, there would be no wars*, he used to say to nobody in particular. Still, while everybody deserved to be fucked a little more often, it didn't help the fact that if Ron started in on fucking and eating everybody–or even just the blonde–somebody would pull a weapon. Yes, even on a plane. If Ron were going to eat somebody, it couldn't be here. And his stupid conscience was telling him he couldn't really eat people who didn't deserve to be eaten, he could only eat people who were already dead. Not literally dead, because that would be like eating rancid meat, but dead as in *You Are Living A Very Non-Productive Life*. Ron laughed. Non-productive? Surely there were a better term for it; a lot of people who didn't deserve to be eaten were non-productive. Hell, most human beings are non-productive, really. How about *You Are Living A Destructive Life*? Ron didn't know what to call, but he knew what it was when he ran across it. Kenny Jones, for example.

"Are you going to Vegas to win?" The blonde was full of questions, and Ron didn't mind. Her breasts certainly gave her license to ask whatever she wanted, and it took his mind off of his erection and his stupid conscience.

"Yes. To win. Make money." Ron lied. "And you?" That should temper her questions a little. At the same time, it was designed to get him some more breast time. He could always use a little more breast time. With or without an erection.

"I'm going to work." Work, Ron thought. What a concept. Ron's only job these days seemed to be figuring out who to eat and when. It was a long way from his pre-KILLZ days as a government worker, sitting in an office all day, crunching numbers and taking on projects. Ron always thought working in an office all day, dressing like a drone, answering to The Man, was just about like being a zombie.

"Hooking?"

"Yeah."

"Your job?"

"Yeah. But I'm not very good at it, as you can tell."

"On a plane?" Ron thought she might have better luck on the ground, in Vegas. With a human.

"Should I have waited? Do people not want to join the mile high club?"

"No. Do it. In. Vegas."

"Yeah, you're right. I was just trying to get a head start on things." She moved over to Ron's seat again and sat in his lap. "Thanks for the advice, Kenny." Her boobs were now in his face and his erection was now poking her ass cheek. It was a very nice ass cheek. Ron wished he could eat it, among other things.

"Uh, sure."

Bambi kissed Ron hard on the mouth as the intercom buzzed. "Ladies and Gentlemen, uhhhhhhhhhhhh, this is your captain, and uhhhhhhh, we're starting our decent into Sin City. We're arriving 15 minutes earlier than we thought, so drink one for me!" The passengers erupted into a cheer. People going to Vegas tend to be happy. And/or drunk. But Ron was happiest of all. Bambi was sitting on his lap sticking her tongue down his throat, and he was starting to give less of a shit whether or not he ate her after fucking her, so he appreciated the interruption. It helped reset his focus. And, frankly, kept him from doing something that his conscience was telling him he'd live to regret. If he lived at all.

She went back to her seat. "Oh, Kenny. Come see me in Vegas and I won't charge you. You're sweet." She quickly lifted up her tank top and showed Ron her breasts, without anybody else noticing. They were as Ron thought they would be: lush, beautifully shaped and plentiful, like two lush, beautifully shaped and plentiful harvests. They were, Ron realized, the Most Fantastic Breasts he had ever seen, even when he was alive...and he had seen his share of breasts. Ron felt himself blush...if zombies can actually do that.

CHAPTER

-4-

Ron caught a cab from the airport and checked himself in to the Casino Royale hotel. He considered not getting a room, because he knew he wasn't going to sleep–and he'd gone entire Vegas weekends without a room before–but decided that he'd fit in better if he actually had someplace to go at night. Or he might need a dining room. Or he might need a place to clean up after dining. Really, it was just good to have a home base. Besides, Kenny Jones had a Casino Royale Players Card in his wallet, so Ron took that to the front desk...and Kenny got comped for three nights. Ooh, big spender. Three free nights at what was obviously not the Palazzo or Venetian or, hell, even the Flamingo. What the hell, right? Sure, it was a bit of a dive, but so was Ron. And a Vegas dive has its charms, and so did Ron. They'd fit well together, and free was always a good price. Three nights would also give Ron a chance to try to settle in to his new life here. His new undead life? His new deadness? Ron couldn't figure out what to call it, so he called it nothing. That's what it was so far, right?

Whatever it was, now that he was in Vegas, Ron wasn't quite sure what to do next. He had spent so much energy getting here that now that he was here, it was a bit of a letdown...but nobody had noticed him so far, which is why he was here. So far, so good. Except for the fact that he was exhausted. He wondered if he could take a nap. Haha! Of course not! Zombies don't sleep! Sleeping, really, was one of the things that Ron missed about being human. It's funny, if you think about it. The undead missed the part of humanity that left them unconscious for six to nine hours a night.

But the undead drink. Ron had found that drinking alcohol helped his energy level between dinings and helped calm him down. He was still a little freaked out by the fact that he was a zombie. Well, really, he was a lot freaked out by the fact that he was a zombie. Who wouldn't be? It does something to the brain, which is ironic, because all he wanted to do was something to other people's brains. But right now, Ron's brain needed a drink, to help with the stress of wanting to eat all other brains. It's a vicious cycle. A zombie *Catch 22*.

He took the elevator down to the first floor and wandered through the casino towards the front door on the Strip. It was daytime outside and warm, even though it was October. Vegas in October is July in most other parts of the world. Ron put on his sunglasses before he went out. Most zombies prefer to come out at night–it's the domain of zombies, really–but Ron had figured out, through strenuous research that involved several rounds of brain freeze–the byproduct of going out during the day without sunglasses–that all he had to do was put on decent sunglasses to shield his eyes and he could go walk around during the day. If only every other stupid zombie had figured that out, maybe they would have survived the Zombie Extermination. The Zombie Extermination occurred mostly during the day because, well, the zombies all went to Zombie HQ during the day to shield themselves from the sun. The humans had figured out where Zombie HQ was and, well, taken advantage of the knowledge. Stupid zombies, Ron thought.

But really, he had something more important on his mind at the moment. Drinking.

Next to the casino was an outdoor circular bar, Carnaval Court, whose motto was *Getting You Drunk Enough To Find Each Other Attractive,* that Ron knew about. Hell, he more than knew about it, it was his favorite place in the whole world. When he was alive, he knew all the bartenders there. He'd fit right in now, because most people sitting around the bar were usually completely shitfaced or completely taken with either the flair bartenders–who were quite entertaining in their own right–or the house band, The Whipits, a New Wave cover band.

Today The Whipits were just starting up with, yes, New Wave cover songs. They were always good, Ron thought. He knew many of the songs, he knew much of their shtick, and he knew the audience would be into them enough that he could probably sit there and drink in relative peace. Sure, he could have found some dimly lit bar in some off-Strip casino and probably been by himself with his drink, but he didn't want to take the time to shuffle off the Strip. That might take days, at his pace. Besides, Ron could see that Flippy, Rob, Charlie and Robyn were tending bar at Carnaval Court, and they were his four favorite bartenders of all time. Ron grabbed a seat at the bar. As much as a zombie can grab anything.

"Ron! My brutha from another mutha!" Flippy was his usual flair-bartender crazy self, with his bald head and his constant laughter. "How ya been?" He shook Ron's hand with the vigor of an old friend.

"Flippy! Good!" Just the fact he was in Vegas and could smell alcohol increased his ability to speak properly.

"You look like shit, my man," Rob said. Rob also had a bald head. Ron wondered if bartending causes hair loss, and decided it didn't matter. Instead of bringing that up, he was going to start a conversation with Rob the way he normally would.

"Fuck you, Rob."

"Fuck you, Ronny! I wasn't going to say anything, but...haha-haha! What're ya drinkin' today?"

"Brains."

Flippy cocked his head and looked at Ron like a puppy. "What?"

"Gin and tonic."

Rob laughed. "As usual. Hey, where's your friend?"

As Rob and Flippy started throwing bottles of alcohol and mixers in the air while they made his gin and tonic, Ron realized he wasn't ready for this question. He hadn't thought about his best friend Jim in some time. Ron and Jim used to go to Vegas and Carnaval Court regularly. Jim was a high school buddy who grew up, went to college, got himself a corporate job and a wife and two kids...but he and Ron maintained contact over the years, and they both liked to escape to Vegas whenever they could. Whenever Jim could get a hall pass from his wife–a concept Ron never quite un-derstood, but married guys seem to have their sets of rules–he and Ron would meet in Vegas, sit here at the Carnaval Court for two or three days listening to new wave songs from their glory days and laughing at bartender antics, and escape from it all. It was the deepest friendship Ron ever had. And it saved his life. Well, his zombie life, anyway. When the Zombie Extermination was in full swing and Ron found himself behind a Starbucks with 12 other zombies, munching on a financial trader turned barista–he wasn't as delicious nor as caffeinated as Ron had hoped–two KILLZ guys showed up and started shooting zombies through the head, per KILLZ protocol. Ron, like the other 11 zombies, thought he was going to be dead again. Permanently. Dead, undead, dead, it's also a vicious cycle. But then he looked up from the barista's bicep–the kid was built, and his biceps were like Thanksgiving dinner to Ron–and he noticed that the lead KILLZ guy was Jim. And Jim noticed that the only zombie still moving was Ron. And he let Ron go. Somehow.

"I dunno." It was true. He had no idea where Jim was. It was probably better this way, because Jim knew Ron was a zombie. And if they ran across each other again, there was no way to know if Jim would be as lenient this time. Still, Ron missed his friend. He downed his drink. He thought about pouring some of it out for Jim, like rappers do, but he hoped that Jim wasn't dead, honestly, and Ron thought that gesture was only for the dead. Maybe he should have poured some out for himself. *For my zombies*. Ron smiled at this thought.

"Hey, party animal, you ready for another?" Charlie smiled and started throwing a bottle of gin in the air like it was a volley-ball. Ron loved this place, because nobody judged him if he drank fast. And they didn't judge him if he looked like he had a nasty hangover. They just asked if he was ready for another and started making another. He and Jim used to get hammered here and shuffle back to their room–much like a couple of zombies–when they were no longer ready for another.

"Yeah."

"Run a tab?"

"Brains."

"Tab?" Charlie lifted his eyebrows as if to say, *Whatever you just said, your secret is safe with me*. Ron imagined that Charlie–and all the bartenders here–knew more secrets about people than anybody. It's a quality that a good bartender has to have. People get drunk, they start talking or acting crazy, and the next thing you know you see something or learn something that you probably don't really want to know. A good bartender is a confidant, so they have to keep those things secret. It's part of their job, really.

"Yeah. Tab. Thanks, Charlie. It's good to see you."

"You too, Ron. Even though you look like shit."

"Fuck you."

"Fuck you too, buddy." Charlie and Ron fist bumped, like usual. Ron hoped his fist felt alive. Alive enough to feel like a human fist, anyway.

All of a sudden, Charlie started blowing his whistle, making Ron jump with fright. What the fuck did he do wrong? Did his dead fist give him away? Then every other bartender in the place blew their whistle and Ron could see that Robyn, the lone female bartender in the place, was balancing five drink glasses on her head and a bottle of Jägermeister on top of the top glass. It was time for some flair. Ron relaxed. The whistle wasn't for him, it was for everybody. He loved this place. This place was for everybody.

Robyn walked around the bar, showing off her balancing skills to the gathered throng of drunks and ne'er-do-wells. The Whipits had stopped playing music and were chanting her name. Truly, it was the band's job to sell as much as alcohol as possible. Hell, it was everybody's job to sell as much alcohol as possible. And when a hot bartendress with a nice rack is dressed in a tight black tank top and has alcohol balanced on her head, a lot of alcohol is sold. Funny how that works. Again, target market and demographic. These people knew the drill. They could sell bullshit to a politician.

Ron took a gulp of his new gin and tonic. He probably would have downed it, but he didn't really want to drink that fast. Once he and Jim had come here and gone on total benders and gotten kicked out, which was honestly hard to do at a place like Carnaval Court. Ron knew alcohol didn't affect him as fast as it did when he was alive, but he didn't really feel like attracting that kind of attention today. Besides, he liked to sit at the bar and watch people. At least, he used to, when he was alive. Now he liked to sit at the bar and watch dinner. Ron looked around to see who he wouldn't have trouble eating.

As the Jäger went into somebody's mouth and the Whipits launched into a song, Ron saw a typical tourist couple across the bar. He knew the type–from the Midwest. The middle aged couple had obviously never been here before, because they ordered the giant plastic cup shaped like the country of Brazil that had a neck-drink-holder attached. $25 for $3 worth of booze in an oversized plastic thing made by Chinese slave children makes you a typical tourist, Ron thought. The man was wearing a Hawaiian print shirt, unbuttoned enough to show his chest hair. On his head, his hairline was non-existent; on the rest of him, however, his beer belly was very existent. His face was red from being out in the Vegas sun and he was taking a cell phone picture of his wife...who was going down on a cock-shaped whipped cream straw thing that Flippy was holding between his legs. Flair and all that. Ron couldn't eat either of these two, because they were just tourists...but Flippy might eat the wife later, Ron thought. The flair bartenders must get so much pussy or penis, depending their preference. Get the couples drunk, get the wives all horny, slip 'em a little flair after hours. Ron always thought that if he lived in Vegas, he'd work here.

To his left, Ron saw a bachelorette party amble up to the bar. He wondered if any of them knew what the word *amble* means. No matter–they had obviously been drinking already and were obviously bent on drinking some more. And they were wearing the typical Vegas Bachelorette Party Uniform of short shorts and pink tank tops emblazoned with the bride's name across their chests–*Lisa's Last Days*, in this case. Ron liked Vegas bachelorette parties. And bachelorette parties and Carnaval Court went well together, because they could all order a drink and go dance to the band or just hang out all day and get shitfaced. Ron didn't think he could eat any of them–they all appeared so young and innocent–but he'd sure like to fuck them all. If that were ever possible. Hell, he'd fuck them all at the same time, given the chance. He wondered if zombies had that kind of stamina. He sure did back when he was a human.

Ron saw a commotion just outside the bar. A damn commotion taking his attention away from his bachelorette party orgy fantasy really irritated Ron, so he looked over to see what was going on. A man was arguing with a woman. Nay, he was pushing her around just outside the bar. The words *stupid whore* and *money* were apparently at the center of the argument, because they were the words Ron heard. And the woman in the argument getting pushed around was Bambi.

CHAPTER

-5-

Ron gave up his valuable bar seat–which wasn't literally valuable, really, because it was just a plastic and metal thing, but as in real estate, location, location, location!–and shuffled towards the commotion. Nobody noticed him walk away, and nobody else noticed the commotion; they were too busy watching Beer Belly's wife deep throat Flippy's whipped cream.

"You need to be making me some money, bitch," the Commotion Man said. Bambi apparently had a pimp. And her pimp was apparently angry. Ron felt semi-astute once he had these two things figured out. Maybe zombies aren't so stupid after all. Ron started calling himself Zombie Fuckin' Einstein.

"I'm not very good at this," Bambi said through tears. Her mascara had succumbed to the tears as well, making her look like a sad clown.

Just then, her pimp slapped Bambi hard on the face, right where her mascara was forging a path. Oh, no, you don't, Ron thought, realizing he sounded like a sassy teenager. But you don't. You don't hit a woman. That was against all rules, zombie or otherwise. You don't hit a woman. You eat her and you fuck her but you don't hit her. Never. Neh–ver.

Her pimp slapped Bambi again. "You better get good at it, bitch, cuz I needs my money!"

Ron shuffled over to the pimp, who wasn't dressed like a typical pimp at all. No big floppy hat, no goldfish filled platform shoes, no flared polyester slacks, no nothing. He was just a white kid who looked like a rapper. White t-shirt, new blue jeans, white sneakers, dyed short blond hair. Is this what pimps looked like these days? Ron thought it would have been more fun to be a pimp if you had goldfish in your shoes.

"Hey!" He hollered at the pimp. He was still 10 feet away from the guy, but he really wanted him to stop hitting a woman. Hitting a woman was truly against everything Ron believed in. He had had his troubles with women–especially blondes, go figure–but he had always respected them. And he had never hit a single one. His daddy had taught him well.

"Leave us alone, old man." Old? Ron found this hilarious. Do I look old? Well, compared to you, Eminem Wannabe, maybe.

"Leave her alone." Ron was standing right next to the pimp now. He was obviously moving faster than he used to. Either the alcohol or the anger was fueling him. It was hard to tell at the moment.

"She's my ho." Vanilla Ice got in Ron's face.

"She's..."

"She's what, fuckface?" The pimp had a way with words. Ron, on the other hand...

"My friend."

"Oh, she has friends now?" He turned and slapped Bambi again. She slumped to the ground next to the wall outside the casino. They were far enough back from the Carnaval Court and far enough away from the entrance to the casino that nobody even noticed them. "She don't need no friends. She needs dicks! Cuz I needs my money!"

"I have money. I'll pay you." Ron's speech was coming as fast his movement was now. He sized the guy up. Yeah, he could pay for Bambi. She didn't deserve this. Ron could see that she was probably just some small town girl trying to make a living. Or something. And she was a nice girl, based on Ron's experience with her on the airplane. No matter–you don't hit a woman.

"Oh, really, old man?"

"Money, my room. How much...you need?"

The pimp looked at Bambi, sitting on the ground a few feet away. She had stopped crying, but now her face looked like a demented highway. Her mascara was the highway's outside lines and her snot was the divider. "She ain't made me shit today, so I need five hundred dollars."

"Done. In my room. Let's go."

"Oh, hell no, I ain't going with you. What if you're a cop?"

"Hahahahaha!" Ron managed a good chuckle. A cop. You have no idea, Justin Bieber. I'm not a cop...but I'm much worse. "Do. I. Look. Like. A. Cop?"

"No, you look like a zombie, actually."

"HAHAHAHA!" Ron laughed louder. Yeah, this was all kinda funny...for a few more minutes.

"Yeah, you're right. You ain't a cop. You're too ugly to be a cop. Let's go get my money."

"Let's go."

The pimp looked over at Bambi. Her sad-clown-demented-highway face was now red on one side, where her pimp had hit her. "You stay here and wait for me, bitch."

"Yeah, wait, bitch," Ron said, as he winked at Bambi. Then he and the pimp laughed.

"Now you get it, old man! Let's go get my money!" And those were the last words the pimp ever spoke in public.

CHAPTER

-6-

Riding up in the elevator at Casino Royale with the pimp–Ron had a room on the fourth floor and the Casino Royale elevators were about as slow as an act of Congress–Ron asked the pimp his name.

"Joaquin," the pimp said with a bit of nervousness in his voice.

"Huh, that's a good name."

"It is. You ain't a cop, is you?" Joaquin's command of the English language was not much of a command, really, Ron thought. Is you? Is I? Fer shizzle!

"No. I'm a zombie, remember?" They both laughed, for entirely different reasons. Ron took great pleasure in realizing the humor in the divide in perceptions of that sentence. To you, Ron thought, it's a joke. To me, however...

"You really a friend of Barbie's?"

"That her name?"

"Somethin' like dat."

"Yeah, we friends, yo." Ron wondered if adopting Joaquin's less-than-educated-vernacular was helping anything. Perhaps he could get Joaquin to be comfortable. It would certainly help what was coming. Ron hated to fight with his meals, if possible. It made the meat tough. And he forgot to bring the *au jus*.

"Where'd you meet?"

"What, meat? Oh, sorry, *meet*. On the plane."

"Join the mile high club, huh?"

"Yeah, nigga." Ron wondered if zombies were allowed to say that word. If he recalled correctly–and he felt like the recall portion of his brain still worked–calling a white kid pimp who looked like Eminem *nigga* was probably okay. He hoped it would bring him closer to Joaquin, in a metaphysical sense. Metazombical sense? Anyway, it would help later. Stupid humans liked to fight back if given the chance. And he didn't want to give faux Justin Timberlake a chance.

"I'm down, yo." Joaquin said as he offered Ron a fist bump. No, Ron thought, but you're soon to be, as he fist bumped Joaquin back.

The elevator stopped at the 14th floor. They got out and turned left towards room 1413. Ron pulled out his card key and opened the door.

"You first," Ron said. He was being polite, among other things.

"This is a swanky place," Joaquin declared, as he walked in the room. There was no accounting for taste, Ron thought. If I had wanted a swanky place, fucker, I would have eaten a banker and stolen his credit cards.

"Thank Kenny Jones."

"What? Who?" Joaquin was obviously confused. Fine, Ron thought. Be confused. Get lost in your thoughts. I need a moment to prepare. And let the meat rest. It was something he learned in a cooking class.

"My brains. Uh, business partner. He paid."

"Oh. Hey, nigga, you got my money? Motherfucker better not be ripping me off." Oh, that's not what's happening here at all, Ron thought. I mean, I might be ripping off your arms...your legs...your head...

"Sure, nigs. Let me get it, yo." Ron walked over to the closet, where the safe was. He reached in, put in the safe code–666, which Ron made up and thought was funny–and opened the safe. He grabbed his money and a large blade steel hunting knife he had purchased from some McCarran Airport shop earlier and turned to face Joaquin with the knife hidden in his right hand. He handed Joaquin some hundred dollar bills with his left hand.

"Here you go, motherfucker," Ron said, as he plunged the knife deep into Joaquin's stomach with his right hand. "You will never, ever, EVER hit a woman again." Joaquin stumbled back and fell onto the bed.

"WHAT. THE. FUCK," Joaquin yelled.

Ron pulled the knife out and showed it to Joaquin. "This the fuck, asshole. Never hit a woman again." He plunged the knife hard into Joaquin's chest, below the heart. Sure, this all might end a little more quickly if Ron simply stabbed him in the head or throat or heart, but Ron didn't really want to make a mess of Joaquin's head or throat or heart with a knife. He wanted that damage to be more organic. He wanted to do it himself. With his teeth. It tasted better that way. At that moment, Ron realized he had a lot of rules as a zombie. Maybe that's why he was still around. He was like a vegan organic zombie, who shops at Whole Body.

"WHATTHEFUCKMOTHERFUCKERIMAKILLYOUASS-MOTHERFUCKERCOCKSUCKER." Ron was always amazed at how people at the sudden end of their lives could only speak in curse words. Loud curse words. Really, Ron thought, couldn't we all be a little more polite when the end is near? "Say, old chap, you've stabbed me and I'm about to die. Might we have some tea and crumpets prior to me passing on?" Ron said all this out loud, with his best zombie British accent. Somehow, Joaquin was not amused. Somehow, Joaquin had found a gun. Somehow, he was pointing it at Ron. Hmm, Ron thought, I wonder if he knows I'm a zombie. I wonder if he knows he needs to shoot me in the head.

Ron wasn't about to give Joaquin the time to even think that far ahead. He leaped at Joaquin, still on the bed, and took Joaquin's gun away from him while sinking his teeth into his face. Damn, Ron thought, I am fast. Lunch is motivating.

If you're a human–and if you're reading this, you probably are–you might consider what dining does for a zombie. Say you, as a human, could eat the finest meal at the finest restaurant on the planet and say you could have the best wine with this meal and say you could order the best fucking dessert the earth has ever produced and say you could have an earth shattering orgasm for an hour straight while eating the unbelievable meal. All this while draped in silk and being fed grapes by your boss's wife. That's what dining is like for a zombie. And you wonder why they always appear to be so joyous about their meals.

For a white rapper pimp with a funny name, Joaquin tasted like everything Ron liked. It had been a while since he had dined, obviously, but Ron wasn't sure Joaquin wasn't the best thing he'd ever tasted. His biceps were like hot butter on a medium-grilled flank steak, his quads–when eaten with muscle tissue bits–reminded him of the homemade chicken and dumplings his grandmother (RIP) used to make. And his brain? Well, Ron thought, for such a dumbass, Joaquin's brain went down like a slutty sophomore girl on prom night. It tasted like oysters on the half shell from some restaurant in Boston that Ron couldn't remember the name of. Now he wished he had some *au jus* to wash it all down with. Actually, Ron thought, he did. He had blood. Which, frankly, was everywhere. Ron took a piece of Joaquin's brain out with his teeth and dipped it into blood sauce on the floor and slurped it down. Yeah, like oysters. Which might still be alive. Joaquin's body twitched. He moaned. Ah, well, Ron thought, he'll be dead soon enough. I need to dine. And if Joaquin is fresh, he'll taste better. Nothing worse than stale human to a zombie. Ron wondered if he could invent born-on dating for humans. Then, when he opened his freezer at home to take something out for dinner, he could check to make sure he wasn't eating a human past his/her prime. *Nope, this tibia has been in here for more than 6 months. I better throw it out.*

Joaquin moaned one final time as Ron reached into his chest and pulled his heart out. "Who says pimps don't have heart," he asked nobody. "I say pimps don't have heart!" he exclaimed as he took a bite of Joaquin's heart with his full mouth, like eating a head of iceberg lettuce straight out of the crisper drawer. "Joaquin, you sure is delicious, motherfucker. Fer shizzle!" He took another bite and pondered the word motherfucker. He was quite happy he could say it–four syllables!–but as a word, it doesn't really make any sense. Who really wants to fuck their mother? Sure, you could claim somebody else does, but do they really? Maybe that's why it's a derogatory term, Ron thought. "I hope you really didn't fuck your mother, like I implied, Joaquin," Ron said out loud. "Cuz that's just sick." He took another bite of Joaquin's heart.

As Joaquin's body stopped moving and Ron dined on various parts–kidney, tendons, biceps–he thought that, at this moment, every part of every human was delicious. This was a smorgasbord of the best flavors on earth, he decided. Hell, he wished there were other zombies around so he could start a business delivering sides of lawyers to their houses. Put the lawyers' bodies into freezers, dine for months at a time! As he poured the blood from one of Joaquin's legs into a hotel room glass, Ron congratulated himself on his ingenuity. He raised his glass. "A toast to me! I'm a fucking entrepreneur! And that's a big fucking word!" Too bad he hadn't thought of this idea when there were other zombies around. Ah, well, Ron thought, as he sipped the blood like a nice glass of Chianti, more for me. Hell, Ron thought, if I could eat EVERY pimp in Vegas, I'd be a happy zombie. If there really is such a thing.

CHAPTER

-7-

fter dining on most of Joaquin, Ron slowly washed his hands in the hotel room sink. He felt energized. He felt...alive, even, and he wanted to savor the feeling for as long as possible. Who knows how often he would get to dine in Vegas? He washed his face with the hotel soap–it smelled like hotel soap lavender, which is to say it didn't smell like lavender at all–and a washcloth, and then slowly looked up to study his face in the mirror. Even with the crap fluorescent light in the dim bathroom, Ron looked about one hundred times better than he did before dining. No, he thought, a thousand times better. Hell, at this rate, he thought, I may not need to find a football field for a few weeks. In fact, I look mostly human. Very human. And I feel like singing and dancing! If this were a Broadway musical, Ron thought, he'd break into a song about how great it feels to eat another human being. "Oh, this feeling has been delivered, because I just ate this man's liver," Ron sang in Broadway musical jest. Not that he knew much about musicals. He had had a girlfriend at one point–a brunette–who was into musicals, so he saw *Rent* and a few others, but he wouldn't say they were his favorite delivery mode for entertainment. But still, he could break into song and dance right now, for sure. Dining as a zombie gave him a feeling that was better than just about any feeling he ever had as a human. Except for sex, of course. Nothing could top that.

He turned towards the hotel room, still singing. "Oh, if only the world could see us, cuz I just ate your pancreas," he sang to the room, stretching out the E in pancreas to make the rhyme work. It's amazing how much dining helps a sense of humor and vocabulary, he thought. If only Ron could eat more often. "If I ate every day I'd be in no pain, and I'd enjoy an *hors d'oeuvres* of your brain!" Man, this was fun. So fun, in fact, that Ron thought he should go do some karaoke. Next door in Harrah's casino was a lounge that had karaoke every night at 6:00. Ron and Jim used to go there and sing after they'd get drunk at Carnaval Court during the day. Yeah, that'd be fun. Sure, there is probably a big difference between a singing, dancing zombie in his own hotel room and one in public, so Ron checked himself in the mirror one more time. Yeah, he looked alive. And yeah, he was going to sing karaoke. What the hell, right? Sometimes you gotta live it up.

First, though, he needed to finish cleaning up the room. He doubted this hotel had a nightly turn-down service, so he wasn't worried about anybody from the hotel coming in to his room this evening, but just in case he was going to dine in his room again, he didn't want his previous meal to give his intentions away to his new meal. It might make it difficult to prepare the new meal. There's truly nothing harder to contain–as a zombie–than a human who knows what's coming, Ron thought. When you get to that point, you spend as much energy getting the meal prepared as you might get from the meal, so what's the point? Gotta keep your meals in the dark, so to speak. Time to clean the room. Just in case I get lucky again, Ron thought. Although, given the way he was feeling right now, if he ate again today he might run back to Colorado and climb a fourteener (a 14,000 foot tall mountain) and be back in Vegas before sunup. He had that much energy. He was like a teenager during his first cocaine binge.

Good thing, too, because there was a bunch of work to do. Blood on the walls, guts on the mini-fridge, bones on the windowsill. Ron Zombie sure didn't eat very neatly. Then again, Ron Human had the same problem. It was something his girlfriends complained about, both blondes and brunettes. They'd go out for barbecue–Ron's favorite–and Ron would have to wear the Pig Bib–so named at his favorite barbecue joint, Los Pulled Porks–because he made a mess. "What the hell are you supposed to do," Ron wondered out loud, "when they make the ribs so succulent?" Ron spotted one of the Joaquin's ribs that he had missed by the Vegas Kickass Visitor's Guide by the window, reached down, and sucked the meat off, spilling blood on his shirt in the process. "See what I mean?"

Ron took Joaquin's undershirt–a wifebeater, ironically–and fashioned a bib out of it, in memory of The Pig Bib. Tying it around his neck, he said, "A Zombie Bib. For messy eaters. I bet I could have sold a ton of these during the Zombie Penetration."

With his bib on, he ate the remaining gut bits on the floor and licked the blood off the walls in quick fashion. For zombies, this was dessert. And this being the Casino Royale, no one would notice the slight stain the blood left behind. The shit lighting would hide it. Or if somebody were to actually replace the lightbulbs in this place, Ron thought, they'd never see it because it was everywhere. Hell, he had redecorated the place, honestly. The carpet was a jumbled mess of a pattern anyway, so you couldn't see where the guts ended and the darker shade of vomit green paint on the walls began. Maybe next time he'd paint the walls with vertical blood stripes, like a boutique hotel in New York or something. Ron briefly considered, for one comic moment, asking the front desk if he could apply to be the Casino Royale's interior designer. "We'll go with a red color scheme."

The bones, however, were a different manner. If he were out at Los Pulled Porks–whose theme song was "You Down With LPP?"– he'd just drop the bones on an adjacent plate, or the floor, or the table, or on his girlfriend's lap, and somebody else would take care of it. But now? This might just be Ron's responsibility. Damn. He looked around the room and spotted his carry-on bag. That would probably work. In eating the pimp, Ron had separated every bone from every other bone, so he was literally in pieces. Small enough pieces to fit into a bag, probably.

"Rest In Pieces, Joaquin," Ron muttered as he sat on the bed. Although, surely, Joaquin was not his real name. He was a white kid who looked like Eminem/Vanilla Ice/Justin Bieber, there was no way Joaquin was his real name. Do pimps have stage names? No matter, Ron thought, although now he was singing 'Walking In LA' by Missing Persons, a song from the '80s. "Joaquin in LA, nobody walks in LA!" Maybe Joaquin was his business name. Yeah, Ron could see that. *Joaquin girls, Joaquin up and down the Strip, just for you!* That'd be pretty funny. Ron took Joaquin's skull and, using his own hand, made it talk. "Hi, Ron, I'm Joaquin, I have girls for you. Direct to you! Well, I did have girls for you, until I hit one of them and I became your dinner. Best meal of your motherfucking life! And now Joaquin is no longer walking in LA OR Las Vegas!" Ron laughed so hard he dropped the skull on the ground and fell off the bed. Oh, it felt good to laugh.

After staring up at the ceiling for a moment from the floor, reveling in his good mood and energy, Ron decided to get moving. It was getting to be almost 6:00, and he really was in the mood for some karaoke. Couldn't waste all this zombie charm on the bathroom mirror and skulls, right? Hell, he was in Vegas! Anything could happen! Ron laughed, as he had already proven that. Anything COULD happen. Like dinner. And breakfast. And lunch, why the fuck not?

He gathered all the small bones and put them in his carry-on messenger bag, which was filling up quickly. Humans have a lot of bones, he thought. Still left on the floor? The skull and sternum bones. Damn, Ron thought, I don't know if those are going to fit. He picked up the skull and stuck it in the outer zipper pouch of the bag, and it made it look like the bag was pregnant. Then he took the sternum and tried to force it into the bag, but it stuck out like a sore thumb. Ron chuckled. When was the last time a sternum looked like a thumb? Oh, what a crazy life. Or post-life, as it were. Corpses never had it so good.

A pregnant bag with a sore thumb wasn't going to go far without attracting attention, so Ron decided to address the situation. First he set the skull and sternum on the carpet, atop a stain. He grabbed the floor lamp next to the bed and brought it down hard on the skull, breaking it into 457 distinct separate pieces. Then he did the same for the sternum bone, which broke into 291 distinct pieces. The floor was covered in 748 human bone fragments, which would easily fit into the bag. Before loading the bag with bones, however, Ron had an idea. He went over to the table in his room, grabbed the digital camera he had stolen from Kenny Jones, lay face up atop the sea of bone fragments, and took a picture of himself, smiling. It was the world's first Zombie Selfie.

CHAPTER
-8-

Slipping through Casino Royale with a carry-on bag was no problem. Sure, it made a crunchy noise when he touched it, but Ron wondered if that was in his imagination. Or, really, if anybody else could hear it. It was probably like a phantom phone ring, in that it wasn't real but somebody thought it was. Hell, in that way, Ron thought, it was a lot like reality television. No matter about the crunch, Ron thought, it's so damn loud in here that if anybody hears anything but slot machines, I'd be really surprised. And I'd have to eat them. Ron wondered if having very powerful ears would qualify somebody to be his late night snack. Hell, he was making the rules, why not?

He found his way back to the parking garage behind the hotel/casino. Ron figured somewhere out here he'd find some dumpster where he could dispose of Joaquin's bones. He had heard that Vegas generated so much trash that the trash collectors never notice when bodies end up in dumpsters, so he figured this was his best shot at disposing of the remains of his dinner. "Ronnie didn't clear his plate, but he tried," he said to no one in particular. All of a sudden, he wished he could find a dog to take care of his scraps...

but being that dogs generally don't hang out on the Vegas strip, a dumpster would have to do.

Sure enough, behind the back portion of the hotel parking garage, behind where the underused Vegas Monorail runs, Ron found a row of metal trash dumpsters. This would do. He looked around to make sure he was by himself, opened a dumpster, and opened the bag and put 1/6 of the bones inside the dumpster. He then repeated this five more times at five new dumpsters. Even if somebody found the bones and figured out who his dinner was, Ron was convinced they wouldn't bother investigating it very far. Joaquin was a pimp, after all. Ron imagined the Vegas police force had far better crimes to investigate than prostitution. Hell, if they spent all their time investigating prostitution, there'd be no cops to look for rapists and burglars and such. Hooking is a big business in Vegas. And Ron figured that cops probably looked the other way when it came to hooking crimes. Really, if this worked, pimps might be the only thing on Ron's menu for a very long time. And if they all tasted like Joaquin, it'd be like repeatedly dining at one of Mario Batali's fancy Vegas restaurants. Or maybe one of Bobby Flay's fancy Vegas restaurants.

After dumping Joaquin's remains–and his carry-on bag–into the dumpsters, Ron headed back towards Harrah's, which was right next door to Casino Royale. Time for some karaoke. He hoped the crowd was fun tonight. After dining, Ron was full of crazy energy. Crazy enough that he might even sing "Don't Stop Believin'," everybody's favorite karaoke song. "Just a small town boy, born and raised in South Detroit," he started singing as he walked through the parking garage.... Out of the corner of his eye, he saw something move. Ron stopped and shifted his gaze toward a corner of the garage. Surely nobody had seen what he had done, right? That would be bad. He stood still for a minute, looking intently towards the corner. Surely nobody knew he was a zombie, right? That would be more than bad, that would be a disaster. One minute you're thinking about singing some karaoke and making some new friends and the next minute you've got a SWAT sniper congratulating himself for blowing your head off from 100 yards. And Ron didn't want to lose his head–not in that way, anyway–so he stood still for a moment, making sure whatever he thought he saw wasn't real. That it was a phantom phone ring.

"Who's there?" Ron asked to nobody in particular. It was a ridiculous question. If anybody was there, certainly they weren't going to answer, right? *Oh, hi, we're here, we just watched you eat and dispose of another human being and we wanted to see what you are going to do next. Is karaoke in the evening's plans?* Right. Really, no matter how many times the question is asked, it is answered exactly 0% of the time. After a few moments, Ron shuffled again towards the casino. Fuck it, he thought, there's nobody there. Still, he was slightly unsettled. If somebody were watching his movements, he could be in a lot of trouble. Or he might have to eat again. Tailing me certainly puts you on my snack list, Ron thought, with a bit of unease. Surely if somebody is following me, he thought, it'd be harder to get them on my plate than if I were following them. He spun around quickly to see if anybody was following him, but the Casino Royale parking garage on a Tuesday evening in October was empty. Apparently. Still, as he shuffled along he kept his eyes peeled...which was funny, because the skin around his eyes was literally peeling.

Inside Harrah's, Ron could hear karaoke music playing from the lounge. Somebody was butchering "Total Eclipse of the Heart." God, he hated slow songs at karaoke. He wondered if *crappy karaoke singer* could put somebody on his plate. Hell, if that were true, Ron could eat himself! He laughed, just as he passed the tank-top bachelorette party from Carnaval Court today, standing at some Kardashian Kaos slot machines watching one obviously drunk member of their party try to line up pictures of one of the Kardashian sisters on the reels. Okay, so now he was horny, too. Not because of any of the Kardashian sisters, but because the bach-elorette party consisted of entirely 100% Grade A Hot Brunette Female, Ron thought. Then again, his standards were low as a hu-man. How high could they be as a zombie? He hoped the tank-top bachelorettes were coming to sing some songs tonight. That would make this day perfect, as far as zombie days go. And give him a chance to try out his zombie charm.

Ron went into the karaoke lounge, a low-lit bar, basically, to grab a seat. CJ, the karaoke host, recognized Ron. "Hey, Ron, how's it goin'? You and Jim going to do "Fight For Your Right" tonight?" Boy, for only coming to Vegas three or four times a year, Ron and Jim sure made an impression on people, Ron thought. Although, honestly, they had been coming here three or four times a year... okay, six or seven times a year...okay, eight!...for many years, so maybe they were regulars, as much as visitors to Vegas could be.

"Nah, CJ, Jim's not here." The words flowed from him like a hu-man, Ron thought. "But I would like to sing some White Zombie. Do you have that?"

CJ chuckled. "Wow, that's different. Sure, we have that, I think. Let me check." He went to check his Big Karaoke Book. CJ had been running this particular Vegas karaoke night for many years and, thusly, his list of songs was as big as a dictionary, times three. And it was all in one giant yellow binder with yellow Karaoke Cau-tion tape all over the cover.

"We have that one White Zombie song that people like," CJ yelled over to Ron. "You wanna sing that one?"

"Yes," Ron yelled back, as best he could, as he sat down.

"Great," CJ said. He started in with his karaoke shtick. He'd been doing this so long that it was a science. "Welcome, friends, lovers, and alimony seekers, to the best karaoke show on the Vegas Strip! Well, the only karaoke show on the Vegas Strip! That starts at 6:00 in the afternoon! And is located here, inside Harrah's casino!" Ron laughed. Some things never change...most of all, the shtick.

It was funny. Ron came to Vegas to escape, but after being here for six hours, he felt like he was at home. "We have three hours to fill with music and I know you singers are out there, so come on in and fill out a paper with a song you want to sing and we'll get you hooked up. And maybe, if you're lucky, you'll hook up with me later." CJ was always a perv, but the crowd loved him, because, well, he was a lovable perv and because, well, the crowd was nearly always drunk. A day of hanging in Vegas will do that to a person. And a zombie. As CJ launched into his usual get-the-crowd-going song, "Viva Las Vegas," Ron pondered the thought. Was he drunk? No, not really. He had just a sip of his gin and tonic earlier, and he had a few quarts of blood after that. The average human adult has nearly five quarts of blood in him, and Ron figured he probably spilled two of those in the room. Meaning he had probably had three quarts of blood. No wonder he felt high. Or drunk. No, high. It was a feeling he recognized from shuffling around Colorado, where secondhand marijuana smoke is a part of daily life. Ron scanned his mind, decided he felt well enough to keep drinking, and ordered a gin and tonic from the waitress as CJ sang.

"Bright lights city gonna set my soul..." Ron looked around the room. To his left, close to the karaoke machine, he saw a middle aged woman who was always here whenever Ron and Jim were here. She was a good singer, took her singing seriously, sat by herself, and appeared to drink water the entire time she sat in the lounge. Really, she was the exception to the rule. Most karaoke singers in Vegas were there to drink and show off and get a little crazy. Ron fit into that crowd, even as a zombie. He was gonna put on a show tonight!

"There's a thousand pretty women, waiting out there..." So far, the crowd was light, but Ron could tell it was going to get better as the night went on. He had that feeling...or maybe it was just the aftertaste of Joaquin's blood in his mouth. Damn, did he forget to brush his teeth after dining?

"Next up, we have an old friend of the karaoke, doing something different tonight. Ron, c'mon up!" Ron grabbed his gin and tonic off the waitress's tray as she walked by and went up to the karaoke stage. Not much of a stage, really, more like a space between a piano and the first row of tables in the room. The room's big money maker was dueling pianos later with hot blonde twin women playing piano, taking requests from the audience, so the piano had to stay and the karaoke "stage" was an afterthought. Hell, karaoke was really a second class citizen in this room, Ron thought, kinda like zombies in a human world. He dropped a five dollar bill in CJ's tip jar and approached the microphone. Joaquin's money was going to a good cause tonight. That cause? Gettin' crazy. On a Saturday night. In Vegas. Nothing more than that...or so Ron thought.

CHAPTER
-9-

White Zombie's song "Thunder Kiss '65" came out in 1992 on the album *La Sexercisto: Devil Music Vol. 1.* Ironically–in the context of our story–its B-Side was "Welcome to Planet Motherfucker," which is exactly where Ron felt he lived sometimes. Upon examination, "Thunder Kiss '65," which was not popular until it was aired on *Beavis and Butt-head,* is not discernibly about thunder or kisses or 1965. In fact, its lyrics are about as unintelligible as anything since REM's first record came out. In fact, "Thunder Kiss '65" sounds like a zombie, grunting over a heavy metal groove. It is the perfect song for a perfect zombie to attempt at perfect Las Vegas karaoke.

Ron didn't really know "Thunder Kiss '65" very well, but when considering songs to perform at karaoke he had to take into account his condition. Certainly, in his condition, Ron knew that Led Zeppelin songs–his favorite–were probably out of the question. His voice was noticeably lower than it was when he was alive, and Robert Plant's vocal gymnastics always went into a higher range than he was probably capable of these days. So he was going to sing "Thunder Kiss '65." Ron Zombie sings White Zombie, a band led by none other than Rob Zombie. The irony was not lost on Ron Zombie, not for a minute. His real name was Ron Watson, anyway. He just called himself Ron Zombie in his head...probably because it sounded like Rob Zombie.

The music started and Ron closed his eyes. He used to get nervous at karaoke, but he discovered that if he closed his eyes for a moment when he got on stage, he could get over it. And he usually delivered a good performance...he thought. Truth is, he couldn't always remember his karaoke performances, because he was often drunk. But he was told, after the fact, that he was a damn fine karaoke singer. When he was human.

He opened his eyes as the vocals kicked in and realized he had no idea what the lyrics to the song were. Damn. And, for some reason, the karaoke machine was not showing lyrics on any of the three giant screens on the walls of the room, like usual. Shit. It's a good thing "Thunder Kiss '65" is not an intricate song, because Ron started singing, in place of whatever the real lyrics are, the only lyric he could think of at that moment: *Brains.* So it sounded like this:

"Brains brains brains brains brains in brains brains on a brains," guitar lick, "Brains brains brains brains brains in brains brains on a brains," guitar lick. Eventually the chorus kicked in and Ron sang, "Brains, yeah, ow! Brains, yeah, ow!"

To his surprise, a crowd was gathering just outside the open wall of the karaoke room, where the casino was. And the crowd was enthralled by Ron's zombie "impression." At least that's what Ron hoped they thought he was doing. Really, Ron thought, this was a damn funny song to sing at karaoke. Not much in the way of lyrics, just a bunch of grunting, and everybody knew the song. Ron couldn't believe this shit was actually played on the radio in 1993. And, more so, he couldn't believe this shit was drawing a crowd in Vegas this year. He and Jim used to say, "Vegas doesn't have to make sense," and here Ron was, proving it.

"Brains, ow, yeah!" Ron tried dancing. He always found that karaoke made him want to dance, and when he danced he danced crazy, like a headless chicken with no sense of rhythm. It was his shtick, really. Ron was a fearless showman who could work a karaoke crowd...when he was alive. Now? Now he felt like his dancing was more like shuffling. Or like the dancing his great- grandparents used to do at family weddings, when they were in their late 80s. Very slow and deliberate. The Palm Tree at one-eighth speed. Still, Ron was half-timing his dancing to the music–moving on every other beat instead of every beat–so it looked deliberate. Almost like slow motion. Or the Palm Tree at one-half speed. Which is four times the speed his great-grandparents could muster. It's funny the times you think about your great-grandparents, Ron thought.

As he grunted along to Thunder Kiss and shuffled along to the guitar solo, the tank-top bachelorette party from Carnaval Court walked in and, without even finding a table, started dancing in the small dance area in front of Ron. Oh, this is good, he thought. Seven young slabs of pure hotness gyrating together just in front of him...all of a sudden, he was moving at full speed, rocking the karaoke room like he did when he was human. He thought his brain might explode from the excitement, which would decorate this room like his own hotel room. He stuck his tongue out at the girls and struck his Zombie Pose as the song ended and the room went a little crazy. Maybe it was a lot crazy, Ron thought. It's hard to tell when you're a zombie and you're singing karaoke for the first time as an undead. Whatever, Ron thought, they love me. He held his Zombie Pose for a moment as the bachelorette–judging by her tank top, which said *I'm getting married, so buy me a drink*–from the bachelorette party came up and said, "You're so cool! What do you call that thing you're doing?"

Ron thought for a moment, came up with nothing, and said the first thing that came to his zombie brain. "I call it Zombie... ing."

"Zombieing! Yes!" The bachelorette toasted Ron with her drink and, as he sat down at his table with his own drink, he realized he was home. Las Vegas was a good place for a zombie.

The bachelorette party went on stage, all seven of them, all drunk as shit, and butchered "Don't Stop Believin'" by Journey like it was a pig after a spit roast. Small town girls, indeed, Ron thought. I guess I don't get to sing that song today. Although, truthfully, this was the kind of display that CJ lived for, because it drew a crowd. Nothing better if you're walking by the lounge than peering in and seeing seven hot drunks chicks destroying the number one karaoke song in the world. That's the kind of entertainment that might make you stop and order a drink or three. And tip the karaoke master handsomely.

"Thank you." Somebody sat at Ron's table. He turned to look. A blonde.

"Bambi? Bambi!" She stuck her tongue down his throat, just like on the plane...and somehow, Ron didn't mind. In fact, he was excited to see her, and excited to have her tongue down his throat. Sure beat eyeballs.

"You saved me today." She had retreated from the kiss, but her tits were still there, barely restrained behind a pink tank top. Hello girls, Ron wanted to say, but he didn't want to be an asshole. Would saying hello to a hooker's tits make him an asshole? Where exactly was that proverbial line in the hooker's tits sand?

"I–what?"

"From Joaquin."

"Brains. Oh, yeah." She sure looked nice, Ron thought. Her face didn't show where Joaquin had hit her, she was wearing a pair of boot-cut blue jeans–Ron's favorite kind–and her breasts looked amazing in pink. Ron thought he better stop calling them tits.

They had met twice now, so they should be a little more formal. Breasts from now on. Yeah, it was a funny second date rule, but it was Ron's funny second date rule. And he was far enough along in his nascent zombie-hood to have rules that didn't involve tibias, blood or football field chalk. Call it maturation.

"You're funny."

"Duh." Ron was surprised he could reincorporate, much less remember their earlier conversation, after all these hours. His brain functionality was clearly improving.

"And sweet."

"Buy you a drink?" Ron figured he could make up for his earlier reluctance. Besides, she was wearing boot-cut jeans. And full on Grade A countrified boots. A girl in those jeans, pink tank top, and countrified boots deserved a drink. Especially when she was sitting at Ron's table.

"Yes, please." Ron signaled for the waitress to come to their table. Bambi's breasts ordered a light beer and Ron ordered another gin and tonic. Well, really, Bambi herself ordered a light beer, but she looked very hot doing it. So maybe her jeans ordered it. Or her boots. Ron couldn't decide which part of Bambi was the hottest–or the best at ordering light beer. Really, all of her was hot. She was like the sun of women, radiating her hotness onto all the other lesser women planets. Ron wondered if his similes were forever fucked up.

"Are you hurt?" Ron really wanted to know, because he was still pissed that Joaquin hit her. That man had no heart. Literally, now.

Bambi touched her hand to her face. "Nothing a little foundation won't cover up."

"Or football field chalk."

"You ARE funny, Kenny! Football field chalk. Hahaha."

She was cute when she laughed. Hell, Ron thought, she was cute all the time. She wasn't nearly this cute on the airplane, he thought. Or maybe, on the airplane, he wasn't ready for this attention. Or maybe he wasn't ready to notice. Or maybe he was hungry then. All he knew was that she was extremely cute now, and, while he was full in his belly, he was feeling a different kind of hunger in other places. No, he wasn't feeling in his dick for once, he was feeling it in the blackest of places: his heart.

"You're funny, Bambi. And cute."

"Was Joaquin looking for me after you paid him?"

"What?"

"After you gave him the money? I owe you, by the way."

"Oh, uh, I don't know if he was looking for you." He might have been, Ron thought. He might have been looking with his eyeballs that went into Ron's belly like skinned grapes. Yeah, if he could see through intestines and skin he might have been looking for you. He might be looking for you right now.

"I left. I don't want to be a hooker anymore."

"You shouldn't."

"Be a hooker?"

A fat balding man was on stage, making "Bad Moon Rising" his own personal off-key theme song. Ah, singing tourists, Ron thought. People come to Vegas and get drunk and think they're Frank Fucking Sinatra.

"No, you shouldn't be a hooker."

"I won't. But what if Joaquin finds me?"

Oh, he's not gonna find you, Ron thought. Not unless he re-animates in the six different trash bins behind Casino Royale. Even then, Ron ate enough of him to know that he's be merely a smashed skull and little else. Ron smiled at the thought. Then he burped. Ah, Joaquin tasted good coming up, too. He thought about sharing this with Bambi, but thought better. Zombie discretion and all that.

"Are you laughing at me? And do you need a piece of gum?"

"I'm not laughing at you. And yes, I'd like a piece of gum. I forgot to brush my teeth when we got here."

"I can tell. What'd you eat? It smells like steak."

"I did have steak." Tartare, if you must know. Ron didn't like this line of questioning, so he changed the subject. "Do you sing?"

"Do I sing? Of course I sing. That's what brought me in this place. I took off after you saved me, went home and took a shower, and decided I was no longer going to be a hooker. That realiza-tion–that moment, Kenny, thanks to you–gave me so much life, so much energy, that I had to get out. So I came down to Casino Royale to apply for a job and then here to see CJ."

"You know CJ?"

"Hell yeah, this is my karaoke bar."

"This is my karaoke bar, honey." Ron grabbed Bambi's hand. His black heart told him to. And he was smart enough, even in his state, to know when to listen to his black heart.

"Oh, it's honey now, is it?" Bambi put her arm around Ron. "You're cute, Kenny. Maybe we should sing a song together. I saw what you did with that White Zombie song, and you're good."

I'm good, Ron thought. Little do you know how good I am. I saved you from a life of fucking random guys for money and had a good meal, to boot. Yeah, I'm good...and getting better all the time.

"You think so?"

"I know so. I see a lot of bad karaoke singers. You're good."

Ron was surprised she thought he was good. He didn't think he was very good, in spite of his internal bravado. Maybe he was evaluating himself on the wrong scale, though. Maybe he was eval-uating himself on the human scale, and he should have been using the zombie scale. Yeah, he was probably pretty good for a zombie. Jeez, what scale was Bambi using?

Bambi grabbed one of the karaoke request papers on the table and a pencil and started filling it out. Ron took a swig of his drink and put his hand on her bare arm. "What are you going to sing?"

"What are we going to sing?"

"What?"

"We, silly. We're going to duet. It's my karaoke bar and it's your karaoke bar, so let's see what we got." She got up and took the paper to CJ. Ron watched her boot cut jeans wiggle across the floor atop her countrified boots and counted his zombie blessings. Bambi had a fine ass to go with her fine breasts. Even a zombie recognized that she was a fine woman. She sat back down next to Ron and purred into his ear. "You ready to sing with me, honey?" Somehow, she made it sound like she was going to fuck his brains out. If this was singing, Ron was all over it.

"Oh, hell yeah. This is my karaoke bar."

The tank-top bachelorette party was just finishing up butchering "Pour Some Sugar On Me" by Def Leppard, but Ron barely noticed. A group of tank-top bachelorettes didn't stand out so much when you had a hot blonde purring in your ear. Perspective and all that. He took a drink and heard the opening beats of "You're the One That I Want" from the *Grease* soundtrack.

"Ron and Bambi, you're up!" CJ called them to the stage. Oh, wow, Ron thought, she was serious about singing together. Okay. He wondered, for just a moment, how many syllables were in the song, and then Bambi grabbed his arm, rubbing her amazing left breast against it, and led him to the stage. All of a sudden, it didn't matter how many syllables were in any song in the world, because Ron had a hard-on and he was going on stage with the most beautiful woman in the universe. Breasts rubbing against your arm have a way of making your perception go that way.

"I got brains, they're multiplying..." Ron could see the words on the screen as he grabbed the microphone, but he was still throwing out the accidental *brains* once in a while, sort of like a possessed Tourette's Syndrome patient. He simply couldn't help it. And besides, he had an erection that he was hoping would go unnoticed, and that took his focus off of singing. He looked down and realized Kenny's pants were loose enough that his erection was barely noticeable and he also noticed that the height of the bar in front of him hid his erection from the room anyway, so he relaxed.

"You better shape up..." Bambi was swaying in her pink tank top and jeans, singing directly to Ron, and she was radiant. Truly, Ron thought, if she truly quit hooking today, it gave her some life. Or maybe she was always like that. Nah, she looked a lot more... human than she did on the airplane. Human and hot.

"You're the one that I want, ooh ooh ooh, honey!" They sang the chorus together, and Ron thought he sounded very nearly human. It was a long way from White Zombie, but maybe Ron needed to warm up with that. Hell, while Bambi sang the chorus, Ron even went up a third above it and harmonized with her. The bachelorette party was up dancing again, the bachelorette herself was Zombieing, CJ was clapping his hands, and Ron was looking over at Bambi, incredulous that his first day in Vegas had gone so well. At this moment in time, Ron had no doubt in his undead mind that coming to Vegas was the right decision. He had made a good decision...for once.

want to thank you again, honey. I start tomorrow as a Dealer-tainer at Casino Royale. I just got the text." They were driving east, away from the Strip, on one of Las Vegas' many nondescript asphalt roadways. It didn't matter which one, Ron thought. They were all the same anyway, especially at night.

"Brains."

"Yes, darlin', I did use my brains, thanks for noticing." Bambi had her hand on his leg, so it wasn't really brains that were on Ron's mind, but whatever. He was still happy for her. He was hoping to be happier for himself at some point tonight. And her calling him darlin' sure didn't dim his feelings–he loved it when a woman got all down-home with him.

"Congratulations."

"If you hadn't saved me from Joaquin, I never would have grown a pair of these," she gently grabbed Ron's balls, "and found the courage to start a new career as Marilyn Monroe."

Ron found it difficult to talk with his balls being caressed. "Mar.....ilyn?"

"That's who I'm impersonating as a Dealertainer. I'm Marilyn and I'm a dealer. Get it? Entertainer AND dealer?" Oh, Ron got it, all right. He hoped the fact that Bambi's hand was still in his crotch was a good sign that he might really get it later. It was a good thing Bambi's blue 1967 Ford Mustang was an automatic. Sure, it was a little down on its luck, for a Mustang, but it was a good *grope my balls* car with an automatic transmission, Ron thought. No shifting, all caressing. A 1967 Ford Mustang was a sexy motherfucking car, especially right now.

"You're funny."

"Before we get to my place, I have a confession to make." Oh, really, Ron thought. A confession? This is interesting. I'm a zombie, and she's confessing to me. What could possibly top being a zombie, confession-wise? Did she used to be a man? No, no way. If that were true, her surgeon had a highly refined appreciation for the finer parts of a woman's body and was an artist, to boot. Was she running from the law? Ha, Ron thought. Aren't we all running from something? Was she a zombie as well? No, no way. Ron saw her breasts on the plane. Those weren't zombie breasts. If they were, Ron should have been dating zombies his whole life. Then again, did he even know what zombie breasts look like?

"Okay."

"I don't live alone." Oh, there it is. She's married. Maybe I'll eat her husband, Ron thought. Ron hoped he was an asshole so he had an excuse.

"I live with my brother," she continued. "More for convenience than anything. I fly to Colorado to visit Emily–my daughter–as often as I can, and I don't like coming home to an empty house. So I live with David."

"Okay. A daughter?"

"Yes. Emily's seven. I lost custody of her a few years ago, and she lives with my parents in Colorado Springs. Her father passed on."

"I'm sorry."

"Yeah, me too. The best laid plans and all that."

"And all that." Certainly, all that, Ron thought. The best laid plans go awry for just about everybody, don't they? Everybody has a story, everybody has a confession, everybody goes off track at some point. They call it life. Or death, as it were.

"Do you have a confession for me?" She was looking Ron in the eye, when she really should have been driving, but the truth was they were on the outskirts of Las Vegas, heading east, and there was no traffic, and the road was as straight as a math major at Harvard. So the Mustang pretty much drove itself while Bambi made googly-eyes at Ron. He liked googly eyes.

"Not yet." That wasn't a lie, right? He did have a confession, certainly, but he didn't want to confess anything to her just yet. He didn't want to ruin his chances. Still, she was going to find out, he realized. Probably when he had to take off his clothes. Ron wondered if Bambi liked to do it in the dark. That would certainly help.

Ron's half-assed answer didn't seem to faze Bambi. "Here we are." They turned into the parking lot of a three story run-down apartment building with a courtyard, out by where the desert turned hilly, east of Las Vegas proper. The parking lot appeared to be full of nothing but late 1970s American made muscle cars in various states of decline. A 1969 Camaro sat wheel-less, on concrete blocks. Bambi parked next to it.

Ron looked up at the building's sign and read out loud. "The Acapulco Arms." Why the hell does it seem like everything in Vegas is named after vacation destinations and/or body parts? What's next, *The Bermuda Breasts*? *The Panama Peckers*?

"This is the place. It's not the Bellagio, but it's mine. Well, ours. Mine and David's. We like it. People don't bother us here, and it's far enough away from the Strip that I never accidentally run into somebody I've...well, you know."

"But you're done with that now."

"Yes. I'm done with everybody but you. I owe you one." She leaned over from her bucket seat and kissed Ron on the cheek. Then she opened her door, stepped out, and turned before Ron got a chance to admire her ass in those jeans one more time. She looked at Ron. "Are you coming in? Or do I have to do you right here in Lustang?"

"Did you say Lustang?"

"Lustang the Mustang. She's my baby. She's been with me since high school. C'mon inside. I don't want Lustang to see how I'm going to repay you for saving me, because it's gonna be"–Bambi purred the next word–"naughty."

Ron got out of the car, adjusted his erection, and closed the door. A 1968 Plymouth Roadrunner next to him nodded its approval, in Ron's mind, of what Ron was about to do. Ron was sure a 1968 Plymouth Roadrunner had seen plenty of action in its own time, so he nodded back. This was probably gonna be good...as long as the 'zombie thing' didn't get in the way. Ron wondered exactly how many instances of zombie-human relations there had ever been in the world. Would this possibly be the first? If it happened at all? What exactly were the chances of being a zombie taking down a zombie-human relationship? Ron wondered if he could bet on that in a Vegas sportsbook. Yeah, I'd like to put $100 against the 100-1 odds that a zombie might actually be able to fuck a hot blonde human woman.

Bambi's apartment on the second floor at the back of courtyard was straight out of the 1950s and hadn't been remodeled since. Laminate floors, wood paneling, an electric stove in a tiny kitchen–...but Bambi and David kept it up like it was a 21st century castle. Everything was immaculately clean, the walls were painted bright colors, and there was a dog. Not that that was part of Ron's 21st century castle thought process, but it sure interrupted that when it came up to Ron and started barking at him. A Black Lab, Ron guessed. He wondered if dogs had a zombie sense.

"Killer, sit." Killer? Ron laughed. "He's friendly, honey, once he gets to know you." Sure, Ron thought, that's what they all say. *He's friendly once he gets to know you.* Ron knew for a fact this wasn't true, because many of his girlfriends had had dogs that never liked him, even after they got to know him. *I don't know what's wrong with Fluffy*, the girlfriend would say after a few weeks of dating. 'She liked all my other boyfriends.' Maybe that's why Ron had few lasting relationships with women. Their dogs didn't like him. Stupid dogs.

"Hi Killer," Ron said. Killer came up to Ron, who had his hand out, and licked it. And licked it again. Then he sat down and wagged his tail. Great dog, Ron thought. Maybe this stood a chance after all.

"Wow, he really likes you," Bambi said. "He's never liked any of my other boyfriends much. Not that you're my boyfriend or anything."

"I have a way with dogs," Ron lied.

"I guess so. Do you want a drink?"

"Where's your brains?"

"What?"

"Your brother, sorry."

"Oh, he's at work. He works security at Excalibur. Drink?" Bambi was holding a bottle of bourbon.

"Yes, please." Was this really happening? She looked good in jeans, she drove a Mustang, she was nice, and she liked bourbon. She might have been the perfect woman, except for the color of her hair...but Ron had a feeling he could look past that small detail.

Bambi went to the kitchen and poured two cups of bourbon, neat, and handed one to Ron. "Here you go. Let me show you around. By *around*, I mean my bedroom." She led Ron by the hand to her bedroom, which was decorated in a distinctly neat and clean 21st century IKEA style. Ron decided a neat and clean IKEA bedroom would be just fine for what he hoped was about to transpire.

Sure, Ron thought, I could be picky about decorating choices and bag the evening, but *I can't stay and fuck you till you're sore because I don't like furniture made out of Swedish particle board and laminate* wasn't going to please Bambi. Or Ron's erection. Besides, he didn't really give a shit about furniture. Maybe he should, being a grown up and all, but when you've been dead and undead, furniture falls off the *I Give A Shit About This* list pretty fast.

"This is nice," Ron said. Bambi closed the door behind him and went into the bathroom attached to the bedroom. "Make yourself comfortable, I'll be right back." Make myself comfortable? I'm a zombie–how comfortable can I possibly be? I'm constantly worried about humans figuring out my true nature and killing me, I'm always looking for somebody to eat, I have a damn conscience so that whoever I eat has to deserve it, and I've got an erection that would scare the people at Viagra. Comfortable? Riiiiiight. That's gonna happen.

Ron could hear Bambi taking her clothes off in the bathroom, so he took off his shirt and looked in the mirror over the dresser. Damn, he thought, I really do look like a zombie. Shit. He put his shirt back on and turned off the light, turning the bedroom pitch black. This might work, he thought. If she can't see I'm a zombie, maybe we can just do it and I can leave before the light goes back on. But Ron didn't want to leave. No, he wanted to stay. And he wanted Bambi to know the truth. Somehow, Ron's zombie conscience was driving this train, and there was only track to be on: the truth track. Ron laughed. The Truth Track? *C'mon down, you're the next contestant*! Surely, there was a better metaphor somewhere. Ron wasn't sure he had time to think of it, though. At this moment, he was more concerned with how he was going to deal with the next few minutes than with metaphors. He enjoyed a good metaphor as much as the next zombie, but depending how the next few minutes went, he might get laid. And Ron had his priorities. He hadn't been laid as a zombie and wasn't sure it was going to rival human sex for sheer stupid pleasure, but he sure as hell wanted to find out. He turned the light back on.

Bambi opened the door from the bathroom and stepped out wearing a white cotton bathrobe and nothing else, Ron hoped. She looked angelic and slutty, all at the same time–just what every guy wants. Ron's erection verified that.

"Bambi, remember when you made your confession?" It was now or never, Ron thought. If I fake it and do this with the lights off, I might get laid once. But somehow, once wasn't going to be enough with this woman, Ron thought. This isn't just about my erection; it's about my zombie soul. I need to tell her the truth and have a clear conscience going into it. Maybe both my boner and my heart can get some action.

"Yes, honey," Bambi purred. "You didn't have one." Her bathrobe opened slightly to reveal the top of her right breast. Ron remembered that breast in detail from the airplane. Damn, he hoped telling her the truth was a good idea, because he was going to be highly disappointed if this led nowhere. Hell, Ron thought, of course this was going to lead nowhere. I'm a fucking zombie. Who hoped to soon be a zombie fucking. Dammit. Nothing good could come of this.

"I do have one."

"Of course you do, honey." She kissed him gently on the cheek and let her left breast fall out of her robe. It rubbed against Ron's arm softly as if to say, *Hi, I'm here. Need a roommate?*

"I–uh..." All of a sudden, Ron had goosebumps and was very nervous. Were zombies supposed to be nervous? Weren't zombies just brimming with confidence all the time? Seriously, Ron thought, he never experienced any trepidation when slurping on somebody's gizzard, why now? He could go out with a bunco of zombies and gorge himself on tibias, fibulas, and all the other -ibias and -ibulas parts of the human body without so much as a moment of hesitation, and now he was nervous? This made no sense.

Except it did. He thought he was about to have sex with somebody he really liked. All humans know that the first time you have sex with somebody you really like the entire event and everything around it is loaded with small, volatile bits of fear, especially if you're about to do something stupid, like tell a truth that will put an end to the night for good.

"You what?" Ah, shit, Ron thought, she was paying attention. Ron had had several partners and girlfriends who wouldn't have even heard what he said. Of course, this time he was with somebody who was listening. Shit. No wonder he liked her.

"I, uh."

"You what? You have a daughter, too?"

"Well, yeah. Stella."

"It's okay, honey. I bet Stella's beautiful, like you," Bambi purred. Her left breast had moved in and was now taking over Ron's arm, like a roommate who couldn't keep her shit out of the living room of a shared apartment. Ron's arm started writing a passive aggressive note to Bambi's left breast, but thought better of it and just decided to enjoy the moment. How often do you have a shapely breast as a roommate?

"But that's not it." Ron thought the daughter thing was big, but Bambi had a daughter too, so maybe it wasn't as big. Either way, he had something bigger. And he wasn't going to end that thought with *in my pants*, either. "I'm…"

"You're what? Married?"

"No."

"Gay?"

"No."

"Mommy issues?"

"No."

"Alcoholic?"

"No."

"HIV positive?"

"No."

"Tranny?" Bambi felt down and grabbed Ron's erection. "I KNOW that's not it." She took a sip of her bourbon and looked at Ron like he was a dictionary with no words in it. He had to tell her. "I'm a zombie." Ron stared her deep in her eyes and held his breath. There it went, just like that. Sometimes words come out of your mouth that you wish you could take back, like dropping coins on the ground and bending over to pick them up. And this one was an entire bank full of quarters, Ron thought. I'd like a refund, please. A do-over. Ron all of a sudden he wished he was a time traveler, too, as well as a zombie. Then he could back time up, turn the light off in the room, and already be diving into Bambi's thighs with the fervor of a man looking for buried treasure. That's kind of how he felt about vagina; it was treasure. And in this particular instance he felt like he just sank his own pirate boat, just a few feet offshore of an island marked with a giant X. *I'm a zombie.* Good idea, Ron. That's gonna get you some.

"I know." Bambi grinned a sly grin. Ron lifted his eyebrows.

"What?" He thought maybe she was joking. Surely she was joking. Ha ha ha and all that.

"I know you're a zombie. I've known since the plane."

"Wait. What?"

"I have a sense about such things." Ron was shaking, but Bambi's arms showed up and wrapped themselves around him. She stared into his eyes.

"Is it obvious?" Shit, Ron thought. What if everybody could tell he was a zombie? Surely that wasn't possible, right? They wouldn't have let him fly. Or sing karaoke.

Bambi let go of Ron and stood up. Her bathrobe barely contained her body, but Ron didn't notice this time. She was hot, but this idea that somebody could recognize his true self was hotter at the moment, much to Ron's disappointment. He'd rather be making Bambi scream than dealing with *this*. What was *this*, anyway?

Bambi poured herself and Ron another glass of bourbon. "My husband–Emily's father–was killed by zombies during the Penetration and turned into a zombie himself. I…" She took a long swig of the drink. "I kept him around as long as I could. I recognize zombie behavior."

"Wow." Ron downed his drink in one swig. "I'm sorry."

"Don't be," Bambi said. She poured another glass of bourbon for each of them. "He was a good man, and he was a good zombie man. That's what I called him. 'Dan the Zombie Man.' It was cute... then."

"What happened to him?"

"He went out to eat one night and ran into a bunco of zombies and they were all wiped out by humans. It was on the news. That's how I found out."

"Sorry." Ron took a drink. The bourbon made him warm.

"So when I saw you on the plane, I knew I liked you." She downed her drink. "You remind me of him–Dan–a little bit." She paused. "I started hooking after Dan was gone and they took Emily, because I was lost, but you saved me today. Made me see the light. You know?"

"Right place, right time."

"Just like now." She sat back down on the bed and kissed him on the cheek. Ron took this as a sign that the evening might still go well, so he pulled her face to his and kissed her on the lips. She tasted as good as Ron had imagined she would. Sure, people tasted good when they were being eaten, but they tasted even better when they were merely being kissed. In fact, Ron thought, if I could just be a sex zombie and avoid the whole *gotta eat humans to survive* nonsense, I'd be a happy zombie. If I were a sex zombie, I'd just have to get kisses regularly to survive. I could handle that. Ron wondered if he could re-wire himself to become a sex zombie; it sure would make things easier. Hell, if everybody were a sex zombie, the world would be a beautiful place.

He pulled away from the deep kiss he and Bambi were sharing. "You're delicious," Ron said. Bambi laughed.

"Is that a zombie joke? Are you going to eat me?" Not in a violent way, Ron thought.

"No, sorry. I–I mean, yeah, you'd probably be delicious, but I can't eat you. This is more fun anyway."

"Why can't you eat me?"

"You don't deserve it."

"Is that why you ate Joaquin?"

"You know?"

"You're wearing his shirt." Bambi slowly removed Joaquin's fluorescent yellow *Girls Direct To You* shirt from Ron's body. He marveled both at her tenderness and the fact that he made a rookie zombie mistake. He usually did wear clothes from his meals, but he never ran into anybody who recognized the clothes. Then again, he didn't know he'd ever see Bambi again, so maybe it wasn't a mistake. Still, he thought he should probably try to be more careful. But, hey, at the moment, Bambi was kissing Ron's neck, so he needed to stop thinking about being careful and start thinking about enjoying this moment.

"You're delicious," Bambi said. "Maybe I should eat you."

"I don't think you're qualified," Ron joked. "Do you have a zombie frequent diner card?" Bambi laughed at this joke and stuck her tongue down Ron's throat. Really, Ron thought, if I had a choice between Bambi's tongue down my throat or Joaquin's eyeballs down my throat, I'd have to go with Bambi's tongue. He wondered if he was really a zombie at all. Wasn't it more of a human desire to have tongue over eyeballs?

"Oh, I'm qualified, honey." Bambi pulled out of the kiss, sat back, and her robe. "See?"

"Oh, I see." And Ron could see–thankfully, his zombie status didn't diminish his eyesight at all, for there in front of him were his two friends from the plane. And they were magnificent in every way. "But let me check your qualifications." He reached over and cupped her right breast with his left hand–yep, they were natural. Just the way Ron liked his breasts. Natural, with a bit of plumpness in all the right places. Kind of like buying chicken at the organic market, but much sexier. Ron leaned down and put her nipple in his mouth. No, this wasn't like buying chicken at all...not anymore. This was more like slurping...eyeballs...Joaquin's eyeballs. Ron jumped up, aghast that his thought process–his conscience–had led him to this place. This place where a gorgeous woman was naked in front of him and he was thinking about eyeballs?

"What's wrong, honey?" Bambi stared up at him with her doe eyes. Bambi–doe. Yeah, it would have been funny at any other time, Ron thought, but right now he needed to clear his head. He shook his head quickly and looked at her.

"Uh, nothing, sorry. I–you're just too gorgeous to believe." Ron always had the lines for the ladies. He was happy that hadn't left him. This line was true, Ron thought. Maybe he liked her so much that his brain couldn't let him do what he wanted to do to her tonight, even though his penis obviously did. Brain versus penis: the oldest battle in the male book.

"You're sweet. Now get back down here and believe it." She grabbed his shoulder and pulled him to her, where her lips met his. Ah, tasty, delicious lips, Ron thought. Lips. Tongue. Breasts. Eyeballs.

"FUCK!" Ron jumped up.

"What?" Bambi covered up her breasts with a blanket from the bed. Dammit, Ron thought, that was never a good sign. Especially when you were just getting started. She could cover up all she wanted to after they were done, but beforehand a woman covering up was the sign that you were an idiot. Or your brain wasn't into the proceedings. Eyeballs? Really?

"Nothing, really." Ron thought back to all the women he had loved in his human life. Yes, maybe this was where his brain needed to be. They came in all shapes and sizes, mostly brunette, a few blondes–like Stella's mom–and they all had eyeballs, right? And breasts and lips and skin. Yeah, Ron thought, everybody has eyeballs. And their eyeballs were all delicious.

"Motherfucking brain!" Ron frantically paced across the room, holding his head. This wasn't happening...this wasn't happening. All he could think about was Joaquin's delicious eyeballs going down his throat like oysters on the half shell, and Bambi was ready to be plowed silly, Ron thought. His erection was losing steam, because, frankly, his penis didn't get all that excited about eyeballs like sushi in his throat. Dammit.

"I can't do this." Ron raised his eyebrows at Bambi, who was sitting on the bed with a blanket over her. Damn, she still looked hot as fuck, though, Ron thought. If only my penis could take over my thought process for just a few minutes. It wouldn't take long. Three minutes max. Maybe thirty seconds max. It had been awhile.

"I can see that." Bambi was staring at Ron's crotch, which had recently gone from looking like a wrapped breakfast sausage to now being flat as a board and twice as uninteresting. "Is this a problem?"

"No. It's not that." Ron went over to Bambi and sat down next to her. "I–I'm sure you can get me going, if I'm in the right frame of mind. You're delicious." Ron realized that probably wasn't the right word at the time.

"Then eat me, silly."

"I can't. Not tonight."

"Did I do something wrong? Is it because I worked for Joaquin?" There it is again, Ron thought. Joaquin's name. Delicious eyeballs. Dammit.

"No, it's not that. I really like you. I just–I'm having trouble showing it right now."

"So, really, Kenny, this is the opposite of what usually happens. Usually, I fuck guys on the first date and never see them again...like the stereotype. Or, if I really like a guy, I don't fuck him on the first date...and still never see them again. This time, *you're* not going to fuck *me* because you like me?" Nailed it, Ron thought. I like you...and eyeballs. He did like her, after all...he just didn't really want to share the fact that Joaquin's eyeballs were getting in the way of their sex life. That didn't seem like it would go over well. "Yes," Ron said, with all the sincerity he could muster without blurting out EYEBALLS! "I like you too much to fuck you–to make love to you–right now. When the time is right, we'll make love–or I'll make you scream and peel paint. But tonight I can't." God, Ron thought, he sure sounded like an actor in a romantic comedy. What the fuck was wrong with him?

Bambi snuggled up next to Ron, and he wondered about the word *snuggled*–was it a verb? Really? Ah, fuck it, Ron thought, I'm going to try to make the best of a bad situation. He put his arms around her bare back.

"Okay, Kenny, honey, I guess I can wait. I like to scream and peel paint, but you're being a woman in a romantic comedy. Will you spend the night with me anyway?"

"Yes, I probably can't catch a cab back to the Strip from out here anyway." He smiled at her.

"Fucker." She lightly hit Ron in the shoulder. "It's good to see you're taking this seriously. I'm going to call you Limpy until you make me scream."

Limpy. Huh. As Bambi turned off the light, Ron wondered if everybody in Vegas had a name ending in a vowel. Everybody except Joaquin...and his damn eyeballs. Maybe Ron should eat everybody whose name ended in a consonant. That would be so random it'd be funny.

Bambi lay down naked on the bed as the light of the moon bounced off the muscle cars outside and came in through the small bedroom window, illuminating her body as she faced away from Ron. She sure had the curves–ass as pear-shaped as a shapely pear, legs as long as the commute on the Strip during rush hour, and blonde hair that could have belonged to a supermodel's secret lesbian girlfriend. She turned to face him. Her stomach was as tight and flat as a laminate countertop in a 1950s diner, and her breasts were...well, they were Ron's best friends. He hoped they would be soon, anyway. Because they were outstanding. He had never seen their equal, and he had seen a lot of breasts.

Ron kept his clothes on as he lay next to Bambi in the moonlight and shadows. No sense in seeing how his zombie body looked at the moment, anyhow. And if Bambi actually had to touch it, who knows how freaked out she might get, even though she obviously had experience with zombies. Maybe, Ron thought, I am just having a bout of self-doubt. Even though he chuckled internally at the stupid rhyme he just made, Ron wondered if that were true. He certainly never had self-doubt when he was with women as a human, but he had not been with a woman since he was killed. Maybe he was starting over. He *was* a zombie virgin.

"Thanks for saving me today," Bambi purred as she faced away from him again, putting her fine ass up against Ron's body. "Maybe one day I can save you." Save me from what, Ron wondered, as they drifted off to sleep under the moonlight. Eyeballs?

CHAPTER
-11-

But Ron didn't sleep–he was a zombie, so sleep was impossible, even though he wanted it, more than anything this side of being human again (and Bambi). He was tired. And he was anxious–being a zombie in a world full of humans is not as easy as it sounds. Actually, that's not true, because it doesn't sound easy at all.

Bambi was snuggled up against him, and Ron could think of nothing sexier–and calming–than spooning her like she was a bowl of rice pudding. Not that you'd spoon rice pudding the same way you'd spoon a nude blonde with an ass to rule them all, but rice pudding does require a spoon. Ron looked up at the ceiling and wondered why his brain was betraying him. Not only were his metaphors completely fucked up, tonight he also was presented with an opportunity to be inside the hottest woman he'd ever seen and he couldn't do it...because his brain was more interested in the eyeballs he'd slurped from Joaquin's head earlier today. Man, they were delicious...fuck you, brain, Ron thought. Sure, they were delicious, but I bet Bambi's vagina was even tastier, and you wouldn't go there. Piece of shit brain. Asshole brain. Motherfucking brain.

Ron wished he were human right now, more than ever. Right now, if he were human, he'd be fast asleep, his spent body crushed up against the fantastic body of Bambi, and he'd probably be dreaming something nice. That's really what he missed most of all about the sleeping–the dreaming. No longer were his nights spent dreaming of millions of dollars, orgies with super models, fast cars, world peace and endless summers, not necessarily in that order–no, these days, he stayed awake at night, thinking about where his next meal might come from, the Zombie Penetration, and Stella.

Ah, Stella. Stella was the product of a relationship between Ron and a pretty blonde named Erika. He met Erika at a cooking class he had taken specifically to meet women, and he and Erika hit it off specifically over seared scallops and ended up spending the next five weeks specifically in bed. She and Ron were boyfriend and girlfriend, or lovers, or whatever name people wanted to give it, and then, because of those five specific weeks spent specifically in bed, Erika was pregnant, Stella showed up, and everything changed. It's a known fact that throwing a child into the mix of a relationship can take that relationship a variety of different directions, and Stella did just that to Ron and Erika. At first, they were proud and ambitious parents, excited to provide their daughter with the best. They even used cloth diapers until they came to their senses. Then, after Stella grew into a precocious seven-year-old girl and, frankly, the parenting became easier as it often does after the baby years, Ron and Erika didn't have baby-rearing to tie them together and discovered that they didn't really have much more in common than seared scallops–and even that was debatable, because Ron took that class specifically to meet women. He didn't have any specific fondness for scallops and neither did Erika, as it turns out. She was just taking that class to meet a sensitive man. And, as Ron and Erika soon found out, when your relationship starts on a funny premise and a cooking class taken for all the wrong reasons, it doesn't necessarily last very long.

Bambi stirred and rolled over, showing her front side to Ron. He certainly enjoyed this view. Now here's a relationship starting off on a funny premise, Ron thought. If this was a relationship at all. He burped and caught another taste of Joaquin–how long would that fucker linger? Does Bambi have any mouthwash in her place?–and wondered if a relationship started with a hooker on an airplane stood any kind of chance at all, or if he could just fuck her and walk away. No, shuffle away. But obviously he was incapable of that, because eyeballs! Eyeballs! He certainly did like her and she certainly didn't have a problem with his condition, but still. Ron seriously doubted this could be called a relationship. Humans had a hard enough time with interracial or homosexual relationships, how was the populace at large going to handle a human-zombie relationship? And why the fuck was Ron even thinking relationship? His brain corrected itself; he certainly liked Bambi at the moment, but he had bigger issues to deal with, ultimately. Eyeballs and Stella and blending in with humanity and staying out of trouble, for starters. Ron's to-do list was epic, to say the least. And he knew he needed to pay attention to it, even while Bambi's fine breasts were calling his name from six inches away. *Ron, we're lonely!* If breasts actually called names, Ron realized, it'd be a hell of a lot easier to tell which women were interested in you. You'd be in a nightclub and you'd just wait for your name to be called. It'd be like a DMV for sex.

Morning came quickly, as it often does when a brain is preoccupied. Ron saw the moonlight through the window turn to the beginnings of sunlight and the horizon turn a brilliant blue and realized he hadn't noticed such natural beauty since, well, since he became a zombie.

The front door to the apartment opened and somebody came in, dropped something on the front room floor, opened and closed the refrigerator, and went into the other bedroom and closed the door, according to Ron's ears. Bambi's brother, he presumed. Or a burglar who knew his way around the place. Ron's stomach growled. A burglar would make a fine breakfast. Especially if there were english muffins in the kitchen. Burglar Benedict, anyone?

"Kenny?" Bambi was as beautiful waking up as she was going to sleep and still precisely as naked. Ron felt a stirring in his loins to go with his stomach growl. Never trust a fart, Ron's grandfather used to say...and now Ron realized that he couldn't trust his boner, either. If he followed that to its natural erection–ur, end–he'd just think of eyeballs or tendons or delicious quadriceps and the moment would end. So Ron ignored the stirring, even chanting a mantra of *baseball baseball baseball* to try to keep the stirring down. That worked when he was alive and worked even better now that he was dead. Baseball is a slow game even for zombies, apparently, judging by how fast his stirring disappeared.

"Hi."

"You're funny," Bambi said in that just-waking-up voice that sounded like whiskey, sex, and a warm blanket and was always sexy as hell. Nothing hotter than a woman waking up next to you, especially if she's naked, and using that voice. This was one of Ron's favorite parts of sex. Or non-sex, as it were.

"Ha ha."

"Come here." Bambi grabbed Ron and pulled him close to her. *Baseball baseball baseball.* "Still not interested, huh?" she asked.

"Oh, I'm very interested. I just..."

"Don't worry about it, honey. You're cute. I'll make you some breakfast and maybe we can try again later." She rolled off the bed slowly and walked towards the closet, her ass and her back swaying like a sexy serpentine. Ron watched and wondered if he'd really get to try again later. That would be nice.

"Your brother came home a bit ago, I think."

"Yeah, he usually gets in around seven. Did you meet him?"

"And leave you here naked all by yourself?"

"I'll introduce you. Don't, uh…" Bambi paused and looked directly at Ron with one of those *this is fucking serious* looks. "Don't tell him you're a–uh, dead. He doesn't like zombies."

"Duh. What human does? Besides you, of course."

"No, Kenny, I'm serious. Don't say anything. In fact, go into my bathroom and put on same makeup. You look like shit. I'm going to put on a pot of coffee."

"Thaaaaanks," Ron said with intended sarcasm. Damn, now he had to dress up to go out in public? Well, hopefully she has something better than football field chalk. He better look human if he was going anywhere.

Bambi put a Las Vegas Wranglers hockey jersey over her naked body and looked at Ron with bad intent. "I still like you. But you do look like shit."

"Are you going to wear that jersey all day? Cuz it's going to make me crazy."

"Too bad you can't seem to do anything about that," Bambi purred as she came up to Ron and put her hand on his limpness. Baseball seemed to have done its job a little too well. Ron wondered if they made zombie Viagra. "And no, silly, I'm not going to wear it all day–I have to dress up as Marilyn Monroe and go to work in a bit. I'll leave it here for you, if you want to stay. It'll smell like me."

"Torture," Ron replied.

"Payback, sweetie." Bambi whispered.

"Oh, it's sweetie now?"

"Go get yourself all pretty, Mister Kenny," she said, smiling, as she left the room to go make a pot of coffee.

Still naked, Ron walked into Bambi's bathroom and was instantly happy she didn't share a bathroom with her brother. First of all, he could walk into the bathroom naked, and second of all, Bambi had a lot of makeup. And it was all out on display. If she had to share a bathroom with her brother, Ron imagined it wouldn't be quite this fun. Mascara, eyeliner, blush...Ron knew of these things, because many of the women he'd dated wore these things, but he had no idea how to use these things. Still, Ron thought, I can successfully put football field chalk on my face and fly to Vegas and fool everybody into thinking I'm alive, I can do this. How hard can it be?

Very hard, as it turns out. As it turns out, mascara, eyeliner and blush are not the entire oeuvre of makeup. No, as Ron soon learned as he looked around, as it turns out there is also foundation (a base for something cool, Ron thought), primer (like Rustoleum, he thought, not bad), concealer (to conceal the fact I'm a zombie, okay), rouge (whatevs), blush (like how my face looks when I can't get an erection), counter powder (um, what?), highlight (like a fluorescent yellow pen?), bronzer (I'd rather have golder, like the Olympians), eyebrow pencil (does it have an eyebrow eraser?), lipstick (does it come in zombie red?), fingernail/toenail polish (does it come in zombie black?), something called permanent waves (isn't that a Rush album?), and hair color. Ron, being the industrious and naive guy that he was–and in this instance, 90% of guys would be naive, because the oeuvre of makeup is more complicated and delicate than anything us guys are capable of comprehending, much less utilizing–used a little bit of everything. He thought he looked elegant and dashing, like a zombie James Bond.

When he was done, Ron walked out of the bedroom wearing Kenny's jeans, Joaquin's shirt, and Bambi's makeup, and feeling pretty good about his efforts and his debonair appearance. Hell, he might even go get a martini–shaken, not dead...ur, stirred. He saw David standing in the kitchen, putting milk into a porcelain Sahara Casino mug that Ron assumed held a cup of coffee. It did, until David lifted it towards his mouth and saw Ron and spilled it all over the laminate counter.

"Wow, sis, your *date* is awake," David said with a stupid grin. Bambi appeared from around the corner and Ron heard David say under his breath, "Bringing home drag queens again, huh?"

"David, this is Kenny, Kenny this is David," Bambi said as she grabbed a mug to make Ron a cup of coffee. "Kenny is my friend."

"Where did you find her? At that La Cage show?" David said it like *bird cage*, Ron thought, not like the French *La Cage*, but Ron knew what he was getting at. Apparently Ron wasn't very good at putting on makeup. When it wasn't football field chalk, anyway.

"Shut up, David, Kenny is just not a morning person, are you Kenny?" She handed Ron a cup of black coffee without asking Ron whether or not he took cream or sugar. Ron figured at this moment it didn't matter if he took cream or sugar. And he preferred blood, anyway, but that probably wasn't in Bambi and David's refrigerator.

"You have some fucked-up friends," David said as he turned to pour himself a bowl of Frosty O's cereal. Nothing better for breakfast than a generic version of crap passing as cereal, Ron thought. Stupid humans will eat whatever's cheap and accessible–which was ironic, because even Ron didn't always eat what was accessible.

"Pleased to meet you, too," Ron said, teeth clenched, trying to hide the sarcasm that his brain felt. He didn't really want to upset the delicate balance that this situation had, because he still wanted to get laid at some point. And sarcasm might just be the thing that capsizes the sex boat this morning...if eyeballs hadn't already pushed the sex boat back to drydock, anyway. Hell, at this point the sex boat was a raft, and Ron wanted the full luxury liner. Hell, at this point Ron wanted to be Captain Stubing of his own Love Boat.

"I never said pleased to meet you." David was a little slow on the uptake, apparently. Perhaps sarcasm was going to be an ineffective weapon against this opponent. Was he really an opponent? Ron realized he always assumed brothers of women he liked were opponents, until they proved they weren't. Which wasn't very often. Dog and brothers of his dates never liked him.

"I know. Sarcasm."

"Oh, really. We have a smart ass transvestite, I see."

"David, don't be an ass." Bambi said. "Kenny, let's go fix you up." She grabbed Ron's hand and they went back to her bathroom. Bambi washed Ron's face gently while her hockey jersey rubbed up against him in all the right places. He hoped he'd see that hockey jersey on the floor again at some point soon and that he'd be scoring a hat trick, so to speak. In the five-hole. Maybe he'd get called for a major penalty and have to spend five minutes in the box. He chuckled.

"You really do look like shit, ya know." Bambi was almost done washing his face. He looked up at the mirror at his clean zombie face. Yep, it was still all there. Pale skin, bloodshot eyes, a couple of scabs from the truck grill, and a long booger hanging from his cheek...wait, that wasn't a booger at all. Ron reached up; it was a strip of skin. Shit. Ron was about to celebrate the fact that he was all still there, but those plans were all of a sudden deferred to a later time, as he was apparently not all still there. Shit.

Bambi noticed Ron's booger skin thing hanging from his face, turned away from him, lifted up her hockey jersey to show Ron her elegant ass–in Ron's eyes, it was elegant AND refined, so fuck you–opened her bathroom cabinet, and grabbed a bottle of spirit gum.

"Let's fix you up."

"Sorry."

"I'm going to glue you back together and make you cute again. Who did your makeup before?"

"Who did my makeup before? You mean the football field chalk on my face when we met? That was me. I did that. You liked it?"

"Oh." Bambi started gluing his booger skin thing onto his face and applying mascara to Ron as he heard David turn the television on in the living room. He apparently liked the television loud, because Ron could hear it all the way in Bambi's bathroom.

"Welcome back." David was watching some morning show, apparently, with some vapid female host. "We're discussing zombie culture this morning." What the fuck? Zombie culture? "The Washington Redskins are finally changing their name from the offensive Redskins to The Washington Zombies, and people everywhere are Zombieing. Bob, it's like the planking craze or the Tebowing craze of a couple of years ago. Zombie Style!"

Bob was the vapid male host of the morning talk show. Bambi continued to work on Ron's face. "Oh, wow, Linda. So people what, go to the tops of mountains and stand like a zombie?"

"That's right, Bob, and we have pictures." Ron HAD to see this. He walked out of the bathroom.

"Kenny, I'm not done!" Bambi said as Ron headed to the front room. David was there on the futon couch with his cup of crap coffee and his bowl of crap cereal, most of which had already gone into his crap stomach. He saw Ron.

"You, uh, wow. She does have some fucked-up friends." Ron wondered if eating the brother of a girl he couldn't properly fuck for psychological reasons was appropriate. Because at the moment he was starting to get hungry, and David was an asshole, by all indications. An asshole with bad taste in food, based on his breakfast choice. Maybe he should *be* breakfast, Ron thought. Then again, if I eat him do I eat everything that he ate? Ugh. Ron realized if he was worried about that he shouldn't be out here on the outskirts of Vegas in a cheap apartment surrounded by muscle cars. No, he should be hanging around the exit of the fanciest restaurants on the Vegas Strip. Mario Batali and Bobby Flay's customers probably had some good food in their bellies. Choices, choices.

Ron looked at the television. There, on the screen, were pictures of people doing zombie poses in interesting places: At football games, at the Eiffel Tower (both the one in Paris and the one in

Vegas), in New York City. Seriously? We're a thing now? Don't you fucking humans realize you wiped us all out (well, all of us except one)? And now you're going to make fun of us? Ron realized this was the American way, really. Native Americans had been fighting this battle for years. And now it was our turn.

The television screen went back to Bob, who was holding a Zombie Pose atop his desk in the news studio. "And now I'm zombieing, Linda!" Fucking humans. They must be really bored with everything to resort to making fun of us, Ron thought. What, did you fuckers run out of reality television ideas? Did all the Kardashians die or something? Ron thought he should pick up an issue of *People* magazine so that he could catch up on his junk food pop culture–maybe then he'd know what the hell was going on. Normally he wouldn't have given half a shit, but if zombies were part of the pop culture conversation these days, Ron thought it might be good to know about. For reference.

"Mother fucking zombies." David looked at the television like he wanted to kill it.

"Kenny, honey, come back into the bathroom and we'll finish up." Bambi was standing in her bedroom doorway, motioning for Ron. A hot blonde in a hockey jersey (and nothing else) affects certain parts of the brain that trash television just can't get to, so Ron followed her into the bathroom.

"What was that about? You said he doesn't like zombies, but he's a bit intense about it." Ron had never seen a person try to kill a television, but David sure looked like he could.

Bambi was cleaning up the mascara on Ron's face. She spoke quietly, below the volume from the television in the other room. "Well, honey, zombies ate his girlfriend during the Penetration. He retaliated by killing an entire bunco of 'em...and he's never gotten over it. He was going to ask her to marry him."

"Oh, shit," Ron whispered. "Make me look extra human then, would ya?"

"I will," Bambi said, with a smile. "Either that or extra transvestite-y. He seemed to buy that, too. After I finish, I gotta go to work. Wouldn't want to be late to my first day."

"At the Casino Royale? I doubt they care," Ron said, as Bambi smoothed the makeup on his face out like she was wiping a baby's ass. All tender and shit. Ron really enjoyed it when women were all tender and shit.

"Well, still, it's a job, and I want to make the right impression, so I don't get fired and have to go back to Joaquin."

Ron smirked. "There's no Joaquin to go back to." He burped. "He was delicious, if that helps."

"I figured. Thanks for that, by the way." Bambi kissed Ron hard on the lips. "Well, then, honey, I gotta keep this job. For that and other reasons." Bambi gently colored his lips with what could only be called lipstick, without the red. Pink, like real lips; Ron found this impressive.

"Other reasons?" Ron couldn't ignore the temptation to ask. When somebody says something like *and other reasons*, it's like a fastball over the plate. Can't not swing at that.

"Well, yeah." She moved her hockey jersey clad body out of the way so he could see himself in the mirror. Not bad, truly. He'd gone from looking like death warmed over to something closer to leftover death casserole. He really should thank her. Or fuck her properly. When the time is right.

"Yeah?" Again, she left a meatball over the center of the plate–he had to ask.

"If I can have some stability in my life–place to live, regular job, that sort of thing–maybe I can get custody of my baby again. I mean, she's not a baby anymore, but..."

Ron understood this completely. Stella was 17 now, but she'd always be Ron's little girl. "Why did you lose her?" he wondered out loud. He wanted to wonder that to himself, but it came out, somehow. So now it was out there, cocked and loaded, ready for somebody to pull the trigger. Stupid mouth.

Bambi obliged. "They–the authorities–figured out I was keeping a zombie in my house and took her away to my parents in Colorado." Bambi looked sad for a moment, then quickly composed herself as she put the makeup away. "I gotta get to work."

Bambi went into her room and stripped off her Wranglers jersey and threw it on the floor. She was naked and her gorgeous ass was staring at him like Ron had raised his hand in algebra class to answer a teacher's questions but actually had no answer in his head. He felt awkward, but then her ass stared some more and awkward changed to horny. Exceedingly horny. His pants hurt. Bambi looked back at him. "I have a few minutes if you think you..."

"I can."

And with that, Ron and Bambi had a quickie. Since the invention of the quickie, there have only been five quickies that were rated the most passionate, the most pure. This one left them all behind. And Bambi still got to work on time.

CHAPTER
-12-

Ron had post-sex hunger. Bambi was at work, David was taking a nap, and Kathy Lee Gifford was on the television, talking to Ron. Well, not directly to him, but mid-morning talk show hosts always seem like they're trying too hard be in your living room both physically and spiritually, and Kathy Lee is the queen of trying too hard. So to Ron, it felt a little like she was talking to him...or trying to. And Ron might have been paying more attention if his stomach hadn't been complaining so much. Hunger Pangs 1, Kathy Lee 0.

"This morning on Wall Street–did you hear about this?–they had a bunco of zombies ring the bell for the opening of the markets." All of a sudden, Ron was paying attention. Hunger Pangs 1, Kathy Lee 1. "Well, not a real bunco, of course, because that would be dangerous, right? And all the zombies are dead. Of course. It was really a bunch of actors playing zombies, and they rang the bell. It's part of the Stock Exchange's effort to get more young people interested in the market, and with zombies all the rage these days..."

Rage? Honey, Ron thought, you don't fucking understand rage, not for a moment. Rage is living amongst you fucking idiots as a zombie, trying to fit in. All of a sudden, Ron was pissed off. He decided to go find somebody to eat. Sure, people aren't supposed to eat when they're angry because they tend to eat way too much, but Ron wasn't sure he could even gain weight, so fuck it. He was hungry. Hunger Pangs 2, Kathy Lee 1. He declared Hunger Pangs the victor in a lavish ceremony in his head, turned the TV off, put on his sunglasses and went outside.

The sun shines in the desert like a dysfunctional father: unrelenting, angry, hotter than anything else in the room. Ron wondered if he could get sunburned, then decided that would be impossible with all the makeup he was wearing—he saw the SPF markings on the bottles. He boarded the #178 bus back towards the Strip, using some of Joaquin's money to pay the fare. For a few moments, he was the only one on the bus (except the driver). Bambi truly did live on the edge of town. And the edge of Las Vegas is about the edge of the planet, truly. Even the bus driver looked like he was from no man's land. Good, Ron thought, I'll fit in on this bus perfectly.

After a 45 minute bus ride, stopping at every godforsaken intersection and picking up every form of humanity along the way (most of whom looked much more like zombies than Ron, he thought), the bus arrived on the Strip. Ron got out and walked the half block to Carnaval Court. Sure, it was predictable, he thought, but it's what he knew. And, really, he could trust the bartenders there, should he need to. It was truly a *live and let live* establishment—or maybe *live and let eat*—and that was important. Ron needed to find somebody to eat, and if he didn't have to worry about people wondering who or what he was, it'd be that much easier. A foundation from which to spring, of sorts.

Charlie and Flippy were working again, and Charlie greeted Ron as Ron sat down. "Hey, buddy, you look MUCH better today!"

"Thanks, fucker," Ron said. Funny how fucker could be a term of endearment, but truly, Ron thought, calling somebody 'fucker' meant you loved them. You loved them so much you could call them fucker. "My girlfriend did my makeup."

"Whoah! Girlfriend? Makeup? All right! Gin and tonic?" Flippy was his usual jovial, dependable self. Pretend to care about the customer's personal life just a little and then sell them a drink. He could sell anything; hell, he could sell water to a drowning man.

"Please." While he waited for his gin and tonic, the guy sitting to Ron's left said something to somebody that made him Ron's next meal.

"I'm a CEO on Wall Street."

CHAPTER
-13-

C EOs are delicious, as it turns out. Jeffrey–the CEO–was a little more plump than Joaquin, probably because CEOs sit on their asses all day and pimps walk around all day, Ron thought, and everybody knows a little more fat on meat makes it flavorful–especially when the meat is on the bone, like Jeffrey's was. It was the first rule of BBQ. Or ZBQ. So Ron really enjoyed feasting on Jeffrey, even pausing for a brief moment in his Casino Royale hotel room to revel in his good fortune and to take another picture, this time of himself with a large amount Jeffrey's blood on his chin as a beard, like a demented member of the Duck Dynasty family. Someday, Ron thought, I'll show these pictures to my zombie children. Ha! *Do as I say, children, not as I do. Unless you're really hungry.*

As Ron gnawed on Jeffrey's left butt cheek–damn, CEOs have plump butt cheeks–he sensed movement outside the hotel room door. He paused, letting a drop of butt skin juice drip down his chin, and looked over to the Casino Royale hotel room door. Seriously, this place is a dump, he thought, if I can sense movement outside in the hallway. Jeez. Maybe next time he needed a place to crash he'd choose a less distracting hotel to do his business in. He'd stayed at the Mirage a few times and really liked it. Yeah, he thought, as he buried his face in Jeffrey's rump, that's where he'd stay next.

Bam! The front door splintered open like a piece of college ruled paper being pierced by a razor blade. The barrel of what was obviously a huge gun entered first, followed by three guys dressed to kill, literally. They looked like foot soldiers in an urban war, all dressed in black. Ron remembered guys like these from when he was a zombie. Wait, he was still a zombie. Shit. He darted from the bloody body of Jeffrey to behind the bed, hoping he was fast enough to not be noticed. He hoped wrong. One of the MF Guys—Ron preferred to make up simple nicknames for guys like these, because it made it easy to keep them all straight in his mind, and MotherFucking Guy was perfect right now—saw him move and dove onto the bed, shoving the barrel of his gun onto Ron's head. "Don't move, motherfucker." It was a simple command, and Ron intended to follow it. Mostly because the huge gun was pointed at his head and he knew that his head was his last line of defense against certain death. Real death. Post-zombie death.

By the front door, the two other MF guys had noticed the bloody body in the middle of the room. Well, it wasn't much of a body anymore and it would be impossible to not notice it, because it wasn't much of a body anymore—it was more of an art installation. A bloody, full room art installation—blood and guts all over the walls (Ron was a messy eater, remember?) and a carcass in the middle of the room, on the floor. Like something you'd see at the Museum of Modern Zombie Arts. The Artist's Statement would read:

My art is environmental, exploring the relationship between a human's insides and a human's outsides. With influences as diverse as Kathy Lee Gifford and the interior design of the

*Casino Royale hotel, new insights into insides and outsides
are crafted as a mirror to our zombie culture, man's inhu-
manity to man, and to the fact that I was fucking hungry,
you fucking motherfuckers.*

MF Guy #3 looked at it like somebody had gotten all the meat
they could have off of one of those pre-cooked rotisserie chickens
you buy at the grocery store, but bloodier. He left the room and
vomited in the hallway. Not that adding vomit to the room itself
would have violated any sort of societal rules. It wouldn't have
changed the look or the smell of the room, honestly.

MF Guy #1 pushed his gun farther into Ron's temple. "Where
the fuck is he?"

"Who?" It was a legitimate question, Ron thought. If they
weren't here for me, who the fuck were they here for?

"You know who. Is that him?" #1 motioned towards the rotisserie carcass in the middle of the room.

"Is that who?"

"Him." Ron thought this whole thing was beginning to feel like
a Three Stooges skit. Him? Who? 3rd Base! Fuck you!

"It was a him." Ron's sarcasm earned him only more gun to the
temple. "Ouch!"

"Is that—was that Jeffrey Skidmore?"

"I dunno. I just got here." Ron did know that that was Jeffrey
Somebody, because they had struck up a conversation at the Carnaval Court over gin and tonics, but he wasn't sure if it was Jeffrey
Skidmore. Last names weren't important when you were drunk or
hungry, as it turns out.

"Shut the fuck up!" MF Guy #2 was apparently playing Bad
Cop today, because he was now leaning over Ron, screaming at
him. "We followed Jeffrey Skidmore up here—he came up here with
you! So where the fuck is he?"

MF Guy #3 had come back into the room and was examining Jeffrey Skidmore's wallet, which was in his pants, which were bloody and on the floor, right next to the body. "It's Skidmore. Here's his wallet."

#2 spoke. "C'mon, get up. You're coming with us."

"But weren't you looking for *him*?" Ron held out a glimmer of hope that they'd just let him go...zombie optimism? Zombtimism? Was that possible?

"We were, but you see his condition. And you did this to him. You have the right to remain silent, you have the right to an attorney...."

Oh, great, Ron thought. I'm fucking going to jail. Or worse.

CHAPTER
-14-

Jeffrey Skidmore had been running a Ponzi scheme where he bilked rich investors out of millions of dollars over the last 20 years, and the cops had been looking for him for nine months. Apparently, he had come to Vegas to blend in, too. Ron learned all this from his Clark County Jail cellmate, a large black man named William who had been arrested for running a Ponzi scheme of his own. William idolized Jeffrey Skidmore, so he knew all about him... and he talked all about him, too. It was sort of a Ponzi Scheme Admiration Society.

"He was the master–he even had professional athletes involved. Ath-a-LETES!" William was quite impressed that Jeffrey had athletes, apparently. "So what did you do to him?"

Ron didn't want William to think he had done anything to his idol–he was a large man, and Ron didn't want to be his next meal–so he said, "I woke up in my hotel room and he was dead on the floor. I don't even know how he got there."

"Wow. That's just..."

Three men with huge guns, gloves, and gas masks with the letters KILLZ stenciled with white across their guns, gloves and gas masks came to the cell. "Kenny Jones, come with me," one of them said. Ron breathed a sigh of relief. KILLZ were his peeps, his boys, and surely they were all going to hang out together over beers and whiskey, just like the good old days...until KILLZ #1 stuck his semi-automatic weapon in Ron's ribs and insisted that he walk this way. It quickly dawned on Ron that these were not his peeps nor his boys; no, in fact, he was now the enemy of KILLZ. He was the Z in the acronym, and that meant he was a Zombie. And KILLZ was formed to kill zombies. No, there was going to be no catching up with the fellas at this reunion of KILLZ. And what the fuck was KILLZ still doing around? Ron pondered this for a second. As far as he knew, KILLZ was created by the government only to fight the zombies during the Penetration and now that there weren't any zombies, shouldn't KILLZ be extinct? Like zombies?

The KILLZ men kept their guns trained on Ron as they walked this way, seemingly deeper and deeper into the Clark County Jail. Down some stairs, through some doors, down more stairs...all of a sudden, it was a soulless, dark place with a hint of dank moisture, according to Ron's nose. He didn't like where they were going and might try to escape, but all three of the men had their guns pointed directly at his head. KILLZ were trained to do that. This couldn't turn out well.

They came to a big steel door that seemed to be the gate to hell. The walls around the door were much like the walls of the Casino Royale hotel room, post Jeffrey Skidmore–caked with something that looked like blood, smelling just as bad. Ron had a bad feeling about this.

The door opened and the guns–and the men behind them–motioned for Ron to enter, if by *motioned* you mean *they pushed him in with brute force*. Tomato, tamato. The door closed behind him. Yeah, this was a lovely place–concrete floor, walls, and ceiling, a single light bulb hanging from a cord high above him, and a smell of death...or did Ron forget to put on deodorant again?

Out of the corner of his eye, Ron saw a figure move towards him. He braced for a beating or a gunshot or some other violence, but when the figure moved into the light coming from above his head, Ron could see he wasn't going to be beat or killed. No, the figure coming towards Ron was...a zombie. Takes one to know one, right?

The zombie shuffled close to Ron and smelled him, much like a puppy sniffs another puppy's butt. Ron was glad they weren't puppies; he wasn't sure how his butt smelled at the moment. If he hadn't put on deodorant, surely his butt didn't smell any better, right? Ron stood silently, motionless. He wasn't sure how to deal with this. Sure, he was still a zombie, technically, but at the moment he really wished he was back at Bambi's place, hanging with the humans. Even David would be tolerable right now. And then he wondered if other zombies would recognize that he hung with humans. Ron imagined that wouldn't sit well with zombies. When you're a Jet, you're a Jet all the way!

The zombie walked slowly around Ron, sniffing him, sizing him up, as Ron followed him with his eyes. Just when Ron thought the zombie was going to be open his mouth and take a bite, the zombie shuffled away. A door opened in the darkness to his right. Two hands grabbed Ron and he was pulled into yet another room. Ron, at this moment, really missed free thinking and the ability to make his own decisions, as there were certainly a lot of decisions being made for him at the moment.

In this other room, Ron felt himself being attached to a wall with handcuffs behind his back and an eyebolt, attached to the concrete wall. An extremely bright light came on, right in Ron's face. He flinched for a second and then squinted. He couldn't see anything behind the light. He felt...famous. Like he was onstage at the greatest dinner theater in hell.

"Are there more of you?" The question came from the light. A male voice, authoritative.

"Um, more of me?"

"More of you."

"Well, there's just one of me, if that's what you're asking." The barrel of a large gun appeared from the light and planted itself against Ron's left temple. Maybe sarcasm wasn't the best tactic at the moment, but Ron really couldn't help it–he was a sarcastic guy. And, honestly, when you ask a vague question, a naturally sarcastic person can only respond how he/she knows best–sarcastically. Dumbasses.

"Okay, okay, look, more of me? What do you want?"

"Are there more zombies?"

Oh, Ron thought. More of me, duh. Of course. And then, yep, shit, they're onto me.

"Zombies?" Ron thought playing dumb might buy him some time. Or something. Really, he didn't know what the hell he was doing. He didn't remember 'being captured by humans' being part of his 'go to Vegas and blend in' plan, so he didn't really have an exit strategy for this. Stupid zombie brain didn't consider this as an option.

Another barrel of another gun appeared from the light and planted itself against Ron's right temple, as if doubling down on bullets in his brain was going to get him to talk or something. Didn't these humans realize it only takes one bullet?

"Zombies. Like you. Where are the others?"

"Others?"

"We can do this the easy way–you answer the questions–or we can do this the hard way."

"What exactly is the hard way? I'm already dead and you already know it. I'm chained to the wall, you have guns...I don't see that things can get much harder." Ron's sarcasm was unrestrained. He hoped he wouldn't regret it.

But he did. A shot rang out in the dark and buried itself in the concrete wall millimeters from Ron's knee.

"Answer the question, asshole. Or your other knee gets it, too, and you won't be just a zombie, you'll be a zombieplegic." Ron laughed. Zombieplegic was pretty damn funny. "ANSWER THE QUESTION, ASSHOLE!"

"I'm by myself. Nobody else." He chuckled again. Zombieplegic. Funny humans. They should put on a show. *Zombie Comedy. Zomedy, by Cirque Du Soleil.* That would sell a lot of tickets in Vegas.

"Where did you come from?"

"Colorado."

"Colorado?"

"You've heard of it?"

"How did you get here?"

"I took a plane."

"How long have you been dead?"

"How the fuck would I know?"

"Have you seen other zombies?"

"Wait, don't I know you?" Ron listened to the voice behind the gun and thought he did know this person–or did all KILLZ guys sound the same when they were on the job?

"HAVE YOU SEEN OTHER ZOMBIES?"

"Bob?" Ron took a shot in the dark, hoping that maybe the distraction of finding one of their former co-drones in their midst would slow down his inevitable demise. And wasn't there one Bob in every group?

Another shot rang out in the dark and a bullet buried itself in the concrete wall next to Ron's ear. Good thing these guys were bad shots, or he'd be dead.

"HAVE."

The gun had reappeared and was now tunneling into his left nostril like it was a gopher looking for an earthworm. Ron felt like he was a vegetable garden.

"YOU."

The gun barrel was now so far up Ron's nose he thought it could pick his boogers...if he had boogers. Unfortunately for the situation, he had stopped producing phlegm the moment he was brought down to this dank hellhole. It must have been a nervous reaction.

"SEEN."

The gun barrel flinched and Ron felt his nostril rip open, like silk stockings caught on a snag. He thought of Erika and how he'd remove her silk stockings with his teeth, slowly, with no snags, after each cooking class. Yes, she wore silk stockings to cooking class; she was a classy woman. In the beginning.

"OTHER."

"Zombies?" Ron realized he was completing his captor's sentences now. Was this Stockholm Syndrome, or was he just being over-the-top sarcastic? Ron voted for the latter, because he certainly didn't feel any empathy towards his captor. In fact, he considered his captor to be a motherfucker. From Planet Motherfucker.

"YES."

"Only next door."

He heard his captor mumble some things to another captor behind the gun. Perhaps this was a Captor Convention. Las Vegas was a good place for a convention, and a Captor Convention wouldn't be the weirdest convention this town had ever seen, by far.

"What the fuck is this place?" Ron asked, squinting his eyes so he could maybe see what a Captor Convention actually looked like. He couldn't. This convention was audio only, apparently. Audio and gunslinger, anyway.

"Have you infected anybody?"

"Well, now, that's a bit of a personal question, isn't it? I mean, I don't even know that I have any sexually transmitted disea–" The other end of one of the guns came up and hit Ron hard in the face.

"HAVE YOU INFECTED ANYBODY?"

"Ouch, motherfuckers! No! Not anybody who's still walking around today, anyway."

"Have you eaten anybody?"

"Well, you already know the answer to that question, Planet Motherfucker behind the light. How the fuck would you know I'm a zombie if you didn't catch me eating that Skidmore guy?" The light went out and the room was dark. Suddenly his handcuffs were released and Ron fell to the cold concrete floor in a crumpled pile. Ron could vaguely make out that people were leaving the room behind the lights, then the door to the main area–where the zombie was–opened. Ron sat there, determined not to move–he didn't really want to pass himself off as a zombie to real zombies, after all, because there was no way of knowing how that was going to go–until an electrical shock passed through his body. Damn, he thought, they're fucking tasing me! Motherfuckers! He slowly picked himself up off the ground and shuffled towards the door as another electrical shock passed through his body. Dammit!

He made his way out of the door of the room and it closed behind him. He looked around to adjust his eyes and, as he did, a female zombie face appeared in the darkness. "Stay in the dark," the face said quietly, and then it disappeared.

The lights overhead came on. Not one to reject gift advice–he once picked up a woman in a country bar in San Diego because her friend came over to tell Ron that the woman liked him–he slid quietly over to a dark area next to the concrete wall between this room and the interrogation room. Now that the lights were on, Ron could see that there were dozens of zombies in this room, milling about like they had been waiting for 4 hours at the DMV and had to get up to stretch their legs. The room itself was like a basement in a 100 year old brick home that hadn't been maintained for 50 of those years–plaster peeling from the exterior walls, exposed flooring overhead, and a faint smell of moisture. Ron figured this was some kind of KILLZ jail, based on the proceedings of the prior five minutes, even though everybody above ground thought there weren't any more zombies, which Ron now knew was as wrong as giving Milli Vanilli the Best New Artist Grammy. But KILLZ was a government entity, and who else would keep such information from its populace? Fucking government. Now everybody felt all safe and shit, even though there were obviously still zombies around. Maybe. Maybe *all* the zombies were here. Ron wondered how long they had been here and what the fuck they were doing here. Still, he kept himself in the dark, because he was told to. By a female. Ron always listened to his female friends–they were usually smarter than his male friends. Ron, however, didn't listen to his female lovers–that was a whole different animal. Friends and lovers do not mix.

A door on his right opened. He could see brighter light behind it. Two men with the same black outfit and the same giant guns stepped out into the room and grabbed the nearest zombie and dragged him/her back into the room and closed the door. It happened so fast it could only be a practiced event, Ron thought. Surely they did this all the time, if they were that efficient at it. But during those 15 seconds the men were in the room, Ron looked towards the door from his dark spot and noticed that behind that door was some kind of lab setup or hospital room or something... and strapped to a table in the room was a zombie.

The room darkened again. Ron could hear shuffling and moaning sounds but barely see anything more than a foot away from him. Zombies had been exterminated, allegedly, for some time. He wondered where these zombies came from. Had they been in here the whole time? And what were they doing down here? What were they doing alive? Were they alive? Ron wondered how often that door opened and the men with the guns came out and took a zombie into that room with the table. Maybe not very often, but he sure as hell didn't want to hang around to find out. Based on what he saw when the lights went on, there was more room to his right, so he started sliding along the wall–to stay in the darkness, should the lights come back on–away from the door with the zombie patient, or whatever the hell that was.

Ron came to a corner; he could feel it because the wall he was using as a GPS disappeared, so it had to be a corner. What the hell, he thought, I'll follow this around. His instinct told him he should get as far away from where he was as fast as possible, and Ron's instincts were often times right. They weren't right the night he turned his motorcycle into the path of the tractor trailer, but everybody's allowed one fuck-up, right? Maybe that's what this whole thing was about. Maybe, he thought, I'm in some kind of predictable Hollywood movie where something tragic happens but the protagonist is allowed one more chance, by the powers that be, to redeem himself and make something of his life. Yeah, right. Ain't no predictable Hollywood movie that turns zombies back to humans.

He rounded the corner and continued down the wall. This room was darker than the previous one, and Ron was thankful for that. He didn't know who it was that warned him but he did know he saw dozens of zombies shuffling around and he didn't want to run into any of them, honestly. He wasn't even sure he knew the zombie language anymore. Not that there was a language, per se, just a lot of moaning and screaming when necessary, but still. What if this was like a human prison and an entire bunco of zombies was running it and wanted cigarettes in exchange for protection? Zombies smoking cigarettes–there's an image. Ron chuckled to himself.

A door quickly opened behind him, and Ron saw a moment of light. All of a sudden he was pulled into a dimly lit room and the door to the previous area was shut behind him.

"Shut the fuck up," a man said. Was he talking to me, Ron wondered? "Don't make a sound." A pistol was placed to Ron's head. Oh, great, another gun. You fucking humans know no other way, do you? Can't we negotiate? Sit down over a Bloomin' Onion at

Outback Steakhouse and discuss everything? That would be much more civilized. Or, Ron thought, maybe I should just eat you now, you motherfuckers. He looked around the room. There were at least three other people in there, and two of them had guns. Okay, maybe dining right now wasn't a good idea. But later, you assholes, you're going to be my smorgasbord. My Vegas buffet. *Tonight, at the seafood station, we have crab legs, and at the humanfood station, we have Bob legs!*

A female zombie face appeared in front of Ron. It was the same female zombie as before. "You're safe now," she whispered. Now Ron was just confused. "Just be silent," she continued. Seeing as how she gave Ron good advice before, he decided he could trust her for the time being, so he decided to be silent.

Another door opened, opposite of the first door, and the two figures with guns motioned for Ron to exit through the door. The female zombie stayed behind while Ron followed one of the figures out and another brought up the rear. This Ron Sandwich–he'd rather be sandwiched between two luscious brunettes, but desperate times and all that–headed down a dark hallway that appeared to ramp upwards. Maybe they were heading back up to the surface, Ron thought. They had come down many stairs on the way, so he knew they were underground somewhere. Ron stuck his hand out to feel the walls of the ramp–dirt.

Nobody said anything as they went up this ramp that turned back on itself every five minutes or so. Ron pondered his situation. Where the hell were they going? What time was it? Would Bambi wonder where he was? They had made no commitments as to their relationship, so she'd probably get home from work, see him gone, and write him off as an asshole. Great. Not only was he a zombie, he was an asshole, too. An asshole zombie who couldn't get a boner unless there was a hockey jersey on the floor and a time limitation. Out of all the things Ron thought he'd be in his life, this wasn't on the list. Deejay, sure, he wanted to that when he was a kid (Thanks to Doctor Johnny Fever from *WKRP in Cincinnati*). Rock and Roll Star, everybody wants to be that. But Asshole Zombie Who Can't Get A Boner For Anything Longer Than A Quickie? Not on the *What I Wanna Be When I Grow Up* list. Not now, not ever.

They came to a steel door. Ron could see a little bit of light coming in around the top and sides of the door. Had they reached the top? Where the hell were these people taking him?

Ron heard rustling in the darkness–sounds of people removing clothes and putting on other clothes. What the fuck?

"We're going out. Act normal. Do you understand?" Sure, Ron understood. Normal. I'll act normal until I can find a way to eat you fuckers. Nobody orders me around.

The door opened and the tunnel flooded with light. They stepped out into the light and let the door close behind them. It took a moment for his eyes to adjust, but Ron soon realized they had come out at the back entrance to Carnaval Court. As he looked to his left and his right, he realized one more thing. He was with Stella and Jim.

CHAPTER
-15-

The back entrance to Carnaval Court during the day is like the approach to a county fair in hell: It's hot as fuck and you can sense a party nearby, but you can't really see it. All you smell is spilled beer, hot concrete walkways, and popcorn. And those three smells together, when they infiltrate your nose, usually smell like unbridled fun, if you're a Vegas regular, because you know what they mean. This time, however, the mix of smells in Ron's nose wasn't fun. No, it was fear. If Ron was interested in alliteration, he might say the smells were also fondue and farts, but at this moment, he had bigger things on his plate than a bunch of F words. Namely, Jim and Stella.

"What the fuck?" If Ron weren't so surprised to see them, he might have found something more eloquent to say, but in this moment *what the fuck* would have to suffice. He reached up to put his nose back together as best he could and then leaned over and gave Stella a long, long embrace. "What. The. Fuck." This may have been the first time in history 'What the fuck' was used in such a positive manner. This time, it meant 'I'm really happy to see you.'

"Dad." Ron breathed a sigh of relief–Stella knew who he was. Well, of course she did–she rescued him. "Dad." What a great word to hear...it had been a long time since Ron had heard it, and even longer–"DAD!"–since he had thought of himself as such.

Jim pulled Stella and Ron apart. Ron grabbed him for an embrace. "Okay, old buddy, you can have some of this, too!" Jim quickly moved out of the way of Ron's embrace-rush, like a quarterback eluding a tackler, and Ron nearly fell on his face. "What the fuck?" This time, WTF was not positive.

Stella spoke. "We have to move." Ron noticed she was a young woman now, and she looked a lot like Erika. Black hair (Erika was a blonde, but the similarities were striking), blue eyes, pug nose, flawless skin. And she was obviously an alpha creature. "We don't have time for this right now, Dad. They're going to be looking for you. For us. We'll catch up later." She even had the vocal cadence of her mom. She spoke like a woman who knew what she wanted but also knew it was good to be nice to people. Sort of like a very capable kindergarten teacher, trying to keep everybody in line and, at the same time, making sure she wasn't ruining anybody's fragile young self-esteem. It's what Ron fell for the first time he met Erika, and he was impressed it passed to his daughter. *His daughter*. He was with *his daughter*. He had come to Vegas to find himself and he found *his daughter*. If there was any time in his life Ron might have believed in a higher power, this was it.

Might have. A shot rang out from behind them, and Jim crumpled to the ground beside Ron. Stella all of a sudden had a large semi-automatic weapon in her hand and had turned and fired a series of shots back towards the door they had come out of before Ron had even realized what was going on. Holy fuck, his daughter had a gun! Eschewing his fatherly desire to talk to her about the danger of firearms, Ron knelt down to Jim. "Buddy." He could see that Jim, who had greying long hair like Sam Elliot and a weathered face to match, was bleeding from a wound to his chest. "It's going to be okay." Isn't that what they always said on those *CSI* television shows? Going to be okay. Was anything ever going to be okay? Somehow, today didn't seem to be leaning that way.

Stella kneeled down to Ron and Jim. "I took care of one guy coming after us, but there will be others. We really have to move. How is he?" Ron wondered if that was a rhetorical question. How is he? Well, they always asked that question on those CSI television shows, too, so...hey, Ron thought, am I on TV? He'd love for somebody to pop up from behind a camera right now and yell "cut" and then he and Stella and Jim and Bambi could live happily ever after and this nightmare could be over.

Unfortunately, Jim's wound started gurgling, bringing Ron out of his head and back to present tense. Stella leaned over him and took a close look at the wound. "That's bad," she said to Ron. "Shit." Again, Ron resisted the urge to give her fatherly advice–this time, about using such words in public–because she was a young woman now, not a little girl anymore. And, well, the word shit was completely appropriate under the circumstances. Ron realized that while she got her good looks and her kindergarten teacher personality from her mother, she probably got her motherfucking mouth from her motherfucking father. He was so motherfucking proud.

"Shit." So Ron thought he'd add to the conversation. A conversation with small curse words, just like normal dads have with normal daughters. Riiiight.

"Blah me." Jim was making noises below them, on the ground. Ron and Stella both leaned down to hear what he was saying. "Blah me."

"Blah me?" Stella was clearly confused. "What, Jim?"

"BITE ME." Jim was staring right at Ron. And Ron remembered how this went.

"No, you bite ME, motherfucker," Ron said. Just like the old days. A couple of dudes insulting each other in that loving, American male way. At that moment, Ron knew Jim was going to be just fine. "And fuck off, too, bitch," he added, just for effect. He and Jim were always trying to outdo each other in the insult department—it's what guys do. Hell, Ron could remember a time they sat at Carnaval Court and insulted each other's mothers all day long—that was a good day.

"Dad, I don't think that's what he means."

"Of course, Stella, he doesn't really want me to bite him. It's a guy thing. Have you ever had a boyfriend?"

"No, Dad, he—"

"No boyfriend? Okay. Are you a lesbian? I don't care, either way, as long as you're happy."

"No, Dad, he—"

"Not a lesbian and never had a boyfriend? Ya know, honey, I'm proud of you. Too many girls these days get into trouble too early and—"

"Fuck you, Dad. Jim wants you to fucking bite him! Really fucking bite him!"

"What?"

"He's dying, Dad."

Ron looked down. Jim sure was bleeding all over the place. The smell made Ron hungry. Damn. His best friend was dying and he was hungry and his daughter was cussing him out. Was this day going to be okay? "Why would he want me to bite him, honey?"

"Because you can save him."

"Um, what?"

"Bite him and turn him. Into a zombie. Otherwise he's going to die right here, right now, outside Carnaval Court."

"Um, but if he dies won't he turn into a zombie anyway?" That's the way Ron remembered it. And he figured if anybody around here was an expert in what makes people zombies, Ron was.

"No, Dad, the virus has been eradicated. If he dies, he dies. And he doesn't come back. But if you bite him…"

"BIIIITTTTTE MEEEEEEE." Jim seemed to think this was a good idea. Ron looked around. The gunshots had drawn a crowd. People didn't get too close, though. He figured there were a dozen people standing about a dozen feet away. Stupid people. Find something better to do. Isn't Kathy Lee Gifford playing at the Las Vegas Hilton?

"C'mon, Dad, we're wasting time!" Stella gave him a look that said, *You're my fucking idiot father and I'm putting up with you why?* "BITE HIM!"

"But what if it doesn't work?"

"He's gonna die right here or he's gonna die after you bite him. Or maybe he lives. Your choice, Dad." Stella looked towards the door they came out of. "This is Las Vegas. Take a gamble."

Ah, fuck it, Ron thought. His best friend was bleeding out on the walkway behind the Carnaval Court, people were watching, and who knows who was going to come out of that door next. His daughter was right.

Ron bent over his best friend, searching for the best place to bite him. Sure, if he was with a bunco and this was a wartime situation, it wouldn't matter where he bit him. But being that Jim was hopefully coming back as a zombie, Ron wanted to make sure he didn't take a huge gash out of someplace conspicuous, like Jim's face. Okay, no face biting. Oh, shit, Ron thought, what if I bite him once and can't stop? I am pretty hungry, and–

"DAD!"

"Okay, honey! Jesus!" Ron looked up for a moment. He used to go to church on holidays, maybe God or Jesus or Vishnu or whoever the fuck was up there could help him right now. "You up there?" he asked so that nobody could hear. Then Ron realized if he had a God, He or She was probably a zombie God. Which didn't sound nearly as inspiring as a regular God at the moment, and inspiration was really God's strength, as far as Ron was concerned. And shit, his zombie God was probably hungry too.

Ron ripped opened Jim's button down short sleeve poplin shirt, exposing his chest to the air. Wow, Jim thought, Ron had been working out a lot since the last time he saw him. He used to be a bit pudgy, but now his firm, taut chest and abs glistened in the Las Vegas sun. Like a muscle car.

"DAD! NOW! FUCK!"

Ron leaned over, nervous that he might want more than just a bite, and closed his eyes. Baseball, baseball, baseball....perhaps a distraction, in this instance, would help. Baseball, baseball, baseball...he bared his teeth, opened his eyes, and took a bite of Jim's left pectoral muscle. It tasted like Ron imagined a baseball would taste, all leathery and chewy, so the distraction appeared to be working. At least it wasn't as good as Joaquin's eyeballs, by comparison. Jim's pec would have needed some cream or soy sauce to get it to the point where Ron would have called it edible, but fuck it–desperate times and all that. He chewed it up as best he could, keeping his mind on baseball the whole time. He didn't want to realize what he was doing. Then he realized he didn't actually have to eat it, per se–this was more about infecting Jim.

Ron spit out what was in his mouth onto the ground and looked down at Jim, who had lost consciousness. Blood was seeping from the sides of his body on the concrete walkway and Ron wondered if he was dead.

"He's dead," Stella said quietly. Well, that answers that, Ron thought to himself. No sense being a smartass to his daughter right now. She closed her eyes, put her head down on Jim's exposed chest, and stayed there for a second. Ron recognized that basic human compassion–she got *that* from her mother.

"Look, they're zombieing! Let's do that, too!" From about a dozen feet away, Ron saw a tourist–he had one of those big drinks around his neck–put his drink down, lay down on the ground, and play dead. His friend leaned over him and pretended to take a bite of his chest, spilling his own drink all over the first guy. "Yeah, we're zombieing!" All of a sudden, six other people dropped to the ground and six of their friends pretended to take bites out of this chests. Stupid fucking humans, Ron thought. I should go over there and take a bite out of all of you. I'll be McGruff, the Crime Zombie. *Take A Bite Out Of Stupidity!*

"Let's get him to my car. It's in the garage right over here." Stella reached down and grabbed one of Jim's arms, and Ron noticed that she had serious arm muscles. She also got those from her mother. Damn, her mother was full of gifts for her, wasn't she? Ron realized he made a good choice of women to impregnate, back in the day, because his daughter was a total badass.

Ron grabbed Jim's other arm, and he and Stella lifted him up so they could half carry him, half drag him. Ron looked over at all the idiots Zombieing and was thankful for them, for they had drawn a crowd and nobody was paying attention to Ron and Stella, half-carrying and half-dragging a dead guy to a parking garage in Las Vegas. Really, Ron thought as he, Stella, and Jim's body headed towards the Casino Royale parking garage, this had to be a common occurrence around here.

A security guard appeared out of nowhere, right in the path to the parking garage. "Um, is your friend okay?" Okay, Ron asked himself rhetorically. He's dead and I just bit him and he tasted like fucking baseball–do you think he's okay?

"Officer, he's just had a bad morning. A little too much." Stella made the universal hand motion for *this fucker drank waaaay too much alcohol*–sort of a hang loose motion on acid–and continued. "We're going to take him back to his room to sleep it off."

"Yeah, you do that. There are laws–contrary to public opinion, mind you–against public intoxication in Las Vegas. So you do that."

"Thanks, officer," Stella said. "We will."

"Yeah, we will," Ron said, unintentionally sarcastic. Shit, can't I leave well enough alone?

"You a smartass, boy?" Obviously the security guard took his job very seriously–and was confused about Ron's age. Ron was certainly no boy. He wasn't alive, either, but he was no boy. Stupid Rent-A-Cop.

"He's my dad. He's a dumbass. And he needs his meds, which are also back in the room." For a moment, Ron wasn't sure if he should be proud of his daughter for breaking up the tension or pissed at her for calling him names. Then she sweetly smiled at the security guard, and he saw Erika in that smile. Then she kissed the security guard on the cheek and he knew that Stella was smarter than he was. And he also knew that she knew exactly what she was doing.

"Okay, then, you get these two back to their room, ya hear? I don't wanna see Drunk Dude or Dumbass Dad out here again until they're in better shape."

"Thank you, officer." Stella smiled that one-side-of-her-mouth smile that all women have that says, *Hey, good lookin', I'll be back to fuck your brains out later.* Ron recognized it; from any other woman it would have been great. But from his daughter? He started to protest, but realized that the security guard was walking away.

"You're welcome, ma'am. Have a good evening," the security guard said as he went on his way. Probably to bang a hooker after he busts her, Ron thought. *I can get you off if you get me off,* he'd say.

"Good thing he didn't see the blood. Let's go." Clearly, Stella was in charge and, being that she knew exactly what she was doing, Ron was completely okay with that. They dragged/carried Jim to the Casino Royale parking garage, and Stella led them to her car. A 1968 Chevrolet El Camino. Of course. Painted black, like a hearse, with a shell. A fuckmobile, Ron used to call these. You could do things in the back of an El Camino that, frankly, no other car or truck would accommodate.

"This is your car?" Ron asked between heavy breaths. Dragging a 200 pound dead man through Vegas was not easy. He wondered how mobsters did it. They must have had a mobster hand truck.

"Surprised, Dad?" Stella wasn't nearly as out of breath as Ron was.

"Does everybody in Vegas drive a…"

"A what, Dad?"

Ron hesitated. This really wasn't the time to ask her daughter about her fuckmobile. "A muscle car?"

"Everybody who needs muscles does."

"Um, haha?" Ron wasn't sure if this was a joke. Stella dropped the tailgate and opened the back of the shell. Ron noticed that the shell was reinforced with steel plates. Maybe it wasn't a fuckmobile after all, maybe it was…something else entirely.

"Help me get him in here, Dad." She lifted Jim up a bit, all by herself, and waited for Ron to carry his part of the load. He lifted his half of Jim and they slid him up, into the bed of the El Camino. Stella closed the shell window and the tailgate and locked both. Ron noticed that the windows of the shell were made with reinforced glass. It almost looked like this car was built for the military.

Stella hopped in the front seat. "We have to get the fuck out of here, Dad. Get in."

"Where are we going, honey?"

"Somewhere safe, Dad. Get the fuck in."

Ron opened the door and sat down in the front seat of the El Camino. With his daughter by his side and his best friend right behind him in the back of this steel reinforced fuckmobile, Ron realized he had found what he had come to Vegas for. Sort of. Did it matter that his best friend was dead and his daughter carried a semi-automatic weapon and knew how to use it? No, it didn't really matter. He was spending time with both of them. And sometimes you have to appreciate the small moments in life and/or death, no matter the circumstances.

CHAPTER
-16-

Driving away from the Las Vegas Strip, in any direction, means you're in mini-mall hell. Need Chinese Food for a buck a scoop? It's here. Need a paycheck cashed (for only 12% of your pay!)? It's here. Need buildings constructed with nothing but dirty stucco and greedy dreams? They're here. If Martians ever wanted to evaluate whether or not to conquer our society based on Vegas mini-malls, they'd have enough data from one off-Strip Vegas block to realize we aren't really worth the trouble. No signs of intelligent life here.

"Dad, why'd you leave Mom?" They were speeding down some street in Stella's El Camino in some Vegas burb, surrounded by mini-malls. At least if Ron got hungry for food, he could have cheap Chinese food. A buck a scoop could go a long way, as long as the scoop size is decent.

The question made Ron's brain freeze. Um, really? "Um, really? I didn't leave her. It was a mutual decision. We realized we had nothing in common but seared scallops and you."

"And that wasn't enough?" It really was a fair question, coming from the product of a failed relationship. Shouldn't that product have been enough to keep the relationship together? A question for the ages, truly.

"It should have been."

"Damn fucking right, Dad, it should have been." Stella reached up above the El Camino's sunshade and pulled out a pack of cigarettes, lit one with the El Camino's lighter, and took a drag. "You fucked me up."

"You're smoking?"

"It's your fault."

"Oh, please, honey, it's your life. Especially now. I didn't put that cigarette in your mouth."

"Might as well have. But don't worry, I only smoke when I drink." She reached down by the driver's side door and pulled out a flask. "Want some?"

"No, thanks. Wait–you're drinking? You're not even old enough!"

"Just enough to take the edge off. I always need a drink after I shoot a gun." Stella took a medium-sized swig from the flask and passed it to Ron. My daughter's firing a gun, smoking, and drinking, and she's only 17...yeah, all right, Ron thought, I'll take a drink. He took the flask and took a large-sized swig from it. Good whiskey. Stella definitely had his taste in alcohol.

While Ron pondered how the hell he got to this point in his life–or death–Stella gassed the El Camino and anonymous mini-malls seemed to fly by like lost dreams in a lost nightmare. Ron wondered if the Buck A Scoop Chinese Food had any MSG in it. Then he wondered why he even gave a shit. MSG sure as fuck didn't affect zombies.

They both heard a noise from the bed of the El Camino, and Ron realized that there was no glass between the El Camino's cab and its bed–only steel bars. They both looked back and Jim still looked dead.

Ron felt it was time to address the elephant in the car. "Look, honey, I'm sorry we split up. It was better in the long run."

"For who, Dad? For who?" She took a long drag from her cigarette and Ron heard another noise from the back of the El Camino. He turned around and saw Jim stirring.

"Um, honey, he seems to be alive."

"I was alive, too, Dad, the whole fucking time you were gone. I was alive."

"He's moving."

"I was moving, too, Dad, your daughter, and did you ever give a shit about me?" She took a long drag from her cigarette. It relaxed her enough that the look on her face changed from *I want to kill somebody* to *I want to kill somebody in five minutes*. "Did you ever?"

"Of course, honey!" Jim moaned. Ron turned to watch him. "I send you birthday cards and all that!"

"All that? All what? A fucking birthday card once a year from a father I barely knew?" Jim shook like a Polaroid Picture, Ron thought, and chuckled. "Oh, that's funny? God, Dad, you're a prick."

"Honey, I'm sorry, that wasn't a laugh for or at you. Jim is shaking. Like a Polaroid–

"'Jim is alive, Jim is moaning, Jim is shaking'. God, what about me, Dad?" The *I want to kill somebody* look had returned to her face, and she took another long drag from her cigarette. Jim got up on his hands and knees in the back of the El Camino and looked at Ron. Yep, he looked like a zombie. What the hell have I done, Ron asked himself.

"Look, Stella, once your mom and I broke up," Jim started shuffling/crawling towards the cab of the El Camino. Ron watched him out of the corner of his eye. "She didn't want me around anymore."

"SHE didn't want you around, Dad? What about me? What about ME?" Just then, Jim's hand came through the metal bars of the El Camino's cab. Ron thought he might be coming after Ron but then realized he had no reason to want another zombie...no, he wanted live flesh. Stella. She knew it, too, and slid over towards her door, just outside Jim's reach.

"EARGGggHHHH," Jim howled as he grabbed desperately for the live human driving the El Camino. Ron took his left elbow and slammed it against the hand, hoping to scare it off.

"I wanted to come back and be a part of your life–"

"But you didn't." Stella stuck the cigarette in her mouth. With her left hand she steered the El Camino down the endless ribbon of Vegas asphalt, with her right she formed a fist and hit Jim's zombie elbow as hard as she could. "It helps to hit them in the elbow, Dad." Jim retreated to the bed of the El Camino. "And why the fuck didn't you?"

"I…" Ron really didn't have an answer for this question. Why didn't he stick around when he and Erika split up? Was it because he wasn't done chasing brunettes? That answer wouldn't fly with his daughter, he realized. Was it because he was bitter about the realization that he and Erika really had nothing in common? That was quite a disappointment, ultimately. Maybe he was a coward who couldn't face up to his own failures. This thought might have made him tear up if he were human.

Jim came back to the opening between the cab and bed, this time with both hands. "CRRAAAAAAGHHHHHHH!" He appeared to be hungry. At least that's what it looked like to Ron. Sort of like a prisoner in a jailhouse movie, begging for food. With urgency. Both of his hands were swinging wildly in the air towards Stella, and his face had the determined look of the best NFL linebackers.

"I don't know."

"You don't know? You basically fucking abandoned your daughter and you don't know why?"

"SCREEEEEEEEEESSSSSSHHHHHHH!" Jim really wasn't into this conversation.

Ron grabbed Jim's hands and held them close to him so Stella could drive. "It was a difficult time in my life."

"Yeah, well, Dad, you turned me into a 17-year-old runaway who smokes, drinks, and shoots a gun. Congratufuckinglations. You're father of the motherfucking year." Ron looked over, and Stella had a tear in her eye. The advantages of being human.

"AAAAAAAAARRRRRRRRRRRZZZZZZZZZZ!" Jim did not respect the gravity of this conversation, and he was not afraid to show it. Now he had his face pressed up against the metal bars protecting them from him and he was trying to get his hands back from Ron.

"I'm sorry, honey."

"Can you talk to him? Tell him to settle the fuck down?"

"Talk to who?"

"Jim! Who the fuck do you think?"

"Jim? I can't talk to him. He's a zombie!"

"So are you, Dad! Shit, you've always been a zombie to me!" She reached down for her flask and took another small swig. Damn, Ron thought, it's one thing when you think you're a zombie–or when you know you're a zombie–but when your daughter thinks you've always been a zombie, you've been a shitty father. Maybe he *was* father of the motherfucking year.

Ron decided to be pragmatic. "We have some unresolved issues, honey."

"Fuck shit, yes we do, we have motherfucking *unresolved issues*, Dad!" Stella looked at him, tears slowly trickling down her face like the very beginning of the first Colorado summer rainstorm. "Fucker."

"GRRRREEEEEEEEEEEEEEEEEEEEEEEEEEEEEEEEEEEEEEEEEEE ETTTTTTT!" Jim didn't give a fuck about issues or about how Ron felt about Stella or about how Stella felt about Ron or about

Stella's Colorado tears. To Jim, she was a steak. While his arms flailed about the cab and his face pressed up against the steel bars so much that Ron thought he might be putting permanent valleys into his skin, Ron also thought it'd be funny to offer him some steak sauce. Or maybe that'd just be mean. He wasn't going to get to Stella, after all. No matter how much of a shitty father Ron was, it was still his job to protect his daughter, so he reached over and punched Jim square in the face. Jim fell back into the bed of the El Camino and lay there, still.

"Don't kill him, Dad! Talk to him!"

Damn, Ron thought, I can't do anything right. "I don't think I killed him, and I know I can't talk to him. Zombies don't have a language."

"Oh, so, BLAAAAAAAHHHHHHHH doesn't mean 'I want to chew on your ass?'"

"No, honey."

"And   'SCREEEEEENNNNNNNDDDDDDDDDDDDYYYYY' doesn't mean 'I want to swallow your eyeballs whole and feel them as they slide down my throat like grapes?'"

"How'd you know about that?"

"YOU'VE DONE THAT, DAD?" Stella all of a sudden looked like she wanted to vomit. She rolled down her window, turned, and did just that, puking at 45 miles an hour. "Jesus, Dad!"

"What the hell do you think we zombies do when we get hungry, honey?"

"Not you, not–that."

"Yes, that."

"No wonder I'm so fucked up." Stella took a swig from her flask and grabbed her pack of cigarettes from above the visor, all in one motion. "My therapist is going to have a field day with this. 'How are you feeling today, Stella? Tell me about your childhood.' 'Well, Patty, I was raised by a zombie. How's that for fucked up?'"

"Can I have one of those?" Ron hadn't smoked since he was a teenager, but he figured zombie lungs weren't going to develop lung cancer, right? And it might give him some common ground with his daughter. He wasn't having much luck finding any other common ground, outside of whiskey, sarcasm and fuckin' foul language, so what the hell. Besides, he just found out his 17-year-old daughter is in therapy, among other things. That might take a while to digest...about as long as eyeballs.

"Yeah, sure, and light mine for me, will ya?"

Ron took two cigarettes from the pack, stuck them both in his mouth, and lit them with the cigarette lighter from the dash of the El Camino, as the miles of blacktop and buncoes of generic strip malls disappeared underneath its tires and chrome rims. At this moment, Ron wished he could make his past disappear, too...but that was impossible. She was sitting right next to him.

CHAPTER
-17-

No place in the country was hit harder by the recession than Las Vegas. From high above the city, it's a concentric circle: The Strip and downtown are the center, and it radiates out from there until, on the edge of Vegas, you have what were going to be new McMansions, but are now just empty lots. Tons of empty lots. Many of them graded so that from an airplane, it looks like somebody's laid out their brown stamp collection on the ground, in neat, easy-to-read patterns. Ever see a stamp collection that looks like a cul-de-sac? You can, from 30,000 feet over Las Vegas.

Just inside this outer layer of the degradation ring, though, is the Ring of Foreclosure. So named because yes, it consists almost solely of foreclosed homes. Pre-recession, housing prices in Vegas were increasing faster than the heart rate of a bum winning the lottery, and everybody in the country took note. Subsequently, Las Vegas was inundated with people from all over, wanting a piece of that action. Remember, it was pre-recession, so everybody was completely optimistic about real estate. It'll never go down in value, right? Only up! Right? Right.

So developers, as they are wont to do, provided for the demand and built…and built…and built, until the outer rings of Vegas were covered with brand new shiny houses. Which people were buying. Which meant the developers kept building…until it all fell apart. And when it all fell apart, people who had purchased a $480,000 stucco palace in the Las Vegas desert on an office manager's salary lost their jobs and any ability to pay that back (not that an office manager ever had the ability to pay back $480,000, but that's a different story for a different time), and the banks repossessed. Thus, the Ring of Foreclosure. Brought to you by unfettered optimism, unfettered greed, and the American Way. Unfettered, of course.

"Where the fuck are we going, honey?" Ron asked Stella but wasn't sure she was going to tell him. Much of what was happening to him today wasn't explained. Sometimes, Ron thought, you gotta go along for the ride. And when everybody else around you seems to know more than you do about what exactly the ride is, you let them lead you. This method had served Ron well over the years, and he wasn't going to change it now. Really, he was just happy to see his daughter again. Everything else was gravy…which might go well with eyeballs, come to think of it.

"CLLLLGHHHAHKLKJLJLKJKJJJJ!" Jim had recovered from his punch to the face and was trying to destroy the back of the El Camino like he was a cop and it was a doughnut. Wherever they were going, Ron thought, he wasn't sure he wanted to be part of removing Jim from the car, if that's what they were doing. Ron took a drag from his cigarette.

"We're almost there, Dad." By Ron's eyes, *there* was nowhere. They had pulled off the main road leading them out here and were heading west, towards wherever-the-fuck-all. The sun was a huge fuzzy orange ball on the horizon ahead of them and Ron couldn't exactly see where they were going, so 'wherever-the-fuck-all' it was. Again, along for the ride.

Stella steered the El Camino around a turn to the north and Ron could see that they were in a neighborhood of new houses. Spanish tile roofs everywhere, pastel colored stucco, new asphalt roads and concrete sidewalks. Everything as clean as a toddler's rap sheet because it was all brand-spankin' new. Except that there were no cars. Stella's El Camino was the only car on the street. The only car on any of the streets, Ron realized as he looked around. It was almost like a brand new ghost town. Either that, Ron realized, or everybody parked in their garages. But everybody? Did everybody really park in their garages? And leave the garage doors closed? Shit, Ron thought, based on my experience, I'd expect to see nothing but 1960s and 1970s Chevy, Ford and Plymouth muscle cars here. Maybe this was one of those covenant controlled communities, where you weren't allowed to have a car on the street or a garage door open. Ron had heard of such things. He had never lived in one, because he wasn't really a fan of restrictions, but he knew that a lot of people did. Some people need rules to feel comfortable in society.

"Do you live out here?" Ron looked over at his daughter as she put out her cigarette butt in the El Camino's ashtray.

"T T T T T T T T T H H H H H H H H H H H-HHLLLLLLLLLLLLLLLLLLLAAAAAAAAAAAAAAAA!" Jim was obviously annoyed that he wasn't part of this conversation, but fuck him, Ron thought. He should be fucking glad to be alive. Or undead. Or whatever.

"I don't live out here, but I work out here." Stella's face in the setting sunlight had an odd combination of the face of an innocent child and a tough street urchin, Ron thought. She was beautiful.

"Work?"

"Well, not like a job or whatever, Dad, but...you'll see. I just want to show you." What the fuck was this, Bring Your Zombie Father To Your Sort Of Work Day? Stella pulled the El Camino into a driveway and Ron could see that they were at a house just like any other–Spanish tile roof, light yellow stucco–*very* light yellow– a two-car garage in the front, big wooden front door, new fence around the side, faded brown grass in front. Yeah, grass in Vegas is always going to fade to brown at some point.

"BRRAAAAAAAINNNNNNNNNNS!" Jim was hungry, apparently. Wait, Ron thought, that's the first time he's said anything even mildly coherent. He turned to Jim and said, "Don't you mean CLAAAGGGGGH?" Jim looked him straight in the eye, tilted his head slightly like a puppy, and said, "Brains." Ron's eyebrows shot up. Stella smiled like she knew something everybody else in the car didn't.

"Um, honey, why is Jim saying brains? And why isn't he destroying the back of your car anymore?"

"Dad, just come with me." Obviously she knew what the hell was going on, right? You don't ask somebody such an important question and get an answer like *just come with me* without the question answerer not knowing the answer. It was an evasive answer for a reason. It means *I'd rather show you than take the time to explain it to you*. Sort of like the first time you get a blow job. *Um, why are heading down there? Just–just come with me.* So to speak.

Stella reached up above her sun visor and pushed a button and the house's garage door opened; Stella drove the El Camino into the garage and reached up again to close the garage door. Ron looked around the garage. It was brand new and completely empty, except for a trash can in the corner. Stella opened her door and looked over at Ron. "Come on."

"Brains?" Jim and his seemingly endless supply of puppy-dog facial expressions seemed concerned that he might not actually get brains. His concern was probably valid because Stella and Ron left him in the back of the El Camino as they stepped inside the house.

Ron looked back at him. "Sorry, buddy, maybe later." He flashed a peace sign at Jim. "Brains, brother!"

The house was like most suburban homes built in the last 10 years–high end aesthetics, brittle and cheap skeleton. The kitchen was just inside the door to the garage, and the appliances were all stainless steel–the countertop was Big Giant Hardware Store Black Granite, and the cabinets were particle board covered with a beautiful cherry colored laminate. Pretty much what everybody wanted pre-recession, right? White ceramic floor tiles, formal dining room off the right, french doors to what might one day be a landscaped backyard, and a quiet moan.

"What the fuck is that?" Ron cocked his head like a puppy and smushed up his face at the sound...much like a puppy.

"What?" Stella was putting her cigarette out in the stainless steel two bowl sink that the developer probably bought off the shelf at Big Giant Hardware Store and didn't realize would one day be a giant ashtray.

"That sound. That moaning. It sounds...familiar." Ron shuddered. Could it be?

"Of course it's familiar, Dad." She walked over to Ron and gave him a big hug. "It's really good to see you, Dad. I thought I'd never see you again, honestly."

Moan.

"It's good to see you too, honey." Ron returned the hug best he could, but what the fuck was that sound?

"You call that a hug, Dad?" Stella disengaged from the hug and looked at Ron, not like a puppy, but more like a disappointed daughter.

"I'm distracted." Everybody knows men can't show full emotions if they're distracted, right? Ron hoped disappointed daughters understood this harsh truth.

"By the sound?"

Moan.

"Yeah. That sound."

Moan.

"Okay, Dad, let me show you something." She started down the hall from the kitchen to the living room. Ron followed. In the living room Stella sat down at a bank of blank computer monitors and offered Ron a second chair. "Here. Sit." Ron sat down and Stella clicked a few buttons on the keyboard in front of her and every monitor in front of her fired on at the same time. And on those monitors? Zombies. Lots and lots of zombies. Not just zombies–zombies playing billiards, darts, ping pong, and watching sports on television, all the while moaning. What the fuck was going on?

Humans as a species are a chill bunch. Once they do enough with their lives, they're content to build a palace of their own and fill it with the accoutrements of relaxation. It's why we have mancaves, recreational vehicles and basements.

It was obvious to Ron that the zombies on the screen were in a basement, mancave or really great pub. Where else would you have dart boards, big screens and billiard tables? It was like the ultimate night out.

"What the fuck? Where are they?" Ron asked two questions at once, not really expecting an answer to the first. What is the correct answer to *What the fuck* anyway? *Um, this right here – this the fuck?* Riiiiight.

"Downstairs."

"Downstairs where?"

"Downstairs here. You asked about the moaning."

Ron squinted his eyes and inadvertently cocked his head a little. Yes, like a puppy. "Downstairs here?"

"Do I stutter, Dad?"

"You didn't when I left you." Touche! That'll teach her to mouth-off to her father.

"Don't be a dick."

"Those zombies are here in the basement?"

"You're quick, Dad."

"Forgive me. It's been a wild fucking day." Ron figured he might just have won the Oscar for the Understatement of the Year, and when he got to go on stage to accept his award, he'd probably thank Bambi, David, Kathy Lee Gifford, Jeffrey Skidmore, Stella, Jim, Flippy, Rob, Charlie, Robyn, the members of the Academy... and when the music started playing before he was done, he'd eat somebody. Yeah, a meal would be nice right now. A private meal, in a dark hotel room, with nobody around. Good for the stomach, good for the soul. And everybody knew the way to a zombie's soul was through his stomach.

"Why are they in this basement?" Ron thought he'd ask. It was an obvious question, even though nothing about today had been obvious. And, judging by Stella's actions, she probably knew the answer.

"Well, Dad–" The door from the basement opened and one of the zombies shuffled into the living room.

"Holy fuck! ZOMBIE!"

"Dad–"

Ron grabbed Stella and put her behind him as he prepared to fight the zombie to the undeath. No zombie was going to eat his daughter.

"Dad–"

"Stay back. I'll protect you from the zombie, honey!" Ron assumed a typical Kung Fu Pose: one leg up in the air so he could kick if he wanted to, and his hands up in the air like he was hanging laundry. He didn't know any kung fu, but it was the first thing that popped into his head, because he had seen it on some comedy show. He really wished he had a gun. Hey, wait, Stella had a gun. "Where's your gun, honey?"

"We don't need it. He's a friend." Wait, what, a friend? A zombie friend?

"No, he's a zombie. He's fucking dangerous. Stay back."

"You're a zombie too, Dad." Infallible female logic–like most men–it tripped Ron up every time.

"Yeah, but–but–but not totally. I'm re-evolving. I'm revolving." That was a good word, Ron realized. Revolving. It was truly how he felt. Back in Colorado, all he could think about was eating people and now all he could think about was eyeballs...and Bambi and protecting his daughter and daytime television. Well, okay, so daytime television isn't much of an evolution over wanting to eat people, but still. Ron was pretty certain he was revolving. Something was happening, anyway. He sure could think better than before...which wasn't saying much, considering where he came from.

"So is he, Dad." The zombie was now standing in front of Ron, looking him over, like a puppy. Ron felt a little sick to his stomach, but he remained in his Kung Fu Pose, just in case his daughter didn't know what the hell she was talking about. In spite of her often infallible female logic, Ron's also infallible male skepticism remained. And, really, it was his job as her father to remain skeptical. Ron figured it would come in handy when boys came around to take Stella out. *So, young zombie, what are your intentions for my daughter? You're not hungry, are you?* Ron chuckled at the thought.

"Wait, what?"

"They're all revolving. That's why they're here. And they're not dangerous."

"Not dangerous?"

"Brains." The zombie decided to join in the conversation.

"Don't worry, Dad," Stella said. "That's all he knows how to say right now. Well, that and corner pocket. He's a very good pool player. Aren't ya, Ted?"

"Brains! Corner pocket!" Ted smiled. A zombie smiling? Ron realized that he had never seen that before except in a mirror. It made him slightly uneasy, like a man whose daughter is out past curfew and hasn't texted or called. He glared at Ted.

"That is fucked up," Ron said to Ted without returning the smile. He learned a long time ago that not all smiles need to be returned, especially the ones you don't trust. And Ron didn't trust a zombie smile. Unless it was in a mirror.

"He's not fucked up, are ya Ted?" Stella smiled at Ted. What was up with everybody smiling at each other? Ron didn't think this was a time to be smiling, no sir. Zombies wanted to date his daughter! Or something.

"I'm confused." Ron thought maybe it was time to play State the Obvious.

Ted shuffled off as Stella tried to straighten out her father's confusion. "All the zombies here, Dad, are revolving. You, however, are revolving faster than any zombie we've ever seen. It's why we were following you."

"So that was you at in the Casino Royale parking garage?"

"Yep. Me and Jim. Oh, shit, Jim!" Stella's eyes went wide and she headed towards the garage door. "We better get him out of the car!"

Stella and Ron went out to the El Camino. Jim was sitting in the back, quietly looking around. "Hey guys, you gonna let me out of here?" Ron stopped halfway through his walking pace. Did Jim *really* just say that? Wasn't he talking about brains just five minutes ago?

"Sure, Jim, we'll let you out. How are you feeling?" Stella was talking to Jim through an open back window of the El Camino.

"Like I'm hung over." Nobody spoke for a second, and then Jim slowly said, "I'm a zombie, aren't I?" It wasn't really a question anybody needed to answer; Jim was covered in blood and there was still a hole in his chest where Ron bit him. Yep, you're a zombie! Don Pardo, tell him what he's won!

"Let's go inside." Stella opened up the back of the El Camino, Jim got out and they all walked into the house and sat down at the kitchen table. "Jim, you were shot escaping from the Underground and you were bleeding out, so I had my dad bite you. I kinda made an executive decision. I hope you're okay with it." She pulled out her pack of cigarettes and gave one each to Jim and Ron and herself. Ron got up and went over to the stove and lit his cigarette on the flame. He then passed his cigarette around to the others and they lit their cigarettes from his.

"Well, I guess I don't really have a fuckin' choice, right?" At least Jim was a pragmatic person. "Brains." Ur, pragmatic zombie.

"You were gonna die, buddy." Ron tried to help out. At this point, he thought maybe a 17-year-old girl couldn't really calm a zombie. Maybe Jim needed some zombie-to-zombie comforting to fully understand what had happened.

"Okay, then, thank you? I guess? Shit. I'm a fuckin' zombie." Jim put his head in his hands.

"It's not so bad." Ron figured he was the senior zombie here–maybe he could comfort the junior zombie enough to make him see the bright side. Ha! Bright side. In context, that was hilarious. When you're a new zombie, there really is no bright side.

The doorbell rang. Stella reached under the table and pulled out a large gun. "Who the fuck?" Ron was similarly impressed and afraid at the same time. This house at the edge of the world had a large gun hidden in it. And his daughter knew where it was hidden. Shit gets weirder all the time.

Stella went to the front door and looked through the peep hole. "I think somebody's lost. Stay hidden."

Ron and Jim went into the bathroom and closed the door. Ron looked into Jim's eyes and said the obvious thing. "We gotta stop meeting like this."

Jim returned the look and said, "I was really hoping you would have bought me dinner before you bit me, asshole."

They heard Stella open the front door. "Hello?" They heard a woman's voice speak. "Hi, I'm looking for my friend Kenny." Oh, shit, Ron thought, it's Bambi!

"There's nobody here by that name," Stella said, and Ron remembered she had a giant gun. Dammit, what if his daughter shot his girlfriend? Girlfriend? Did they have that kind of relationship already? We had sex, but it was just a quickie, so it didn't really count. He opened up the bathroom door and walked out to the front room.

"Bambi. What are you doing here?" He was looking at Stella, who was looking at him and at Bambi, back and forth, looking for all the world like *How the fuck do you two know each other*?

"I was looking for you, honey. Ur, Kenny."

"HONEY?" Stella seemed surprised. "Honey? Dad, this is your–what–your girlfriend?"

"Dad?" Bambi lifted her eyebrows. "You found Stella?"

"Dad, she fucking knows my name? How the fuck?"

Ron figured it was time to step in, see if he could straighten this out a bit. If that were possible. "Stella, Bambi, Bambi, Stella. She's my daughter, and," he pointed to Bambi, "she's my…my friend."

"Is this the tramp you left Mom for, Dad?" Oh, shit, Ron thought, not this. Not right now. There are zombies in the basement, my best friend is undead, I'm extremely hungry, and all you want to talk about is some misplaced notion that I left Erika for another woman?

"I told you–I didn't leave your mother for anybody. I left her for me. And for her. And for you."

"Don't blame me for this, Dad. I had nothing to do with it." Stella threw herself against the newly textured wall, folded her arms, stuck out her lower lip, and for a minute she looked just like a 1970s punk rock chick–Joan Jett, maybe–all attitude and snottiness and dark clothes and spiky haircut. As if to prove her '70s punk pedigree, Stella pulled a pack of cigarettes out from the pocket of her ripped black jeans and lit one. Ron half expected her to put a safety pin through her lip at the same time.

A thought occurred to Ron, and he looked at Bambi. "Wait a minute, how the fuck did you find me?"

"I, uh…" Bambi, for the first time since Ron had known her, appeared disingenuous. Then her face softened and she told the truth. "I was worried about you, so I put a tracking device in your shirt. Joaquin's shirt. Since you're a zom–wait, she knows, right?" Bambi motioned to Stella.

"Yes, I fucking know my fucking dad is a fucking zombie. Jeez." Stella rolled her eyes and slowly shook her head to say *I'm not a fucking moron*, took a drag on her cigarette, and blew smoke up to the newly textured vaulted ceiling above the living room. "You put a tracking device on me?" Ron all of a sudden had visions of Glenn Close never leaving him alone. "When?"

"After we, you know–you're a zombie. What if you get into trouble? I wanted to be able to find you. I was just worried. I can't imagine zombies in this town are treated very well."

"HOLY FUCK, DAD, you had SEX with her? That's just–fucking GROSS." Stella looked at Ron and Bambi and took a drag from her cigarette as she wheeled around. "GROSS. I never imagined my parents having sex, but this is worse! GROSS!" she said as she left the room.

Ron and Bambi paused as the two of them stared off into space. The gravity of everything they were going through seemed to weigh down the room like an anchor weighs down a boat. Bambi spoke first. "I'm sorry."

"It's okay." Ron really did think it was okay. Truthfully, he was happy to see her. And she was wearing a tank top. In spite of it all, that always helped. Which, Ron thought, made him your average American male. The world can be going to shit, your 17-year-old daughter can be smoking cigarettes, drinking whiskey, and hating your zombie guts–your best friend can be undead, but a nice pair of ample American titties barely concealed under a flimsy tank top can make everything seem momentarily okay. Yay titties! Sorry, breasts. Second date rules.

While Ron was having his mental mammary celebration and rules reminder, he didn't notice David sneak up behind him and put a shotgun to Ron's head. Bambi noticed, but by the time she could warn Ron, it was too late.

CHAPTER
-19-

If you've never had a gun barrel against your head, it feels just how you imagine it feels–like a gun barrel against your head. The cold hardness of metal up against a skin-covered skull is hard to describe, except as *it's like having a gun barrel against your head*. Who knew that such a thing didn't lend itself to metaphorical description?

And David's gun against Ron's head was jarring. Probably more so than usual because David was pissed off and gentle persuasion was not part of his personality when he was happy, so he was treating Ron like he was a cue ball, trying to get it into the corner pocket. Poke, poke, poke...

Bambi went first. "David, what are you doing?"

"Yeah, Dave, ol' buddy, what's up?" Ron turned around to shake David's hand but shortly found the barrel of the shotgun flat against his nose.

"You're a fucking zombie." The look in David's eyes suggested that this was not new information to him. It also suggested he was not happy to be privy to this information.

"Put the gun down, David." Bambi took a step towards David, her breasts jiggling underneath her tank top. Ron realized she wasn't wearing a bra.

"Take one more step and I'll fucking kill him." Wow, Ron thought, way to stop a nice jiggle, asshole. You're going on my menu–I can go low-rent once in a while, fuckface.

"Look, David, whatever's going on–"

"You're a fucking zombie."

"David, put the gun down. He never did anything to you." Bambi seemed genuinely concerned that this might turn into something stupid. Which is exactly what Ron thought about it–it was stupid. I'm a zombie, David doesn't like zombies, it's a stalemate, can I just take my daughter and girlfriend and go home? Wherever-the-fuck-all *home* is.

Another man appeared in the doorway to the kitchen. He was dressed just like David. Big brown boots, big black rifle, camouflage pants, camouflage shirt...like they were going out into the jungle. In the desert. Stupid humans, Ron thought. They probably sell those clothes at Walmart and they were probably made by kids in China who know what a jungle really is. Wearing camouflage clothes you bought at a low low price does not make you a soldier. Or warrior. Or whatever. It makes you an idiot. Who looks like an idiot. If you really wanted to camouflage yourself in Vegas, you'd wear clothes that have pictures of giant casinos all over them. Or, if you wanted to metaphysically camouflage yourself in Vegas, you'd wear clothes covered in unrealistic expectations and shattered dreams.

"There are more downstairs," the second man said. "A *lot* of them."

"Call for backup." Oh, great, Ron thought, there are more assholes like you out there? And you're going to bring them here? Well, hell, maybe this will be my Vegas buffet!

"David, you and your little friends should leave. Before things get ugly." Bambi looked intently at her brother. Ron wondered if intent looks ever convinced anybody of anything. They weren't as convincing as, say, a rifle barrel against your head, anyway, even if they did lend themselves to metaphorical description.

"Sis, you know what we have to do. As sergeants in the Zombie Extermination and UFO Society, it is our job to eliminate all zombies."

"Is that what it's called?" Bambi took a step towards David. This time he didn't move his body or his rifle. Ron started to get a little itch where the metal touched his nose. "I thought it was a Beer and Porn Club, because that's all you seem to do when you meet."

"Wait, what's the Zombie Extermination UFO Society?" Sure, there was a gun pointed at his nose, but Ron was never one to hold back a logical question...and he kept going. "Why aren't you in KILLZ?

David and his friend laughed maniacally, like they'd just been asked if they would like a microbrewed beer instead of their usual piss lager. "KILLZ sucks," David said, pushing his rifle further into Ron's head. "That's why we ain't in no fucking KILLZ, they ain't got rid of all the zombies like we do! ZEUS all the way!"

Bambi looked at her brother like he was a nutcase–which, Ron thought, he was–and asked, "How the fuck did you find me?"

"I followed you because your boyfriend is a fucking zombie. It's pretty easy to follow you out here in the Ring of Threeclosure. You were the only car."

"It's the Ring of *Fore*closure, asshole." Ron thought this was obvious...to anybody with a brain.

Which David may not have had. "What?" God, Ron, thought, this guy was really fucking stupid, and he might be the one to end my life once and for all. It was always the brothers of the women he liked that were the stupidest–every fucking time. It was probably

God's Balancing Act–if you're gonna have two kids, one of them is gonna (Ron was sure God didn't use the word gonna, but he was also sure that his thoughts at this exact moment were going to send him to hell anyway, so fuck it) be gorgeous, smart, kind, and have incredibly beautiful breasts, and the other one is going to be a complete fucking douchebag. Just to even things out. Circle of Life and all that.

Bambi grabbed the gun, pushed it back, and stepped in between David and Ron. "You're going to have to go through me to get to him, big brother." See? Smart *and* kind. Okay, she was also gorgeous when she was taking a bullet for Ron *and* he knew her breasts were beautiful and she had a sense of humor...smart, kind, gorgeous, *and* funny. She was the perfect woman.

"You know I have to kill him, little sister. He probably ate my girlfriend. And if he didn't, one of his ancestors did. So I'ma kill him." He raised his rifle and put it to Bambi's nose. "Don't get in my way."

"But–" Bambi sounded like she was starting to cry. Ron was standing behind her, so he couldn't see her face, but she sure sounded like it. Ron knew that sound–he had disappointed many ex-girlfriends enough to know that sound. "But I *love* him." What the fuck, Ron thought. She's either a very good liar or this relationship was going to a whole new level. Ron realized he didn't have time at the moment to contemplate what that meant, so he stuck in his *to be contemplated later* compartment in his brain. Because yes, this might take some time to contemplate. Love usually does. Even when it's with the perfect woman.

"Shit, you can't love him." Ron could sense that David was about to enlighten all of them with some "knowledge." Or some douchebaggery, anyway. "He's a zombie. Zombies and humans can't fall in love, sis. And if they can, it still ain't right. Love is between a man and a woman–a *human* man and a *human* woman.

And that's it. Society's gotta have rules or the next thing you know men will be fucking dogs out in the street."

The second man laughed. "Hell yeah!" Ron could see that he was dealing with the upper echelon of humanity right here, all gathered in the same area code. Lovely.

"Next thing you know," David continued with his well-thought-out thesis while waving his gun around like it was his cock at a porn shoot, "zombies and humans will be getting married and there will be little zombie babies running around and then men zombies and men humans will be getting married and zombies be having butt sex and being all depraved and shit."

"Gay zombie marriage would be gross," the second man chimed in. "And all them zombies wanna take our jobs!"

"Yeah, what about zombies taking our jobs?" Clearly, Ron thought, these guys had been watching too much Fox News.

"David, you need to let him go." Clearly, Bambi had heard much of this engrossing discussion about the value of traditional marriage before and wanted to move on with her day.

"Nope, I need to kill him. And the rest of the zombies downstairs. So they don't take our jobs. Or our women."

"I'm your sister, David. And you know blood is thicker than opinions. That's what Daddy always said."

David took a breath and his eyes seemed to soften. "Yeah, that's right, God Dammit. Daddy did say that."

"So you need to let him go."

"He ain't blood. He ain't even *alive*. Daddy woulda killed him already."

"But I love him and I'm your blood. I'm thicker than your opinion that he should be dead. So let him go." Ron was amazed at that logic. Bambi really was smart. And people mentioning blood made him hungry, even if that's not how they meant it.

"FUCK!" David was clearly agitated. His gun was still being waved around like it was his cock at a porn shoot. "God Fucking

Dammit! If–IF I let him go, you stay here. Ain't no zombie dating my sister, no matter how you feel. Daddy woulda disagreed with that opinion. So your zombie friend's gotta leave. And he's gotta go far away. To the next state."

"Yeah, to Texas!" The second soldier in this Army of the Stupid had flunked geography, apparently.

"Deal." Clearly, Bambi wasn't going to consult with Ron about this deal. Ron certainly had different ideas. Indeed, while Tweedle Dee and Tweedle Douchebag had been having deep philosophical discussions with his girlfriend he had been working on an elaborate scheme to defeat both of them with his mouth and a few strategically placed bites. Too bad he wouldn't be able to implement the plan, because it would have totally worked. Totally.

"Baby, you gotta leave." David had withdrawn his offer of Gun Up Bambi's Nose and Bambi turned to Ron, repackaging the offer as Here Are My Breasts Now Please Leave to Ron. "Just go."

"But–" But what, Ron wondered. But I was gonna have some finger food? I was gonna make stuffed potato skins with your brother? We were gonna make our own episode of *Chopped* where the secret ingredient was your brother?

"Just go, honey. I'll see you later," Bambi whispered as she leaned over to press her lips lightly against Ron's. "I'll come find you."

"I guess I don't have a choice then," Ron said out loud so every moron in the room could hear. He looked over at Stella, who was standing against the wall in the living room, smoking a cigarette. Thanks for the help, honey. Fucking teenagers.

"You don't, fuckin' zombie. Now go. Mark, let's go downstairs and kill some zombies. Sis, you're coming with us."

Stella walked over with the keys to her El Camino in her hands. "Let's go, I'll drive. We're bringing Jim. And, uh, David, enjoy your stay."

David was clearly confused. "What the fuck?" This time, *what the fuck* was more about confusion than anything else. It's amazing how many ways those three words, in that particular order, can be used.

"It's a nice house–that's all I'm saying." Stella had a twinkle in her eye, a twinkle that Ron recognized. It said, *You're a fuckin' idiot and I'm a good bullshitter, but you'll figure that out soon.* She got that twinkle from her father.

"Uh, yeah, it is a nice house." David was clearly thrown off by this turn of conversation. Or maybe he was a fan of Joan Jett. "Hey, you, uh, wanna go out sometime?"

The twinkle returned to Stella's eye. "Sure, big boy. Look me up."

Big boy? Ron couldn't help but feel overprotective now, and he couldn't hold back. "Hey, motherfucker, if you touch my daughter you're dead."

"Dad, you're already dead, so lay off. Besides, I'm 17, I can date who I want." Stella pushed Ron towards the garage door. "Jim, we gotta go," she yelled. Jim came lumbering up the stairs like, yes, a puppy. Ron almost wanted to offer him a treat, but he had other things on his mind.

"But that guy's a douchebag!" Ron offered.

"At least I'm alive, dude," David chimed in.

"Yeah, Dad, he's alive," Stella said. "And I'm alive. We can bond over that – kinda like scallops and nothing else, right?" Ron realized he probably deserved that. Stella pushed Ron out the garage door and Jim followed.

CHAPTER

-20-

There is a style of teaching in schools known as Gradual Release of Responsibility which, over time, allows for transition of responsibility for the learning process in the schools from teacher to student, resulting in independent students who can handle whatever is thrown their way. In theory. It is also a theory that can and probably should be applied to parenting. Shelter your babies when they're babies and give them the tools and gradual freedoms that they need as they grow into children, teenagers and adults who are capable members of society.

Ron, however, had never heard of this style of parenting. And really, since his role as a father was cut off when he and Erika divorced, his gradual release model was truncated somewhat. Especially when it came to someone wanting to date his daughter.

"Honey, I forbid you to go out with that guy. He's an asshole." Ron was taking the high road, if the high road was a ditch.

"Seriously, Ron, she's a grown woman now–you have no control."

"I'm gonna take parenting advice from you, Jim? You're a zombie!"

"So you are you, asshole!" Jim had a point, as usual. He was always the logical one of the duo. Ron was the one who'd get drunk and stumble around hitting on random women until Jim guided them back to their hotel room. They were Las Vegas' own Batman and Robin. And, as everybody knows, Batman always needed Robin. And Ron always needed Jim. Otherwise his Vegas trips might have ended up in the gutter or, worse, the jail. Ron knew there were public intoxication laws, even in Nevada–just ask the Rent-a-cop!–and he knew that he was publicly intoxicated, in Nevada, more than once. And more than once, Jim had saved his ass by guiding him back to his room to sleep it off.

"Fucker." Ron acknowledged Jim's point the best he could.

"Guys, where are we gonna go?" Stella was ignoring Ron. She was also driving the El Camino out of the Ring of Foreclosure and towards wherever-the-fuck-all they were going next. Which could have been anywhere. Ron was in the front seat, because he called it–"I call the front seat!"–and Jim was in the back, because Ron called the front seat. Calling your seat was never fair for somebody.

"Shouldn't we get some of your guns and go back and rescue all the zombies?" Ron asked. "That fucker's going to kill them all."

"That fucker's crazy," Jim added.

"Don't worry about those zombies, Dad," Stella said. "Your ho's brother isn't going to hurt them."

"Honey, she's not a ho. I mean, she was, yesterday, but she's not anymore."

"Riiiiiight," Jim said. "Once a ho..."

"Shut up, fucker. Honey, how do you know that douchebag isn't going to hurt them? He and his friend sure seemed like they were hot to kill them some zombies. I mean, they were calling for backup!"

"In the Ring of Threeclosure!" Jim laughed at his own joke reincorporation from the back of the El Camino, where he looked like a prisoner who accepted where he was. He was always good at laughing at his own jokes. Somebody had to.

"Stella, honey, I really wanna go back and help the zombies out. Really, if–"

"Dad, don't worry. Those zombies are fine." Stella looked absolutely gorgeous in the fading light of this day, and her beautiful confidence was mysterious to Ron. He was a little shaken by having a gun pointed at his head and at the impending basement zombie slaughter, and his daughter seemed to think the whole thing was no big deal.

"How, honey? How the fuck are those zombies fine? Because they're already dead? Is that what it is? Because they're fucking zombies? That asshole David–your future boyfriend!–and his fuckin' friends are going to go down into that basement and slaughter every last zombie down there, and you think that's fine? I'm a zombie, you know! What if I were in that basement? What if I were killed again? How would that make you feel?" Those zombies have families!"

"Dad, you're freaking."

"Of course I'm freaking! Those zombies have families!"

"Dad, calm the fuck down." Stella reached down for her flask and handed it to Ron. It was heavier than before. Did she refill it?

"Did you refill this at that house?"

"Yes, Dad, I also rescued all the zombies." She lit a cigarette, took a long drag, and, in the fading light of this day, looked to Ron like the smartest, toughest, most beautiful woman he had ever seen. If Ron had had a second child, that child would have been an utter douchebag, he just knew it.

"How? They aren't here, and you only have one car."

"There's a tunnel, fucker." Jim had stopped laughing at his own joke and joined in the conversation. Apparently he knew something about this.

"Yeah, Dad, there's a tunnel. Fucker. There are tunnels all throughout the Ring of Threeclosure–" Stella and Jim giggled simultaneously, "connecting the houses to each other."

"And there are warning buttons in each brains–ur, house," Jim said.

"While you and that hunk of man–" Stella giggled again. Clearly she was joking, and Ron took a breath of relief. "While you were having that deep philosophical discussion about gay zombie marriage or whatever, Jim and I were getting all the zombies to a safe house. They're fine. That dreamy future husband of mine–" Stella giggled like a little girl, "and his friend are going to go down there, guns ablazin', and find nothing."

"Nada," Jim said.

"Zilch," Stella said.

"Not even a bag of chips," Jim said.

"Cuz zombies don't eat processed foods!" Stella and Jim laughed and gave each other high-fives through the bars separating the cab of the El Camino from the bed.

"You two have done this before," Ron said.

"Oh, yeah, many times," Jim replied. "Once in a while some human gets all uppity and figures it out and comes out here with guns ablazing and testosterone on fire and brains! Whoops, sorry."

"What he's trying to say, Dad, is that we hide and protect the zombies until somebody can find a cure for what they–you–have. So when that guy and his friend showed up this afternoon with guns and more balls than brains, we knew what to do. That's why I couldn't really help you–I was busy coordinating the Safe Move."

The El Camino flew down the road like a doomed man trying to outrace inevitable truths. "Wow, nobody knows about this, do they?" Ron asked. "I mean, people think there are no more zombies. But here they are. And they're being protected...by humans."

"It's all your fault, Dad."

"What? Why?"

"You taught me to be a compassionate human being. And zombies are people too. Well, mostly people. They're all revolving and someday, somebody's going to find a cure and we can turn them all back into fully living people. If we want to."

"If we want to?"

"Dad, ever since I started working with zombies, I've enjoyed their company, maybe even more than human company. With revolving zombies, there's no bullshit. No discrimination, no false admiration for you, no leaving you for no reason. Fucker." She glared at Ron. "They're loyal and they know what they want and they're true to that. No false human bullshit, ya know?"

Ron did know. It was something he always struggled with. He had a hard time being fake. Except when he was pretending now to be a human. That was a fairly easy task to undertake. Holy crap, Ron was rhyming in his own head.

"So what do we do now?" Ron was very hungry. He hoped maybe he could find a time to eat soon. Really, it might be a requirement for the near future. If he didn't eat, he wouldn't have the energy to keep up with his daughter. Or anybody.

"Well, we should probably stay away from the Ring for a bit," Stella replied. "Just in case Dumbfuck and his friend Tweedledouchebag are driving around looking for zombies–or us."

Ron laughed. "Tweedledouchebag is what I call him, too, in my head!"

"Great minds and all that. What about your ho...ur, your girlfriend, Dad? She said she *loves* you, whatever the fuck that means. Do we need to go back and get her?"

"She lovvvvvvves you," Jim said from the back of the El Camino. The mock in his voice was strong. Asshole.

"Oh, uh, yeah, that." Yeah, Ron thought, that. What the fuck was that? "I, uh, I think she was just trying to help us. I seriously doubt she meant it. I only met her two days ago. And don't worry about her. She said she'd find me later." Ron paused and looked over at Stella, driving the El Camino in the dusk of the October afternoon. "And besides, I have never really loved anybody since your mom."

The silence in the El Camino lasted a few moments more than normal conversation silence. It was a silence that spoke loudly and echoed off the walls of the mini-mall canyons of greater Las Vegas as they drove.

"I live with Mom here, you know," Stella finally said, after the El Camino had gobbled up several blocks of mini-malls.

"Wait, I thought you were a runaway?"

"I am. Sometimes. When it's convenient."

"I knew you and your mom moved here. You told me."

"Dad, she met a guy."

"A guy? Like, a guy guy?" Ron felt like he was in high school all of a sudden. Does she like me or does she *like* like me?

"Yes, Dad, a *guy* guy. A rich guy. He protected us during the zombie shit."

"Oh. Well, that's good. I suppose. And I think it was called the Zombie Penetration."

"Dad, we—you should really know—we still live with the guy guy. The rich guy. He and Mom are engaged."

"Wow." Ron's mind whirled like a carnival ride. A Tilt-A-Whirl, to be exact. A rickety old Tilt-A-Whirl that felt like it might tilt and whirl right off its tracks at any moment. "Do you like him?"

"He's rich. He bought me this car." Well, hell, Ron thought, he has good taste in cars. "It was my choice, but he gave me the money to buy it." Well, hell, Ron thought, he has enough money to let Ron's daughter have good taste in cars. "He's not my dad, but he's good to Mom. Unlike *some* people." She glared at Ron.

"Hey, should we get a hotel room or something? And some dinner? I'm kinda hungry." Ah, Ron thought, there's Robin to save the day again. Sure, Ron and Stella could have an intense conversation about why their family was no longer together and, honestly, why Ron was such a shithead–because that's where he knew the conversation was going to–or maybe his intrinsic Catholic guilt knew that's where the conversation was going to go–but instead, like Jim said, they should really talk about dinner. And a movie. Yeah, a movie! A George Romero zombie movie would be fantastic right about now!

"I have a hotel room. At Casino Royale. Shall we go there?" Ron figured his room was as good as any. "Oh, but wait, maybe I don't. That's where they found me. They know where it is."

"They?" Stella looked at her dad like he was an idiot. Do all daughters think their dads are idiots, Ron wondered. Maybe this is just the nature of father/daughter relationships, when your daughter is old enough to drink, smoke, and shoot a gun.

"Yeah, they–the KILLZ guys."

"Oh, *they*." Jim obviously knew who they were.

"Oh, *theyyyyyy*." Stella joined in, and Ron realized they were both making fun of him now. Zombie Friend and Daughter of Zombie Cracking Jokes in a Muscle Car in Las Vegas. Could have been the title of a 1950s horror movie, ya know?

"Fuck you two. I was kidnapped. *Theyyyyyyy* kidnapped me." Ron put on his best *make fun of Stella* voice.

"We know, Dad. We saved you."

"We know, Ron, we saved you." Great, now Jim was piling on. Nothing like having your two favorite smart asses in a car with you. They should take a road trip and film it. 'On the Zombie Road' or some shit. By John Zombeck.

"Anyway, the point is, assholes, my hotel room is probably not safe."

They had been talking so long that now they were at the south end of the Strip. It was dark and the Strip was lit up like it always is as night–like the Neon Road of the Damned. Seriously, if you're a neon salesman and you can't sell a neon light in Vegas, you're not a very good neon salesman. It's almost brighter at night than it is during the day.

"How about the Mirage? I know a guy," Stella said. "I can get us a room there."

"Do you have to flirt with him?" Ron wondered out loud. Really, his daughter flirting with men to get what she wanted shouldn't have bothered him like it did, he knew that. She was a grown woman, almost, and could handle herself very well, as it turned out. But still – something about the father/daughter relationship mandated overly worrisome emotions towards his daughter. It was not his fault. At least that's what Ron told himself.

"No, Dad, he's gay."

"Oh, good."

"But he says he'll pinch-hit for my team if I want him to."

"HONEY!"

"Dad, I fucking grew up years ago. Stop worrying. You gave up the opportunity to worry when–"

"I left your mom. I know. Can we talk about something else?"

"Brains! I'm hungry," Jim said from the bed of the car.

The El Camino pulled into the parking garage of the Mirage before anybody had a chance to change the subject, so brains it was. Stella parked the car, and they all got out and walked into the hotel. It was almost like going to Vegas as a human, Ron thought. Almost.

CHAPTER
-21-

In the overall pantheon of Vegas hotels, the Mirage was Ron's favorite. Sure, he'd never stayed at the ritzy places, like the Wynn or Encore or Palazzo, but he'd stayed at Harrah's, the Tropicana, and Flamingo, and he'd gladly pick the Mirage over any of those. It had a great location – right across Las Vegas Boulevard from Carnaval Court–and inside it had a zen-like quality that many of the other casinos in the same price range failed to achieve. And, while Ron liked to come to Vegas to get crazy, he also really appreciated the down time Vegas afforded him. And the Mirage was a nice place to spend down time. Dark and modern with a huge light well in the middle, filled with plants, the Mirage was easily the calmest hotel Ron had stayed in in Vegas. And, as noted previously, it was right across the street from Carnaval Court. That fact might have been–nay, it was–the most important thing about the Mirage. It was like living directly across the street from your drug dealer.

After they cleaned up and put makeup on in their room–no need to check in, because Stella's gay friend left them a key underneath the huge V in the Revolution Lounge sign–Ron and Jim realized they needed new clothes. Ron's *Girls Direct To You* shirt that

Joaquin had donated to his cause smelled like zombie and quickie, and Jim's shirt had blood all over it, so they sent Stella downstairs in the hotel to look for new clothes.

When she returned, she had a huge plastic bag from the Mirage gift shop. "You're going to love this," she said with a smirk on her face so obvious that she might as well have said something stupid like, *I got you both white velour track outfits to wear*!

Which, in fact, is exactly what she got them. In her bag were two white velour men's track outfits with *Mirage* printed across the jacket and across the front pants pocket. "I can't fucking wear this," Ron said.

"It's kinda all they had, Dad," Stella said. "Either these or dolphin shorts and Siegfried and Roy t-shirts."

"I'm not sure which is worse," Jim said, after seeing the outfits. "Jesus."

"Come on, you guys," Stella said with a smile. "You're in Vegas. You'll fit right in."

"Riiiiight," Ron said, rolling his eyes. He was standing in a hotel room in Vegas, having just showered, wearing nothing but a towel, and his daughter was trying to make him dress like Wayne Newton's gay podiatrist...and his best friend was in the same exact situation. This could only turn out well...like everything else.

"Shit, Ron, let's wear it. I'm hungry. I wanna go out. Nobody will know. Everybody in Vegas dresses like this."

"No they fucking don't," Ron said.

"But I'm hungry." Jim was clearly hungry.

"Yeah, c'mon Dad, put it on so we can go out for some food. What are you guys hungry for? Sushi? Pizza? Tacos?" The room was silent as neither Jim nor Ron answered the question. Stella quickly figured out that she had made a mistake. "Oh, no...no, no, no."

"Yes, honey."

"Yes," Jim said. "We are–"

"Zombies, right," Stella said.

"So we must eat–"

"People, right. No. No. Nononononononono..." Stella gritted her teeth, grimaced, and looked out the window to the pool below. Ron realized she clearly hadn't thought this through. Dinner with these two? Ron wondered if she had bit off more than she can chew, then he laughed at his own stupid joke.

"Look, honey," Ron said, "it's what we do. We can't eat pizza or tacos or pulled pork -"

"We can only eat pulled human," Jim said, without a trace of irony. It was no time for irony.

"But we only eat people who deserve it," Ron said. "You know all this, right? I mean, how do you feed the zombies out in the Ring of Fuckclosure?" Nobody laughed. It was no time for humor, apparently.

Stella turned to face her dad and Jim. Her face was shiny and wet from tears. It was the first time since Ron had found her that he'd seen anything besides hard resentment and dialed-in toughness from his daughter. His zombie heart skipped a beat and he felt a tear forming at the corner of his right eye. Instinctively, he wiped the tear away, because that's what dads do.

"I know," Stella said with a deep sadness in her voice, a sadness so deep that Ron thought he could fall into it and never be found. "I just–I never wanted my dad to..."

Ron enveloped Stella in a hug so tight that he thought he might crush her, but really it was only tight with love for his daughter. His newly re-discovered daughter. Even though he couldn't make up for the years of neglect with this one hug, he sure did try, because he never wanted to lose her again. When he finally released her after minutes of mutual hugging and crying and crying and hugging, Jim was standing there in his white *Mirage* lounge outfit with the zipper down to his navel, looking for all the world like one of Liza Minelli's ex-husband's boyfriends.

"Wow, you sure go pimp fast," Stella said, wiping away her tears. "I should have got you some gold chains, too. And some chest hair." She looked at her dad. "Well, get dressed, Dad. We gotta go get you some–well, some food–so you don't starve or whatever. Maybe I'll just go get a salad or something. I really doubt I'll be very hungry after this."

Ron went into the bathroom and quickly put on his lounge suit. It's a good thing it was long-sleeved, because he noticed that the skin on his right arm was peeling. And not like a sunburn type of peel, either–no, this was more like the skin was peeling, and there was no more new skin underneath–just tendons. And muscle. In fact, Ron could see the bone in that arm. It's a damn shame he never paid attention in school, because at this moment he really wanted to know what that bone was called, so when he talked to himself in his head about this problem he could describe it properly. In the meantime, he thought about the peeling skin and realized what he needed to keep it safe–Band-Aids. Or duct tape. Nobody could see it in the long sleeve track suit, but he'd sure like to tape it up anyway. When Ron was a kid, he always–*always*–had to have a Band-Aid on any cuts or scrapes he had, and this obsession had obviously not gone away. Ron made a mental note that next time they were near a Vegas gift shop that had giant Band-Aids or duct tape, he'd pick some up. If such a thing existed in a Vegas gift shop. You could get anything in a Vegas gift shop, right?

Once fully dressed–with his jacket zipper *all* the way up, thank you very much, and his tracking device replaced on his person, so Bambi could find him–Ron, Jim and Stella left the room and headed through the Mirage towards the Las Vegas Strip. They were a motley crew–as beautiful as Stella was and as poorly dressed as Jim and Ron were, they could have easily been mistaken for a hooker and her two pimps. Or a madam and her two gigolos. Right? In Vegas, anything was possible.

"Where shall we go?" Stella asked. "Where do you guys want to–" Stella gagged for a second. "To eat?"

"I think we should go to Carnaval Court," Ron said. "I could use a drink, I know the place and we can find some, uh, food, there." Shit, now all of a sudden Ron was having a trouble talking about eating. His daughter's trepidation about it was rubbing off on him. Shitballs.

"I'm not old enough, Dad."

"Ah, shit, that's true, isn't it?" Jim asked.

"I know somebody," Ron said with a smile. "I can get you in. And I can get you some tacos. Seriously."

"Wait, how the fuck do you know somebody?" Stella asked.

"Honey, I've been coming to Vegas a long time. I started coming here to get over your mother."

"You came to Vegas to get over Mom? *Over* Mom? You left her!"

"Don't fucking start, you two," Jim said. "I'm not in the mood. I wanna partttttay! And eattttt!" Jim threw his zombie arms up in the air, like he just didn't care, and waved them all around. Ron was surprised he didn't start yelling *Hey, ho, hey, ho* and asking people if they were down with OPP right here in the lobby of the Mirage. He had been known to do that occasionally in his previous life. Well, in his only life, really. The word previous isn't really necessary in that sentence.

They walked out of the Mirage to cross Las Vegas Boulevard. Although it was late October, the night was pleasant, like a summer night in Colorado. Ron realized that not only did they look ridiculous in their outfits, they were overdressed for the weather. So, to make up for it, when they got to the other side of the street, he took Jim and Stella into the Harrah's gift shop and bought them all sunglasses with Joaquin's money. Stella's were cool, in a Joan Jett kind of way, black frames and black lenses, while Jim's and Ron's were not cool at all, in a white track suit kind of way. Gold frames and brown lenses–Ron had spent enough time in Vegas to know what went together. As long as they matched stylistically, right? If you're going to dress like you belong in a David Hasselhoff music video, you might as well have the sunglasses that somebody in a David Hasselhoff music video might wear.

While in the gift shop, Ron, to his surprise, found some duct tape. Sort of an emergency pack of duct tape, really–it was small enough to fit into a pocket. Why the fuck is this for sale in a gift shop? And who the fuck would buy duct tape in Vegas, he wondered. A zombie? Ron bought the duct tape, answering his own questions in the process.

As they walked the half block to Carnaval Court, Ron looked around to see if anybody was laughing at their ridiculous clothes... and he noticed that nobody was really looking at them. Young men with saggy jeans and big NBA caps were hanging onto to their girls, older people with gray hair, parrot short-sleeved shirts and Bermuda shorts were singing Jimmy Buffet songs at the top of their lungs, and an Elvis Presley impersonator walked down the Strip unaccosted by anybody. Ron realized that this was why he came to Las Vegas–to blend in. And now he was a zombie dressed like an AARP member on vacation from a Florida retirement home...and he blended in perfectly. Irony sometimes drips like a freshly ripped tendon, Ron thought.

As they walked towards Carnaval Court, Ron also noticed people Zombieing all over the place–in front of the Harrah's gift shop, in front of the Harrah's casino, and even in the karaoke bar, a man was singing "Bad Moon Rising" and Zombieing on stage. Ron really wanted to run in and tell the man he was mixing his monsters, but he was hungry and didn't want to waste any time finding his next meal.

As they approached Carnaval Court, a man holding a bible approached Ron. "Are you saved, young man?" the man asked. Oh, great, religious nutcases in Vegas–perfect. Am I saved, Ron asked himself. Saved from what?

"Fuck you," Ron said. You're interrupting my dinner, shithead.

"Accept Jesus Christ as your Lord and Savior and you can be born again!"

Ron stopped walking and turned to the man. "Born again. Really. I can't be born again."

"Yes, if you accept Jesus Christ you can!"

Ron rolled up his sleeve so the man could see his peeling arm and the bone underneath. "I can't be born again, fucker. I'm dead." Ron had never had much kindness in his heart for hardcore religious fanatics. He believed in a higher power, but he had always believed that that higher power wanted each human to be a good human in whatever way they wanted to.

And these days, he wasn't even sure he believed in a higher power. What fucking higher power would let him get hit by a truck in the first place?

The man gagged and turned, holding his mouth, and then puked into the bushes by the sidewalk. Ron looked at him, said "Sorry, man," and walked fast to catch up to Jim and Stella, who had stopped to get some tacos from the taco truck right outside the front entrance of Carnaval Court.

The Great Food Truck Fad of The Twenty First Century had made its way to Vegas, and it came in quite handy right now. They didn't have to go sit down at a restaurant and make themselves conspicuous by not ordering anything but drinks, although Ron realized that that probably wasn't conspicuous in a Vegas sense. You could always chalk up the fact that you're not eating to a current binge of cocaine or alcohol or whatever. But he didn't want to be the white pimp one-hit-wonder rapper addicted to cocaine while his 17-year-old daughter ate like she'd never been fed before. That might not go over well, even in Vegas. So Ron was glad they had street tacos in Vegas. Now if only they had a food truck that served up pulled people for zombies...

You're not supposed to bring underage people or outside food into Carnaval Court, but Ron didn't give a fuck. He was getting hungry and his underage daughter had tacos and Ron wasn't letting her out of his sight again, so she was coming with him and Jim to Carnaval Court. No matter what. So Ron did what all good Carnaval Court regulars did–he used the side door.

The Carnaval Court side door is not well known and not known at all to newbies, but Ron knew it well. It was rarely guarded and rarely locked, so Ron took Jim and Stella through it, just like that. Easy peasy lemon squeezy, Ron thought as he approached the Carnaval Court bar. Yeah, he was getting excited. He was about to have alcohol–always a nice thing–and, with any luck, he was going to eat tonight. Surely there was a pimp/financier/lawyer sitting at the bar getting drunk, right? Surely. Even when Ron was a human and wasn't interested in eating humans, there were always at least one or two or twelve douchebags sitting at the Carnaval Court bar, especially at night. It was a diverse melting pot of the human race at all times, and douchebags are part of the human race, unfortunately–fortunately, if you're looking to eat one.

Behind the Carnaval Court bar, Flippy and Robyn saw Ron approach and doubled over with laughter...and stayed that way for a good minute. When they came up, both of their faces were wet with tears...laughter tears. Ron stared at them both without moving a facial muscle, like he wanted to burn a hole through Flippy's forehead and Robyn's pierced lower lip. He found this was the best way to fight laughter tears. If you've done something stupid enough to make somebody cry from laughter, you burn a figurative hole through their forehead and pierced lower lip. Fuckers.

"Holy fuck, you are one crazy motherfucker, you know that? And holy fuck! Jim, too! HAHAHAHAHA!" Flippy doubled over again.

"This is my dad, and I dressed him. He needs a drink, asshole," Stella said to the top of Flippy's head. Flippy lifted his head up and looked at her.

"You're Ron's daughter? Ron, you have a daughter?" Robyn was a tattooed bad-ass bartending woman, but her face softened when she realized Stella might be the daughter of one of her best customers.

"Dad, you never told your bartender that you have a daughter?" Stella asked. "God, you're a terrible father. I'm glad you look like an assisted living facility shithead." She put her plate of tacos on the bar. "Gimme a beer, assholes."

"Robyn, I ran out of clothes. Seriously. And I have a daughter, yes. And, yes, that's her."

Flippy looked at Stella. "Is she old enough to order a beer, man?"

"Yeah, she's old enough."

"All right, brutha!" Flippy turned to get Stella a beer, and she sat down at the barstool in front of her, as Robyn came over to give her a bearhug. To their right, two drunk tourists got up and left and Ron and Jim sat down.

"Can we get two gin and tonics, too, Flippy?"

"As long as I don't have to look at you fuckers again. I'm going to bartend with my back to you cuz you're going to make me puke. Do they actually sell those clothes at the Mirage?"

"Flippy, you've worked in Vegas for years and years–you know how bad the clothes here are," Ron said.

"Boy, aren't they?" The man sitting to Ron's right spoke. Ron hadn't even noticed who was sitting there, but he looked over and there was a middle aged man in a nice suit, sitting by himself, nursing a piña colada.

"Yeah, they are," Ron said.

"But I like what you're wearing," the man said. Wow, Ron thought, you have incredibly bad taste. Or you're a fuckhead. "And your friend."

Flippy brought over a beer and two gin and tonics and set them on the bar.

Robyn came back behind the bar after her bear hug with Stella. "Another piña colada, Senator?" she asked the man to Ron's right. Senator, Ron thought? Wow. Really?

"Yes, please, Robyn. And a second round for my friends here, when they're ready," he said, gesturing to Ron, Jim and Stella. "I'm Stephen, by the way. Pleased to meet you."

"I'm Ron, pleased to meet you. And this is Stella."

"Is she your...daughter?"

"Yeah, she's my daughter. Hanging out with her dad tonight," Ron said, making it obvious. "You're a senator?"

"Yeah. I mean, I was. I was the Republican Senator for a certain state, but there was a scandal and whatnot, and now I'm not a Senator of any state. I'm on vacation, really. Or hiatus. Or whatever, until I run again next spring."

"Stephen..."

"Geiser."

"Oh, I know who you are." And Ron did know who he was. Ron wasn't much of a news follower, honestly, but the 24 hour news cycle that had sprung up in the last twenty years meant that some stories were inescapable because they were in-your-face, all the time. For about five days, anyway, then the media moves on to the next toddler who disappeared from a trailer in a Southern state. A trailer that was going to be wiped out by a tornado in the next storm season anyway, so who gives a shit? Ron realized his attitude was cavalier, at best. Toddlers shouldn't have to grow up in trailers in the first place. Fucking asshole parents should get some education and better jobs so they can afford a proper fucking house.

Stephen Geiser was a crusader against all the usual things closet political pervs are crusaders against: Homosexuals, the homosexual agenda, homosexual teachings in school, legalized marijuana, the loss of morals in this great country, abortions, and gun control. He was against all these things until he was caught sticking a rifle up the ass of a naked, hogtied eighth-grade boy in his basement and all bets were off. Funny how that works–the people who are most *against* something are usually the people who are, deep down inside their black souls where truth lives, the most *for* the same thing they profess to be against. So Geiser resigned in shame, his wife left him–rumors had been swirling for years that she was nothing more than a prop anyway–and he vanished from public view. And five days later a toddler disappeared from a trailer in a Southern state and people forgot about Stephen Geiser.

"Ya know, Ron, the media made a bigger deal out of my whole situation than was really necessary," Geiser said with a sly grin. Yeah, Ron recognized that sly grin. It said, 'I'm a slimebucket but aren't we all? Hanging out naked with a young boy and a rifle and cinnamon rolls in my basement is something we *all* do.'

"I'm sure they did," Ron replied. "I really didn't follow it."

"Oh, good," Geiser said. "It was really just a–a misunderstanding." As Geiser said misunderstanding, he looked at Ron's face and squinted. "Are you–are you okay?"

"What do you mean?" Oh, shit, Ron thought, what is going on? "You're peeling."

"Oh, yeah, ha, too much, um, sun. Vegas, ya know. Sun. Desert. I'll be right back." He downed his drink and tapped Jim, who had been talking to Stella, on the back. "Jim, I'll be right back."

"Sure." Jim turned to his right. "Hi Stephen, I'm Jim. Thanks for the drink."

Ron quickly left Carnaval Court by the side door, holding his hands up to his face. Damn, he hoped his face looked mostly normal. He really wanted to stay at Carnaval Court because he was hungry and because he felt that Stephen Geiser was like a steak waiting to be cooked, but he knew if he was having a serious image problem he'd have to leave and go take care of it. Dammit. Dinner was waiting. Oh, God, if you truly want me to be saved, you'll make Stephen Geiser delicious.

He went into the nearest bathroom, in Harrah's, by the poker room. Fortunately he was alone in the restroom, which would make this easier. He also knew that Vegas restrooms don't remain empty for more than a few moments, typically, so he'd have to be cautious. He'd hate to have some drunk frat boy walk in and see something he shouldn't. That wasn't a crime and shouldn't end up with the frat boy being Ron's appetizer, but if necessary...

Ron looked at his face in the first mirror over the first sink nearest the door. Yeah, he was peeling, sort of. It was really more than that and worse than before. He reached up to his cheek and pulled the skin back...and saw cheekbone. Ron gagged a little and felt like he was going to throw up. Sure, it was easy to peel raw muscle off of raw bone when it was a pimp or a stockbroker or anybody else, but when it was your own bone? That was pukeworthy, and Ron threw up in his mouth a little, even though he hadn't eaten food since he became a zombie. He spit what was in his mouth into the sink and saw bits of skin, blood, and an eyeball. He really had to start chewing eyeballs up–they weren't digesting very fast. Ron liked to eat them like he liked to eat hard boiled eggs: in one bite, and one bite only.

A young man wearing an oversized sports cap and a basketball jersey with black jeans walked into the bathroom–a fucking frat boy. Sometimes Ron wished he weren't so damned prophetic.

"You okay, brah?" the frat boy asked. Bra? Was I holding two fabulous breasts in place, Ron wondered? "You okay?" Obviously Ron looked like he was in some kind of trouble, and the frat boy walked towards Ron...towards the sink with the eyeball in it. It would be mere milliseconds before the frat boy could see the eyeball in the sink, so Ron quickly took his hand and slammed it into the sink, smashing the eyeball beneath it. He felt it explode like a grape beneath his palm and closed his eyes. This really wasn't where Ron Watson saw himself going in his life, and for a moment he was disappointed in himself. Then he realized his daughter, his best friend, and his next meal were sitting at the bar just outside the hotel waiting for him, and he collected his thoughts and opened his eyes.

"No, brah, I'm fine. I just – I just had a little too much." Ron reached over and turned on the faucet with his free hand, hoping to appear to be mostly coherent so the frat boy would leave him alone so he could clean up. Having a smashed eyeball beneath his hand and trying to hide it from the world weren't nearly as fun as drinking and preparing to dine.

"Oh, ya, brah, I get that. Totally. It's Vegas, brah!" The frat boy came over to high-five Ron and Ron high-fived him with his free hand.

"Vegas, brah!" Ron exclaimed with all the sincerity of a kid being forced to sell magazine subscriptions door-to-door by his parents.

"Hey, wait you're that guy on the Internet, I saw you!" Clearly, the frat boy was confusing him with Miley Bieber American Idol, Ron thought, and he told the frat boy so.

"Ha!"

"No, brah, you're that guy. Do that thing."

That thing, Ron thought? The only thing I want to do right now is to get to my next meal, frat boy, and you aren't it. Yet.

"That thing?"

"Yeah, that thing. You know...." The frat boy stuck his tongue and his arms out and made his best Zombie Pose. Shit. Ron really didn't want to *do that thing*, as the frat boy so eloquently put it, but it was dinner time and his food was getting cold, so what the fuck, right?

Ron stuck his tongue out, stuck his free arm out, moaned, and shuffled towards the frat boy, who obviously enjoyed it. "Yeah, brah! That's it! You're Zombieing!"

Ron bowed awkwardly, like he was visiting a foreign country and didn't have a fucking clue about the customs in said country. "Thank you."

"Yeah, brah!" The frat boy went into a stall and locked the door behind him. Ron lifted up his hand. The eyeball was smashed into a pasty substance that looked like sour cream. He ran the water over it until it went down the drain and then he looked at his face. The peel looked like somebody had cut a U shape in his face. No wonder the frat boy didn't say anything about it. Ron looked dangerous. But he thought that the skin wouldn't stay even for very long and he didn't have any of Bambi's makeup glue. Somebody was bound to notice his facial Grand Canyon again, so Ron pulled out a piece of gift shop duct tape from his pocket. He took the duct tape, ripped it to length, and put it on his face so that it covered up the peel and held his face together. Sure, it looked goofy, but what choice did he have, really? Either wear a piece of duct tape on your face or risk having the world see your cheek bone. Ron gagged slightly and decided that he'd made the right decision. Fuck it. If nobody laughed at him because he was dressed like Celine Dion's gardener, no one was going to laugh at him because he had duct tape on his face.

The frat boy came out of the bathroom and saw Ron. "Whoa, brah, that's kinda cool. Duct tape on your face! You should write Vegas on it." The frat boy reached into his pocket and pulled out a pen. "Here, I'll do it for you." He went up to Ron's cheek and wrote 'VEGAS' on Ron's duct tape. "Yeah, brah, that's totally cool!" The frat boy admired his writing. "Hey, brah, can I have a piece of duct tape?" Ron ripped of a four inch long piece of the tape and handed it to the frat boy, who took it, stuck it on his face in nearly the same position as Ron's tape, and wrote 'VEGAS' on it while looking in the mirror. You could tell the frat boy had written on his face before because his handwriting, while looking in the mirror, was nearly flawless. "Thanks, Brah! VEGAS! WOOO-HOOOOOOO!" The frat boy struck a Zombie Pose and shuffled out of the bathroom, and Ron wondered if he could get some of what the frat boy had been drinking. Or smoking. Or snorting. That boy was having fun.

Ron looked at himself in the mirror. He looked decent. Like a guy who had been drinking in Vegas and, in a moment of wild inspiration, had written VEGAS on a piece of duct tape and stuck it to his face. Whatever. He checked the sink for remains of eyeballs and went back to Carnaval Court.

Entering through the side gate of Carnaval Court, Ron could see that Jim and Stephen Geiser had become fast friends. They were toasting each other with new drinks as Ron approached. Behind the bar, Flippy was laughing again. "What the fuck," Ron asked.

"You, uh, you have a piece of duct tape on your face, Ron, good buddy," Flippy said with a smile. He always had a smile on his face. "It, uh, has some writing on it. Says Wiggles or some shit. Wasn't that a kid's show?"

"Fuck you, Flippy. Do I get a new drink?"

"It's right in front of you. Your boy Stephen here bought."

"Oh, thanks Stephen."

Stephen Geiser didn't hear Ron; he was busy looking deeply into Jim's eyes. Yeah, okay, this might get a little weird, Ron thought, but he still considered Geiser to be dinner. He assumed Jim thought the same way. Great zombie minds and all that.

Jim turned to Ron. "You and me and Stephen are going to go back to our room for a nightcap. Stella can stay here."

"Yeah, I'll keep an eye on her," Robyn said. "Don't worry, Ronnie, I have a niece. I'll keep an eye on her. Keep the crazy tourists away from her. And later, we'll get tattoos!" Robyn winked at Ron.

"You, uh, okay with this, honey?" Ron asked Stella. Was she okay with this? Was *he* okay with this? Damn, Ron thought, I really haven't thought this through. His daughter was still human and had no business or interest in eating another human—no, she only wanted tacos. Ron, on the other hand...he needed to eat. And tacos weren't on his menu tonight. So what would he do with his daughter while he sucked on Stephen Geiser's sphincter, among other things? Did Ron's zombie restaurant have daycare for 17-year-old human daughters?

"Yeah, Dad, go. *GO*. You need it. I'll sit here and make fun of tourists. Mentally, only, of course. And get tattoos!" Stella stood up and high-fived Robyn across the bar.

"Yeah, Ron, go," Flippy said. "You need it. Stella and Robyn can hang out and make fun of tourists. And I'll sell those tourists lots of alcohol. Your daughter will be fine. And she can call me asshole all night if she wants."

"Take my room key, honey," Ron said while handing over his room key. He tingled with something—either excitement that he was about to eat, or trepidation that he was about to leave his 17-year-old daughter with his favorite bartenders while he ate. He paused. Yeah, he knew Robyn and Flippy. This was okay.

"Thanks, Dad."

"No, thank you. I need to do this."

Jim and Stephen stood up and turned to Ron. "Ready, big boy?" Jim asked with a wink. Uh, yeah, Ron thought, I'm ready, big boy. To eat. He kissed Stella on the cheek and he, Jim and Stephen headed out of Carnaval Court towards the Mirage.

CHAPTER

-22-

Ron's favorite restaurant in Las Vegas was Mon Ami Gabi, at the base of the fake Eiffel Tower in the fake Paris Hotel and Casino. Everything in Las Vegas is fake, really...but to Ron, Mon Ami Gabi always felt real. Walking into the restaurant right off of the casino floor, you were immediately transported to a real Paris. A dark wood entry and waiting area greeted you warmly, as did the hostesses, as you tried to hide the fact you all of a sudden felt terribly underdressed, no matter what you were wearing. It was irrelevant. The hostesses–who weren't French, Ron noticed, but the air of the place automatically gave them sexy French accents and hot Parisian bodies, at least in his mind–grabbed two menus (Ron always had a dining partner) and said, "This way, please," every time.

You were lead to a dining room that could have been borrowed from the Champs Elysees–glass walls supported by faded green steel columns and beams, all leading out to an outdoor patio surrounded by delicately trimmed green shrubs. Small tables with white tablecloths and an impeccable wait staff rounded out a place that could have easily been set in the City of Light...if not for the view of Las Vegas Boulevard from your table and the end-less parade of tourists just beyond the shrubs. This hybrid soup of smooth European beauty and awkward American consumerism could only be achieved in this one place, truly.

But the food at Mon Ami Gabi always brought Ron back to France. It was a breakfast restaurant to him. Rarely did Ron eat more than two meals a day when he was in Vegas, and the second meal was usually some drunken affair at the taco stand outside Carnaval Court or barbecue at a country bar. Also, Ron under-stood that eating good food when you're drunk is a waste of time, because you simply can't appreciate it. So he'd hit up Mon Ami Gabi as the first meal of the day...and what a first meal it was. Lob-ster eggs benedict, freshly squeezed orange juice, and the strongest coffee this side of Paris made for a very good start to each of Ron's Vegas days.

Stephen Geiser, however, wasn't going to be any lobster eggs benedict, and this wasn't going to be fine dining. No, this was go-ing to probably be closer to a very sloppy fast food meal. Such was the reality of trying to eat something that didn't want to be eaten. As they walked towards the Mirage, Ron felt a longing for Mon Ami Gabi, stationary food, and lobster eggs benedict. He won-dered what would happen if he poured hollandaise sauce over a couple of eyeballs, served atop delicately toasted English muffins. Eyeballs benedict? That sounded delicious.

As they walked, Ron saw a guy running up to him out of the corner of his eye. He tensed up and prepared to fight. He wasn't going to go back down underground or wherever the fuck that was and he sure as hell wasn't going to lose this meal. Ron didn't get to eat very often–morals and whatnot always getting in the way–and this meal was already cooking, the plates were set, the silverware was placed, and the timer was about to go off. No way was this get-ting away from him.

Then Ron recognized the guy, because he had a piece of duct tape on his face. It was the frat boy from the bathroom. And he was leading a whole group of similar looking guys and girls, all with strips of duct tape on their face. And all the strips of tape said VEGAS on them. Um, what?

The frat boy turned around to face his posse. At least, that's what Ron called it, in his head. Yeah, it was an assumption...but it was a correct assumption. "Okay, okay, babes and dudes, this is the guy." The frat boy turned around to face Ron. "Brah, you're a double meme now. Zombieing and duct tape! Everybody's doing it! And you started it! Brah!" The posse all stared at Ron with a quiet reverence, removed their giant sports caps, put them over their hearts, and said, in unison, "Braaaaaaaaaaaaah."

Ron didn't quite know what exactly this all meant–what the fuck is a meme, much less a double meme? So he looked over the gathered posse, removed his gaudy sunglasses, bowed like a ninja warrior, and simply said, "Brah." The posse broke out into spontaneous applause, and Ron felt a little like a minor celebrity. Here, on this tiny little piece of concrete pavement in the middle of the Nevada desert, Ron *was* somebody. Not just a zombie trying to avoid getting slaughtered; not just a father trying to understand his daughter; not just a guy looking for his next meal. No, he was *somebody*. Ron paused for a second and realized this was ridiculous. The last thing he wanted in life–or death–was to be a Kardashian: famous for nothing of import, sustainable for no perceptible length of time. No, he was happy just trying to avoid slaughter and trying to understand his daughter. And trying to get laid once in a while.

So Ron looked over the gathered throng again–it seemed to be bigger than before–and, in the interest of getting to his meal, said the one thing that came to his mind. "Now fuck off, you zombies."

"Fuck off! Yes, brah, we'll fuck off! Come on, everybody, let's fuck off! Like zombies! We'll combine memes!" And the crowd dispersed. Not quickly, like Ron had hoped, but slowly, like a pack of zombies–with duct tape on their faces–after a long night of dining on the dregs of society.

"They look just like you," Jim whispered to Ron.

"You're some kind of star," Stephen Geiser said to Ron.

"Yeah, what'd you do?" Jim asked.

"I didn't really do anything," Ron replied. "It just sort of happened. Let's head out."

"You're like a Kardashian or something," Stephen said. "I like that."

Oh, jeez, Ron thought, my dinner likes me. Not as much as I'm going to like him, though. He smiled at Stephen. Might as well keep him on the hook.

But Stephen didn't stay on the hook for very long, as it turned out. Most of Ron's meals went down easy, so to speak, in that they never saw him coming and so, when he attacked, his meals were dead within seconds and he could commence dining. Not Stephen Geiser. Apparently the whole *gun up the ass* incident had wisened him up to the possibility that not everybody was always on his side, so, when Ron and Jim changed the mood in the Mirage hotel room from one of *hey, maybe we're all going to have sex tonight*, to one of, *hey, maybe one of us is going to die tonight*, Stephen picked up on the fact that he was the one who might die tonight and left the room. Inadvertently.

As the door closed behind Stephen, Ron and Jim looked at each other. Jim had blood dripping down his chin from when he tried to bite Stephen and mostly missed, but connected somewhat. "You're not very fucking good at this, are you," said Ron.

"It's my first time, you asshole!" Jim retorted. "It's not like I could go to fucking zombie school and learn how to do this before embarking out. It's sort of a learn by doing affliction."

"Affliction? You're a zombie and you used the word affliction? And embarking?" Ron laughed. "Jesus, what is this world coming to? And why the fuck did you bite him on the cheek?"

"He tried to kiss me. And, oh, by the way, Mister English Lit, I'm still hungry," Jim said, wiping the blood off his chin. "In fact, I'm hungrier than before. I didn't realize humans could taste so good."

"You know what we have to do, don't you?"

"Go back to Carnaval Court?"

"No, you idiot. I think we have to go get Stephen and finish him."

"He *was* delicious, the small bite I got. But he's in public. We can't go get him."

Ron all of a sudden felt like a veteran defensive football player, trying to explain to a rookie that you have to blitz once in a while to keep the offense honest. "We can't *not* go get him. He's out in public, He's going to tell somebody about us, at some point. Even if he's a disgraced politician, he'll tell somebody. His boyfriend, a bartender-"

"Flippy!" Ron and Jim both said it at the same instant.

"Shit," Jim continued. "Flippy can't find out! Where will we drink? Where will we get our next meal from?"

"Let's go. We have to find him before he finds Flippy."

As they headed out the hotel room door, Ron sang the Mission Impossible theme song. Really, this was an impossible mission, wasn't it? Finding a meal that had somehow left the dining room and, worse, knew about Ron and Jim and could probably point them out to a policeman? Or worse? Still, a little levity seemed in order. This was Las Vegas, after all. *Home of I've seen some crazy shit in my lifetime.* If they couldn't retrieve a wayward meal here, they probably didn't deserve to be zombies. They–well, *he*–had survived the Zombie Extermination Movement. Picking a little food off the floor and calling in the Five Minute Rule so he could still eat it is a fucking walk in the park, Ron thought.

As they rode on an elevator full of people down to the Mirage lobby, Ron realized it would be easy as hell to push the stop button and have a smorgasbord. He looked around. Yes, it would be quite the smorgasbord. Some aged beef, some Indian food, some vegetables (those people looked like they were from Boulder) and some greasy Italian. As tempted as he was—and, judging by the look in Jim's eyes, he was not alone in his temptation—he knew that most of these people were probably good people and didn't deserve to be delicious. More importantly, Ron knew that if he made a bloody mess on an elevator and a bunch of people went missing, he would probably never see Stella or Bambi again. There were, he had learned, people in Vegas who could quickly put the kibosh on Ron's existence. Realizing his priorities, he decided to concentrate on the task at hand. Besides, everybody knows a good hand-cooked meal in a nice restaurant—or hotel room—beats a smorgasbord every time. Even in Las Vegas. *Especially* in Las Vegas.

The elevator stopped at the lobby and Ron and Jim got out first. "Where do you think he went?" Jim asked.

"I don't think he's moving very fast. He's not the kind of guy who wants to be noticed," Ron said, matter-of-factly. Like he knew what that was like, even. "I'm guessing he's heading out to the Strip. He did say he's staying at Wynn. That's just down the street. Let's head that way."

"Um..." Jim said. He was staring off towards the casino, like he'd seen a ghost. Or noticed something very, very important. Ron looked towards the casino. Nothing appeared out of place.

"Um what?"

"I can smell his blood," Jim said, matter-of-factly. Damn, Ron thought, all of a sudden being a zombie was coming in handy. Jim pointed towards the Mirage Starbucks. "He went this way." Ron followed Jim to the front corner of the hotel, where the men's room was located, just behind the sportsbook and the Starbucks. "He's in the bathroom."

"Wow," Ron whispered to Jim, "I guess you are pretty fucking good at this."

"What do we do now?" Jim asked.

"We go inside and get him."

"How do we do that?"

"Like this." Ron went in first. He figured he knew how to blitz and the rookie could use a good example. Even John Elway needed a guiding hand his first season, right? Once inside, Ron realized the bathroom was empty...except for one lonely creature in the corner, cleaning blood off of his face. Stephen Geiser. Asshole. Dinner. And yes, his asshole would be part of dinner. As gross as that sounds, Ron was still a zombie. And sphincters, as it turns out, are delicious, in a scallopy kind of way. To zombies.

"Did you really think we weren't going to find you?" Ron asked, in his best Zombie Doom voice. It wasn't his normal voice–that was more of a 'young boy asking for directions voice,' as Ron's voice wasn't always his strongest suit. His girlfriends had often laughed when he let his guard down and spoke in his natural voice, so he learned to lower its register and sound a little more manly than he really was. And, when necessary, he could affect a huge, Barry-White-meets-Clint-Eastwood voice that he thought sounded scary.

And it did sound scary–if you were a bleeding meal, alone in a restroom, facing up to the two diners who thought you were delicious. Ron wondered if Big Macs ever felt fear. Stephen Geiser obviously did, judging by his next action: a scream. Ron just laughed and carried on in his *You're so fucking fucked* voice from hell. "Really? You're in Las Vegas. Just outside this door is a casino where a Black Eyed Peas song is being played at ear-splitting volume. Do you think your pussy little scream is going to be heard above Fergie's wailing and Will.i.am's bland beats?"

Stephen Geiser stopped screaming and looked at Ron with a *this is really fucking hard to believe* look in his eyes. Ron imagined it was because Stephen Geiser never thought, not once, while he was sticking his rifle up a boy's ass or snorting blow off a lobbyist's wife's tits or voting "present" on bills that he should have had an opinion on, that he would ever, ever be listening to a zombie give a dissertation on modern music. It was certainly a stretch.

Just as Stephen was about to start screaming again, Jim lunged at him, mouth wide open, and tore a piece of his face off with his teeth. Stephen did start screaming again, and then he stopped. What the fuck, Ron thought. A quiet meal? Jim chewed on Stephen's skin like it was a piece of beef jerky and Stephen spoke. "Don't do this." Of course, Ron thought, that's what they all say. Don't do this. Like that was going to stop somebody. *Oh, you're right, I shouldn't do this. What was I thinking? I'm really a very nice person. I do apologize for my transgression, old chap.* That *never* happens.

"Seriously, I can help you." Stephen's hand was on his face, covering up the area where there was no more face, and blood was running down his arm. "I *know* people. I can get you the antidote." Ron looked over at Jim, who was no longer standing next to him. Jim had gone back for more and had quickly started to make a full meal of Stephen–ripping the skin off his face with his teeth like he was eating an artichoke. Please pass the melted butter.

"Fucking stop!" Ron yelled, but it was too late. Stephen's body convulsed and he fell to the floor, dead.

"He's so fucking delicious," Jim said, a flap of skin hanging from his mouth. "Goddamn, I love being a zombie. This is the *best* meal I've ever had." Jim slurped the remaining skin into his mouth like a noodle out of a soup bowl.

"I kind of wanted to hear what he had to say, but–"

"He's dead."

"No shit, numbnuts. You killed him."

"I thought that's what we were *trying* to do," Jim said, with a disdain in his voice that reminded Ron of his girlfriends. They always talked like that just after the relationship with Ron jumped the shark. It was a voice of *I can't believe I was stupid enough to ever think you were not stupid.*

"We were, but did you hear that he said antido–"

Ron heard the bathroom door open...well, mostly he heard the Black Eyed Peas get louder, which was never good, no matter the situation. Shit, if some unsuspecting man walked in on them, they were going to have a problem. Well, Ron thought, the unsuspecting man was going to have a problem, not Ron and Jim. As much as Ron didn't eat people who didn't deserve it somehow, he knew he'd have to make an exception when it came to protecting himself and his best friend. He really hoped the unsuspecting man turned in to use the urinals so he wouldn't become dessert. Accidental dessert, really. Sort of like when the waiter at your favorite restaurant brings you a piece of cheesecake meant for a different table. You never sent that back–you just ate it. Was this Ron's cheesecake walking through the door?

Jim stiffened up and made the universal sign for Shhhh with his finger to his lips. For a moment, they heard footsteps heading towards them, then they heard the footsteps turn towards the urinal, somebody unzipping his pants, and the universal sound for *fuck it feels good to pee*, which always sounded like a tiny orgasm to Ron. He motioned to Jim to grab Stephen's body, opened up a stall behind them, and they both dragged Stephen's body into a stall. Jim stayed with the body, and Ron stood out by the sinks. He thought it might be weird–well, weirder than it already was–if the unsuspecting man somehow looked down and saw six feet in one stall. As the unsuspecting man finished up and came towards the sinks, Ron washed his hands slowly.

The unsuspecting man was unfortunately wearing the same white *Mirage* track suit that Ron had on. As he approached Ron, who had his head down in some lame attempt to not be noticed, he said, "God, the clothes here are awful, aren't they?" and began washing his hands.

"Yep," Ron said, as he uncovered some peeling skin from his hands. As he looked over, he saw the unsuspecting man uncovering peeling skin from his own hands. Wait a minute, Ron thought, peeling skin...either the unsuspecting man had been sitting by the pool all day and, thusly, had obtained a nice hand sunburn, or... Ron looked up at the unsuspecting man, and visions of dark rooms and a table popped into his zombie head. That was it! The unsuspecting man was the zombie strapped to the table in the KILLZ dungeon! Which made him not an unsuspecting man at all, but an unsuspecting zombie...or something. Ron's brain slowly assembled all the facts of this situation into a nice order, like a zombie mental spreadsheet, and examined his options. Surely the unsuspecting zombie was a friend, so Ron could reveal that they were each of the same race. Race? Persuasion? Tribe? Sexual orientation? Ron didn't know what to call it, so he called it a tribe. In his head. But, Ron realized, if he and unsuspecting man revealed themselves to each other as kin–that's a good word–and joined forces, they and Jim might legally be considered a bunco (Ron figured that the strictest definition of bunco was probably three or more zombies gathered in one place at one time), and the last time Ron was part of a bunco he was perpetually dodging bullets and morons with guns, so maybe that wasn't the best idea. Plus the unsuspecting zombie had obviously spent some time in the KILLZ dungeon, so it was quite possible that he was being followed or, perhaps, that he wasn't the most stealthy zombie around–considering that he was captured–so hanging out with him might be quite dangerous. While Ron's slow Windows Vista-type brain calculated all the rows and columns in this mental spreadsheet, the unsuspecting zombie-man finished washing his hands, dried them and walked out of the bathroom. Ron realized he was gone and let out a sigh, not that much different from the tiny orgasm he made when he peed with a full bladder. Fuck. He probably should have talked to the unsuspecting zombie.

"You still in there?" Ron asked the bathroom stall. "You're not eating him now, are you?"

Jim opened the bathroom stall. Stephen Geiser was propped on the toilet, like a bloody, dead version of Rodin's *The Thinker*. "I was just trying to be quiet, man. Fuck, that was scary. I like being a zombie, but I don't wanna get caught. I thought that guy was going to catch us."

Ron thought about telling Jim that the guy wasn't really a guy, but then thought better of it. What if the guy really was a guy? There were a lot of zombies in the dungeon and it *was* dark, so how could he be sure the guy was a zombie? He couldn't.

Stephen Geiser's body was bleeding, and Ron noticed that a bloody creek being formed on the floor. In 40 million years it might be the bloody Grand Canyon.

"We need to clean this shit up and get Stephen back to our room," Ron said. "That's the only place it'd be safe to dine."

"Dine? You call it dine?" Jim laughed.

"Yeah, asshole, I try to dignify it a bit, ya know? That way, when I'm eating lower intestine like spaghetti–you gotta either roll it up or chop it into smaller pieces to get it in your mouth–I'm not grossed out!"

"You should really have your own cooking show, ya know? Everyday Zombie, starring Ron Watson. Today's secret ingredient? Sphincter!" They both laughed, then realized they were standing in a Las Vegas restroom with a dead body and a trail of blood. Maybe the jokes should wait for a better time. They looked at each other. "So, how exactly are we going to get him back to our room?" Jim asked.

"It would have helped if you didn't bite his face off," Ron said. "He *looks* dead now. Good job."

"He *is* dead now. And I didn't bite *all* his face off," Jim replied. "Much of it is still there, see?" Jim reached down to Stephen's face and tried to spread the remaining bits of skin around so they covered his entire face, much like a pizza maker working a ball of dough into a circle shaped crust. And, much like a pizza maker who underestimated the size of his pizza pan and overestimated the size of his ball of dough, Jim was not successful. Stephen still looked like spots of his face were tomato sauce.

"Yeah, that–that was, uh, good," Ron said. "He looks *much* better." Ron turned to the mirror to think for a moment and looked at himself. How the fuck were they going to do this? I look like a zombie, and...hey, I know what to do! "I know what to do," he said to Jim. Ron reached into his pocket and pulled out the duct tape. "Let's use this. We'll cover up your dinner marks–"

"My *dining* marks," Jim said.

"Yeah, what the fuck ever, we'll cover them up with duct tape. Then we'll spatter blood–well, more blood–on his clothes and we'll drag him through the casino."

"Um, riiiight," Jim said. "How the fuck is that gonna work?"

"Easy," Ron said. "We're going to tell everybody he was zombieing and he had too much to drink and he needs to go sleep it off."

"Is that going to work?" Jim asked.

"People are stupid. And it's Vegas–people are drunk. It's totally going to work. Besides, we can't leave him here. And we can't eat him here. Too many people need to pee. Do you have a pen?"

"No," Jim said, "but Stephen does." He reached into Stephen Geiser's shirt pocket and pulled out a blue ball point pen. It was stamped with some official government logo, and Ron laughed at the irony. We're going to use his government pen to help us get him to our dining room table. Or hotel room floor, whatever you want to call it.

Ron held the pen in his mouth, took the duct tape and tore off a piece. "Blltthh htttsss fccccce tooooogffffffff," he said to Jim.

"What?"

Ron spit out the pen onto the bathroom floor. "Hold his face together so I can tape him back up."

"Fuck you," Jim said, with a look on his face that said, yes, *fuck you.* "That's gross."

"Who took a fucking bite out of him before the dinner bell, asshole? You *made* him gross. And you think this is gross? Just wait. This ain't shit. Just. Wait."

Jim's face froze in mid-expression. He spoke like a man who had just seen a, well, zombie. "Wait, he's dead, right?"

"You killed him."

"So isn't he gonna turn into a zombie?"

"What, are you all of a sudden afraid of zombies?" Ron said. He lifted his arms up, widened his eyes, and stumbled towards Jim in the universal Frankenstein style. "Woooo-hoooooo, I'm a zommmmmmbie!"

"Seriously, fucker."

"You bit him in the face."

"And?"

"Oh, I forgot, you're new at this, aren't you? Missed the zombie training and whatnot."

"You just used the word 'whatnot.' Did they give you a diction-ary when you became a zombie, or what?"

"Not what. Whatnot." This cracked Ron up and he laughed heartily. Damn, it felt good to laugh. He looked over at Jim, who clearly didn't get the joke. Or was too irritated to laugh. What-ever. "Look, numbnuts–or should I use a big dictionary word like simpleton? Ignoramus? Cretin? Yes, cretin. Look, cretin, you bit him in the face, so he's dead. Anywhere above the neck kills hu-mans dead. For good. With no chance of resurrection. As zombies, anyway. It's why I bit you in the boobie." He reached over and lifted up Jim's shirt, showing him the bitemark. "The titty. The mammary gland." Ron laughed again.

"Obi-Wan, you are so wise," Jim said. "Prick." Ron heard a gurgling sound coming from Jim's stomach. He put Jim's shirt back down. "And I'm still hungry."

"Let's tape his face back together and get him back to our room before he rots," Ron said. "Help me tape him back together."

Jim grabbed Stephen Geiser's face and mushed it back together, like a chef trying to close a calzone. "How's this?" Stephen Geiser's face looked like a fat woman's stomach. Jim and Ron both laughed heartily, like they had both been caught off guard by a fantastic punchline to an unexpected joke.

"There's no fucking way you'd ever be on my zombie cooking show, Jim," Ron said with a smile. "Your calzones would look like shit." In many ways, this was as funny a time as they'd ever had together in Las Vegas. Sure, they'd had some benders, lost some nights to alcohol, and had some great times in Las Vegas, but they'd never worked quite so closely on such an important Las Vegas project like this. It made Ron feel very close to Jim. He'd always been close to Jim, but this moment, this instance, filled his black zombie heart with such love for his best friend that he put down the duct tape, reached over to Jim, and embraced him with as much love as his zombie arms could muster. "I fucking love you, man," he said through his choked up throat.

"I, uh, love you too." Clearly, Jim didn't quite get the gravity of the moment, but Ron didn't mind. Sometimes a moment of clear realization is not shared. Sometimes, Ron thought, it's just for me. He released Jim from the embrace.

"Let's do this, brother," Ron said with a peace in his voice that his voice hadn't owned in many years. "Hold his face together. Like you're making an empanada."

"Oh," Jim said, his face lighting up like a five-year-old on Christmas morning. "Why didn't you say so?"

"I just did, motherfucker." Jim grabbed Stephen Geiser's face and smashed the remaining skin bits together as best he could. Ron picked up the duct tape and stuck it across Geiser's face so that the tomato sauce portions of the face were no longer visible. He picked up the pen and wrote VEGAS on the duct tape. Ron then lifted up Stephen Geiser's face and faced it towards the mirror with his own. Yep, they both looked the same. Jim joined the pose from the other side and they both realized what was wrong at the same moment –Jim had no duct tape on his face. Without saying a word, Ron put Stephen Geiser's face back, grabbed his duct tape, and put a piece on Jim's face. He then wrote VEGAS on that piece of duct tape as well. Now all three of them were very much the same: they all had duct tape on their faces, and they were all dead. Triplets in a world of the damned. Ron pulled out his camera and took a picture.

CHAPTER

-23-

Las Vegas on a Saturday night is many things to many people: fantastic Broadway shows, fabulous celebrity chef restaurants, horny nightclubs and, to many, the early and unwanted end to a long day of drinking. Sure, if you pace yourself you don't have that problem. Or, if you spend the day at the pool and don't start drinking until you get to the nightclubs, you don't have that problem. Or, if you're chemically enhanced–Ron had once gone to Vegas with a sexaholic girlfriend and a truckload of cocaine, back in his true bender days–you don't have that problem. But, if you're underprepared, old or have no sense of pace, sitting around and drinking all day–at places like Carnaval Court–can lead to an early exit from the stage that is Las Vegas. Alcohol always catches up to the optimistic and the unprepared.

Ron understood this phenomenon. Really, he had been on the bad end of it more than once. You sit down at Carnaval Court on a Saturday afternoon, The Whipits are cranking out your favorite tunes, Flippy, Robyn, Charlie and Rob are mixing drinks like motherfucking geniuses and keeping you well-lubricated, the next thing you know you're staggering down Las Vegas Boulevard at 5 pm hoping you can get back to your hotel room to lay down before you fall down on the way.

So passing off Stephen Geiser as just another casualty of the Standard Saturday Las Vegas Drink-A-Thon as they staggered through the Mirage was not difficult. Not once did Ron have to explain that their "friend" had had too much. People just seemed to understand...or they were drunk themselves. Either way, Ron and Jim soon found themselves back in their hotel room with the warm body of a disgraced politician on their floor. This was going to be a good Saturday night.

And it was. A first course of Warm Finger Tips Au Jus, followed by a palette cleansing second course of Lightly Bloodied Forearm Skin Tidbits got the meal off to a rousing start, and Stephen Geiser truly was delicious. Ron thought if people realized how delicious politicians were, they'd limit them to two terms and then serve them up for their constituents to enjoy, buffet style. "Today, we have Prime Rib Of Prime Minister and a Baked Alaskan Governor. Which would you like?" Hell, Ron realized, it might just appeal to a true politician's ego. *I get to rule the people and then have them eat my body and blood like bread and wine, just like Christ*? It'd be surprising, Ron figured, to see how many politicians would actually go for something like that.

A third course of Raw Back Ribs and Diced Earlobe Salad brought Ron back to present, and he dined heartily, savoring every bite like it was a fine wine, thinking about everything that had happened to him since he got to Vegas. Life–or death–was pretty good. He stuck a rib in his mouth to suck on it and looked over at Jim, sitting on the bed, who was like a two-year-old in a high chair, without a bib, trying to eat spaghetti: Blood all over his face, half eaten ribs spread all around him on the bed, bits of earlobe in his hair. Ron laughed and remembered how much fun it was having a two-year-old around.

A noise came from the hotel room door. Ron and Jim both froze. "What the fuck?" Ron said, and dove down behind the bed, where Jim and 3 half eaten ribs had already gone. Metal clicking on metal; it sure sounded like somebody was coming into the room. Did the fucking KILLZ guys or ZEUS guys or whoever the fuck follow him again? Dammit, how could he be so careless? Ron shook his head and whispered, "Fuck."

The hotel room door opened. Ron looked up to the ceiling and hoped for the best, but expected the worst. Really, it was zombie nature to expect the worst, he figured. Jim looked at him, and Ron could see that he was scared. Ron put his finger to his lip and made the universal *shut the fuck up* sign and decided that, since he was the veteran zombie, he would go see who was coming into their room. Not in any courageous way, mind you–there was no fucking reason to stand up and shout *Who the fuck goes there* or whatever– but he did owe it to Jim, who was trembling next to him, to be the semi-brave one. So Ron stuck his head down next to the ground and looked under the bed towards the door. He could see Stephen Geiser's nude half body lying there–the other half was partially in their bellies and partially all over the room, like a two-year-old had just eaten spaghetti there–and beyond that he could see shoes. Black shoes, specifically. Black...Doc Martens. Ron knew those shoes. Fuck, he knew those shoes. He stood up.

There, in the front hallway of the Mirage hotel room, with the door closed behind her, stood Stella.

"Honey, you shouldn't–you shouldn't be here." Ron felt like a father who had just been discovered looking at pornography on his office computer in the middle of the night, trying to explain himself to his five-year-old daughter. Like a five-year-old daughter and pornography, there was no fucking way Stella was ready for this.

She stood there, silent for a moment, surveying the situation. Fingers and toes on the dresser, blood on the television screen, ribs all over the bed spread...and Stephen Geiser's nude half-body in the middle of the floor. Ron felt like a shithead. Couldn't he have become something else? An architect? A lawyer? A meth cooker? Anything but a zombie? At this moment, he felt very much like a failure as an ex-human being. Shame washed over him like ocean waves over sand at high tide and he sat down on the bed.

"I'm..." Ron searched for words, but they weren't there. Like his pride and all of his ex-girlfriends, they had abandoned him at the perfect moment. He felt a tear form at the corner of his eye. Zombies weren't supposed to cry, but fuck it. Rules no longer seemed to apply.

"Dad, I–I wanted to see it," Stella said, slowly and deliberately. "I–I wanted to *understand* it."

Jim sat up from the behind the bed and looked at Stella with a resigned look on his face that said, *yep, this is what we do.* He excused himself to the bathroom and Ron silently thanked him for that. It felt like it was Daddy-Daughter Time, and Ron didn't want to have to worry about Rookie during this conversation. Jim was probably still hungry, but Ron figured that could wait until Stella left the room again. Eating in front of her wasn't on either one of their to-do lists, for sure. Eating humans was something they both had to do to survive, but when you get right down to it, it was nothing either one of them were proud of. In that way, they were both very much like crack addicts, and nobody likes to do crack in front of their 17-year-old daughter. Don't want to set a bad example and all that.

"Understand it? I thought you did understand it, honey." Ron was slightly confused.

"I–I do. But I've never seen it. We have subcontractors who feed the zombies out at the Ring, and I never watch. I never wanted to...until now."

"You don't have to."

"But, Dad, it's *you*. And I want to understand *you*. So I have to understand," Stella waved her arms around the room, "this."

Ron looked at his little girl, his baby daughter, his grown up offspring, and realized he had never felt such a connection to any person in his life. Maybe this is the point where blood is thicker than water–or opinions–or whatever. Ron had a family, and he knew it now. He hugged his daughter like he was hugging a new-born baby. "Dammit, I love you, Stella. Sorry about the blood on your shirt."

"Dammit, Dad, it's okay," Stella said, wiping her shirt with her hand. "I bet that happens. It's a good thing I wear black."

"Good thing. So, uh, seen enough? Jim and I will clean up and we can go out or something."

"No, Dad."

"You want to stay in?"

"No, I want you to finish."

"Finish?"

"Finish eating. You and Jim, finish eating."

"Oh right. And you, what, you'll watch?"

"Yeah. I want to see it. Remember?" Yeah, Ron remembered. He was just blocking that part out of his mind. He was really hoping his daughter would take a look around, enjoy the sights and smells of a dismantled human body in a Las Vegas hotel room, and call it good. That would be so easy, but as Ron was finding out, things in Las Vegas were never as easy as he hoped they'd be. No, oftentimes they were more difficult than he'd ever imagined.

"Oh, and Dad?" Stella asked.

"Yes, honey?"

"Can I–can I try it?"

CHAPTER
-24-

For many families, a meal with family members is one of the simple pleasures of life. Sit down to a scrumptious meal, prepared from scratch by one or more members of the family, pour a glass of wine and enjoy the company of the people that you love. Or tolerate, depending on how you feel about your family. Either way, it's a chance to catch up with your relations and enjoy some camaraderie, and many families make a habit of it.

Ron knew that if he had stayed with his family, he would have had family dinners on a regular basis. He would have insisted on it. His father had insisted on it when he was a kid; therefore, it was in Ron's DNA. If he had any DNA, that is.

This family dinner, however, was going to be unlike anything Ron had ever experienced as a child. Stella stood in the hotel room doorway, looking like a young woman, even though in Ron's mind she was still a little girl. He realized this was one of those difficult parenting moments, where being torn between preserving the innocence of your child and showing them just enough of the real world to teach them a valuable skill or lesson was completely normal. And Ron was torn. He wondered if other zombie parents took this much time to consider things, or if they just moaned and had their zombie kids join in. *C'mon in, the blood is fine! Here, try some of these ribs, honey! Tender and juicy!* Ron shuddered. Were we really going to do this? Was this the moment where you took your kid to visit the prison so he/she could see what stealing a candy bar would lead to? Or was this the moment where you rolled a joint for you *and* one for your kid?

Jim came out of the bathroom. "So, uh, hey, are we going to go out? Dancing? Drinking?" Jim made an awkward dancing move, like he had just invented the Hellbound Macarena or some shit. Clearly, he was uncomfortable.

Ron closed his eyes and shook his head. "She wants to try it."

"Try what? Dancing?" Jim did another awkward dance–the Zombie Hustle, perhaps?

"She wants to..." Ron swallowed hard. He felt like he might puke.

"Eat. I want to eat," Stella said to Jim, looking him directly in the eye. Jim looked at Ron, Ron looked at Stella, Stella looked at Ron, Jim looked at Stella, and Stephen Geiser's dead body looked at the ceiling. Like a Three Stooges sketch in Purgatory, Ron thought. And he didn't mean the ski area. No, he meant the place of temporary suffering between death and heaven or hell, depending. Like Las Vegas right now. This could easily be Purgatory. Ron thought if he had a billion dollars he'd build a casino and base it completely on Purgatory. They already had a casino based on Paris, one on medieval times, and one shaped like a pyramid, why not Purgatory?

"Well, let's go get some food," Jim said, as he reached to put on the shirt he had removed when he started dining. "I could go for some–"

"I want to eat here. Like you," Stella said.

"Oh," Jim said.

"I want to know what it's like."

"Honey, it's really not…" Ron couldn't find the words to finish this sentence. It's really not what? Delicious? No, it truly was delicious. Polite? Well, duh. Legal? Again, duh. Shit.

"Glamorous," Jim said. "It's not glamorous, like all those people" Jim waved his hands towards the Las Vegas Strip "seem to think it is. Being a zombie is not pretty. In fact, it's pretty fucked up. Do you really want to see this?" Jim grabbed a length of Stephen Geiser's intestine and let it dangle, like a rope. Ron thought it looked like fresh sausage links, without the links…and it smelled as good. Damn, he was still hungry. The blood dripping off the intestine wasn't helping, either. That shit smelled like *au jus* to a zombie.

Stella turned her head. Maybe she was going to puke. Ron looked at Jim, rolled his eyes, and shook his head. Damn kids. He knew she wasn't ready for this. And, really, how much empathy can you have for your progeny when they want to do something that you've already shown or told them they're not ready for and they try to do it and, sure enough, they're not ready for it? Ron remembered the time he, at the tender age of 15, stole–or borrowed, as he explained later–his daddy's car and crashed it into the local Dairy King in the small Colorado town where he grew up. His daddy told him he wasn't ready to drive and, of course, his daddy was right. Ron spent a lot of time fixing that mess. And he might have to spend a lot of time fixing this mess, too.

Stella turned and faced him. Her face had the steely look of a warrior. "Jim, I do want to see that, and I want to…" she gulped loud enough for Ron to hear "…eat it."

Jim inhaled a full breath and exhaled slowly, with this cheeks puffed out. This caused a flap of skin on his cheek to flutter, as though it were windy in the hotel room. He looked at Ron. His face said, *What the fuck do I do with this?*

"Guys, it must be like sushi, right?" Stella's voice all of a sudden had the tone of somebody who was trying to get her friends to taste, well, sushi. "I've had sushi. Or, what, Carpaccio? Tartare?

Hell, I've had all of those things. I can do this, right? Give me a bite."

"Honey, I, uh–"

"C'mon, Dad. I want to know what it's like. And I want to...eat."

"We call it dining," Jim said. Obviously, he was trying to cut the tension in the room. Or, Ron thought, he was being a fucking asshole. When there is this much tension in a room, the line between fucking asshole and comedic cut-up is very thin.

"Shit," Ron said, with the accent on the *Sh*. "Okay. Okay. Okay, if you really want. It's your life."

"Holy fuck, Ron, you're actually going to let her do this?" Jim must have thought this *was* all a joke. His face had as much disapproval in it as Ron's daddy's face did when he got to the Dairy King with his car stuck halfway into the side of it. Shit, Ron thought, I can't make anybody fucking happy right now.

"She's an adult."

"No she's not. She's 17. And she's a human, not a fucking zombie."

"Jim, she's as adult as any other human we know at the moment."

"She should eat cooked food. That's what human beings do."

"Should she?"

"Yes, asshole."

"Who says?" Ron's brain was on fire now, and he could feel his synapses connecting and his thoughts coagulating like blood on the floor of a hotel room. In a way, he felt human for the first time since...well, since he was human. Fuck making people happy. Ron was gonna follow this path of connection that his brain was presenting him, because it felt good. So he continued. "Who says eating cooked chickens and cows is better than eating raw humans? Who says eating any living creatures is what we're supposed to do? Why isn't this," he held up Stephen Geiser's bloody left leg, which had been severed at his pelvis by a well-placed bite from Jim earlier, "an appetizer for everybody, not just for you? And why isn't this," he reached down and grabbed Stephen Geiser's head – sans earlobes – from the bed and held it aloft by its base, "part of the Mirage buffet?" Stella turned her head and threw up onto the carpet as Ron put Stephen Geiser's head back on the bed. "Oh, God, honey, I'm sorry."

"It's okay, Dad."

"It was pretty gross."

"It was, Dad."

"You wanna see him talk?"

"Don't even start, fuckhead," Jim said from across the room. "You've done enough. Stella, do you need some water?"

Stella was still bent over at the waste, hands on her knees, next to the nightstand. "No thanks. I'm going to raid the minibar, though." She went over to the room fridge, opened it, found a small bottle of vodka, and downed it.

Jim was still holding Stephen Geiser's lower intestine. He motioned towards Stella. "Do you, uh, still want to try this?"

"Fuck no. In fact, you sick motherfuckers, I think I just became a vegetarian."

"Do you mind if I have some, then?"

"Do you what you gotta do, Jim. Do what you gotta do."

"I'm sorry, honey," Ron said, putting his hand on Stella's shoulder. "I never should have gotten you involved in all this."

"All this? Shit. You know what you never should have done? You never should have gotten a motorcycle, Dad. Maybe you'd still be alive, and we could go out for a proper meal. Like normal fucking families do."

"If I were alive, honey, I might not have ever found you."

Stella's face, for an instant, softened like a down feather pillow. "Touché, Pops."

"Pops...I love it when you call me pops. Reminds me of when..."

"When you were still alive? And still my dad?"

"Ouch."

"Just kidding, Pops. You're here now. That's what matters."

Jim was over by the window, slurping up Stephen Geiser's lower intestine like a 23-year-old corn-fed farm boy at a hot dog eating contest at a flyover-state county fair. It sounded like water draining from a full bathtub. Ron heard it and then heard his stomach growl. He wished he could keep eating, but Stella was more important. He didn't want to upset her anymore, so eating would have to wait. Maybe he could sneak away later and find a corrupt pit boss or something. Hmmm...pit boss. His eyes widened at the thought.

And his growling stomach was apparently loud. "Dad, go eat," Stella said, with a lovely smirk on her face. Her smirks were always lovely. She got her smirks from her mother, whose smirks were also always lovely, until they turned ugly towards the end of their relationship. As smirks often do.

"What? No, I'm not gonna–"

"Yes, you are."

"But–"

"Don't worry about me, Dad. I'll watch, but I don't want a taste anymore. This," she pointed wildly around the room like she were reprimanding an entire class of kindergartners, "is pretty fucking gross. And if I can't handle watching, I'll go downstairs and get a salad. Or a drink. Or both, what the hell."

Ron's stomach was pretty empty in spite of his 3 courses of appetizers; he sure could eat some more. He looked over, and Jim was gnawing on Stephen Geiser's left leg–the same leg that was a major contributor to Ron's presentation a few minutes ago–like it was a turkey leg at the same flyover-state county fair. Ron realized that much of being a zombie was like being at a flyover-state county fair. You ate things you wouldn't eat during the week, everything smelled like shit, and you were occasionally drawn to rides and games like the funhouse, whack-a-mole, and eat-a-senator. Oh, and you never got laid properly. Shit, Ron thought, maybe I should have gone to a flyover-state instead of Las Vegas. I'd fit right in.

"Eat, Dad. I insist." Stella was pushing Ron towards the mess that occupied their hotel room. Limbs over here, tendons over there, blood just about everywhere. Yeah, it sure looked–and smelled–delicious.

"If. You. Insist."

"I insist."

"Okay, here I go." Ron didn't move. He was still hoping his daughter would leave so he could eat his dinner without guilt.

"You go now."

"I'm going." Still, Ron didn't move.

"Go, Dad!"

"I'm going." Ron stood still. "Can't you see me going?" Dammit, he really wanted her to leave. Then again, what the fuck was he feeling guilty about? All this was going to be was Ron getting his nutritional needs met, really. He was a zombie–nothing anybody could do about that (unless they found the antidote). And what do zombies eat? People. It was nature's way, or something. Still, Ron didn't want his daughter to see what he did. It was his fatherly instinct to protect her. At least, that's what he told himself. He also didn't want to admit to himself that eating human beings was also very, very gross. It was. And, like most parents, Ron wanted his daughter to *Do as I say, not as I do*!

Stella put her hand on Ron's shoulder. "Go, Pops."

"Dammit." Ron took a deep breath. "Okay, honey, you asked for it." Ron walked over to the middle of the room and picked up Stephen Geiser's left foot as Stella watched.

"Is that like a chicken wing, Pops?"

"Are we really going to do this?"

"I might want to just ask a few questions."

"You always were curious."

"I still am."

"Jesus. Okay, yes, it's…" Ron spoke haltingly. It was difficult to get the words out "…like a chicken wing. Lots of bones, a small quantity of delicious meat." He tore off Stephen Geiser's big toe with his mouth and held it up for Stella to see. "And the toes are the best part. They're like the muffin tops…if the feet were muffins."

"Wow, feet as muffins. That's so fucking gross, Pops."

"You asked." Ron opened his mouth and took a big bite out of the side of Stephen Geiser's foot. "Umm…yummm…cshfftt… aashhkj….thskkks," Ron said, with his mouth full. Stella closed her eyes and kept her mouth shut. She was probably keeping her puke inside her mouth this time, Ron thought, as he cleared his throat. Then flavor overcame him. "GODDAMN! This is delicious," Ron exclaimed with the enthusiasm of a teenage boy who has just touched his first vagina.

"Yeah, boy, this fucker is goooood." Jim was clearly enjoying his first true dining experience. He grabbed Stephen Geiser's torso, held it up, and looked at Stella. "And this is like the chicken breast," he said, pointing to Stephen Geiser's ass. "The best meat is right here, on the cheek. I'm guessing. I mean, look at it!" He opened his mouth wide to take a bite as Stella puked on the carpet again and passed out on the clean bed. Ron made sure she was breathing–she was–and took out his camera and took a picture of Stella, Jim, Stephen Geiser's ass cheek, and the room. Boy, he thought, this is gonna be fun to clean up.

CHAPTER
-25-

While Stella slept, Ron and Jim finished dining on Stephen Geiser, cleaned up their borrowed hotel room, and laid on the beds, watching late night television. There's really not much on television during regular waking hours, and the television landscape at three in the morning is even more barren and torched...but there are shopping channels. And shopping channels don't sleep.

"Welcome back to The National Shopping Channel, where it's pop culture/pre-Halloween Saturday and we're selling all things pop-cultureous and Halloweenous! Are those words? I hope so." The hostess for the NSC at 3 am Saturday was obviously a fucking idiot. A job like this, Ron thought, required more vapidity and dead soul than any job since, well, politics. A zombie could even do it. "And tonight we're–oh, yes, I'm so excited about this–we're selling the latest, greatest, most fabulous accessory since Silly Bands. Yes, friends, we have..." the hostess reached down by her side and held something gray aloft, "Las Vegas duct tape! It's the hottest thing in Las Vegas. Up and down the Strip, everybody's duct taping their faces, their arms, their legs, and we, here at NSC, have it, just for you. Three rolls of Las Vegas Duct Tape–with a certificate of authenticity, even–for three easy payments of $9.95, plus shipping and handling. Here, let me show you how nice it looks as a fashion accessory." Ron and Jim both watched the hostess take the duct tape, which already had the word VEGAS on it every twelve inches or so, and rip a piece off. She then stuck that piece to her face, with the VEGAS upside down.

"I'd like to fuck her," Ron said.

"I'd like to eat her," Jim said. "Is stupidity enough of a reason to end up in my stomach?"

"Everybody has their own standards," Ron said. "You just have to figure out what you can live with."

"Or be dead with."

The hostess obviously saw that her VEGAS was upside down. She squealed like a little girl and said to the camera, "Oh, it's upside down! It's like I'm drunk in Vegas!"

"Or you're just stupid," Jim said. "Dude, is American culture really this bad?"

"Apparently," Ron said, with raised eyebrows and an air of resignation.

"I never noticed before," Jim said. "I feel like it's gotten much worse since I became a zombie."

"Or maybe you just started noticing."

"Maybe it's amplified. Maybe my Zombie Sense is like Spider Sense, only for culture."

"That's fucked up."

"It is. I really don't want to be this aware of how bad things are."

"Maybe if somebody actually has an antidote, we can go back to being oblivious to it."

"Do you think there's an antidote out there?"

Ron thought for a moment. Surely if mysterious men and/or women were running experiments on zombies in underground tunnels somebody must have found something, right? A cure? Or was it like the HIV virus, where you still had it but you lived with it and you took the right medicine and you lived your life almost like it wasn't there? Yeah, Ron thought, that's probably more what Zombieism was like–you had it, you knew it, but you ate when you could and you went on living your life. Wow, what a fucked-up parallel that was.

"I doubt it, brother," Ron said. "If there was an antidote, I'm sure it'd be all over the news and social media. Nothing like that stays hidden for very long, especially these days."

"We stay hidden."

"Yeah, but–"

"But what?" Jim was sometimes like an eight-year-old boy, Ron thought. He was constantly curious and never stopped asking questions until he was convinced he knew the answers. This, Ron realized, was probably what it was like to have a son.

"But nobody's looking for us. They think we're dead."

"We are."

"She's deader than we are," Ron said, gesturing towards the television, where the hostess was trying to sell a shirt with blood all over it. She called it a Zomb-T, and it was only two easy payments of $19.99, plus shipping and handling! And they'd already sold 472 of them! "Who the hell would take a job like that?"

"Who the hell would buy a shirt like that?" Jim asked. "It's fake! You want a real one?" He reached over and grabbed Stephen Geiser's bloody oxford button down and threw it at the television. "Only 17 easy payments of fuck you!"

"Wow."

"Sorry. I got carried away. I'd still like to eat her, but I bet she's soft inside, like a marshmallow peep...without the yummy sugary flavor."

Stella stirred in her sleep. Ron yawned and reached over and put his hand on his daughter's face. Surely something so beautiful could not have come from him, could it? To have such beauty in your life when everything else is so black and shitty is almost paralyzing. You don't want to touch it for fear of making it black and shitty like everything else. Still, she was Ron's daughter, so he felt compelled to comfort her as she slept, even if it did turn her life black and shitty. He had a deep, confident feeling that he couldn't do that to his daughter. No, she was already past the part of her life where she might get fucked up by her parent's fucked-upedness and was going to be fine. Call it Zombie Sense. Or, more likely, call it parental confidence. Somehow, in spite of this world's worst intentions, Stella was going to be fine. Ron yawned again and smiled at his daughter.

She was going to be fine. Ron knew in his head, his heart, and his balls that he would do everything to make that statement true. But what about Ron? Was he going to be fine? Was a lifestyle of hiding from authority and random meals going to be adequate? Should he take his daughter and his best friend and his girlfriend and move to a farm in the middle of nowhere, where he could be as zombie as he wanted without worrying about any of this? And what about the duct tape and the stupid fucking people who thought Ron was a "brah?" As he contemplated all of this, a funny thing happened: Ron fell asleep.

CHAPTER
-26-

Outside a farmhouse set up against the foothills of the Rocky Mountains, in a neighborhood between Denver and Boulder, Ron pushed his two young daughters as they soared high in the clear blue Colorado sky on plastic swings. Amelia, three, and Julianna, two, squealed as the tight metal ropes held the swings in an arc so they wouldn't go flying off to the nearby rock formations, the Flatirons. Stella was inside the house studying. She was starting her sophomore year at nearby University of Colorado at Boulder, majoring in international business and minoring in social work. She lived in the farmhouse with Ron, Bambi, and her two half-sisters.

Ron stood behind the girls and pushed each swing alternately, so each girl got as much air as she desired. The bigger the air, the bigger the squeal. In between pushes, Ron looked over at the Rocky Mountains and counted his blessings. It was good to be home. From the farmhouse, Ron could see brilliant yellow Aspen leaves set against fiery red oak leaves, set against majestic mountains...and it was 75 degrees on this fine October day. Fall in the Rocky Mountain region is truly something to behold.

From the farmhouse, a question: "Would you all like some lemonade?" The girls cheered. "Yes, mommy! Lemonade!" Ah, yes, Ron thought, Bambi's lemonade. Freshly squeezed from imported California lemons, with a hint of raspberry and basil, it was the drink of choice for the Watson family on nice Colorado days. In fact, it was the drink of choice for much of Colorado on nice Colorado days. Bambi had been selling her lemonade in Colorado supermarkets for a couple of years now and was very successful as a businesswoman. In fact, it was the lemonade that had bought them this farmhouse and land.

The girls began slowing down their swings as Bambi came out of the farmhouse with a tray holding a pitcher of lemonade and some cups on it. She approached the swingset as the sky quickly darkened and blackened. Ron looked up. What the fuck was going on? Amelia jumped off her swing and landed awkwardly on the ground in front of her swing. She screamed, and Ron ran over to find out what happened. As he approached Amelia, he could see a long strip of skin on the ground behind her where she had landed. Oh, shit. Julianna jumped from her swing and landed with her hands in front of her. Ron could see skin from her hands on the ground as her hands slid forward. What the fuck? Bambi handed Ron a glass of lemonade as the sky turned black and stormy. Ron looked at her. She was smiling.

"Oh, girls, you did it again," Bambi said. "Let me get the duct tape."

Ron's eyes widened and he turned to his daughters as they looked up at him with their own wide eyes. Wide eyes surrounded by peeling skin, blood and rotting flesh.

"Braaaains," Amelia said as she reached for her mother's arm. She took a bite as Bambi screamed.

"Bwaaaainnnnns," Julianna said (changing the 'r' to a 'w' as only a two-year-old could) as she reached for her mother, taking a bite as Bambi fell to the ground.

"Aaaaaaaaaaaaaaaaa," Ron screamed and turned to run to the house to find Stella. He had to get her to safety. He reached the house, opened the screen door, and went in, where Stella was sitting at the kitchen table, reading her International Business 102 book.

"Honey!?"

"Yes, Dad?"

"We gotta get out of here!"

"But Dad, we live here!"

"Your sisters are zombies!"

Stella stopped reading Chapter 3: Global Issues, and turned toward Ron with a quizzical look on her face. Her bloody, rotting face. "Yeah, Dad, so?"

Ron woke up screaming.

CHAPTER

-27-

"Dad!"

Oh, fuck, Ron thought, my daughter's a zombie and my new daughters are zombies and oh fuck!

"Dad!"

What have I done?

"Dad!"

How can I fix this?

"DAD!"

I gotta find the antidote!

"Kenny!"

Ron sat up in his bed in his Las Vegas hotel room. Through bleary, slept-too-much eyes, he looked around. Jim was there, sitting on the other hotel room bed–he was watching the same bullshit shopping channel–as was Stella, sitting on his bed, and Bambi, sitting next to Stella, wearing her pink tank top, thank the Lord. That should wake him up.

"What happened to me?"

"You fell asleep, Dad. And then your friend showed up."

"Hi Kenny." Ron looked at Bambi, who was absolutely resplendent in her pink tank top, short shorts, and cowboy boots. All of a sudden, Ron remembered what an erection felt like. A post-good-night's-sleep erection, even. Those are the best kind. Morning Wood.

"Hi." He reached up, grabbed Bambi's neck, and kissed her with his full mouth and full tongue. "I'm so glad to see you. And I'm so glad you're not a zombie."

"What?" Bambi was clearly confused. Obviously, she didn't have the same dream.

"Never mind. Look, I gotta be honest–I've been meaning to tell you this–my name's not Kenny."

"I know, silly. Kenny's your Vegas name. Do you think my real name's Bambi?"

Stella looked over at Ron. "Dad, you woke up screaming."

"I had a bad dream," Ron said, wiping sleep shit out of his eyes. "You were a zombie."

"Oh."

"Don't worry, honey," Ron said to his daughter. "Based on last night, I really don't think you're cut out for zombieism."

"Good thing," Stella said. "It's gross."

"Wait," Ron said, feeling his sweaty hotel room pillow. "I fell asleep?"

"All night," Jim said from the other side of the hotel room as he stared at the television. "You missed all the good shit. They have a football jersey for sale with your picture on it, and the Las Vegas Wranglers hockey team is having a Ron Zombie night!"

"I thought zombies didn't sleep?" Ron had always assumed this was a Zombie Rule. There really weren't many Zombie Rules, as far as humans understood it. Zombies eat people, they stagger around, they don't die unless you shoot them in the head, and they don't sleep. Pretty straightforward, really. Until they do sleep. Then, Ron thought, you've probably fucked the universe up completely and who knows what happens next? Little zombie girls on swings against a magnificent Rocky Mountain backdrop?

"We thought that too, Dad," Stella said. "None of the zombies in the Ring of Foreclosure ever sleep. You must be different."

Different. Boy, Ron thought, first I can't get parenting correctly, and now I'm a zombie fuck-up too. Nobody ever really wants to be thought of as different—we all just want to fit in, right? Be like everybody else? Blend in with the crowd? Isn't this is why Ron came to Vegas?

"Kenny, I have something to talk to you about," Bambi said, as her pink tank top sat on the bed next to Ron. Well, her whole body sat on the bed next to Ron, but her pink tank top sort of led the way. "Wait, what's your real name?"

"Ron. Ron Watson."

"Ron's a cool name. It's sort of a muscle car name."

"Yeah." Ron still couldn't get his head around the fact that he fell asleep, although the pink tank top was trying very hard to change the subject.

"Dad," Stella said flatly.

"Yes, honey?"

"You're supposed to ask her her name now. Jeez, you're so fucking romantic."

Ron glared at Stella. Was he supposed to take dating advice from his 17-year-old daughter? Shouldn't that be the other way around? This world was all kinds of fucked up.

"Oh, so, uh, what's your real name, not-Bambi? Although I do like that name. It kinda matches your..." Your what? Your body? Your personality? Your eyes? "...your–your all-of-the-above." Yeah Ron thought, I am one romantic fuck. Nothing more romantic than an all-encompassing all-of-the-above. Poets could come up with lines about *deep oceans of blue in your eyes* or *your skin is like virgin silk spun from silkworms only found in certain corners of the globe* or *you radiate joy like a joy radiator*, but what do I get?

All-of-the-above. No wonder I'm a fucking zombie. An eight-year-old human boy has more poetry in his body than I do.

"You're silly, Ken-Ron. My real name is Maria. Does that match my all-of-the-above?"

"Wow, yeah, Maria is a beautiful name," Ron said, and it was. "It matches you perfectly." And it did. Since the invention of the female name, there have been only five female names that were rated the most passionate, the most pure. This one left them all behind. Maria.

"But you can call me Bambi if you want. Can we..." She looked over at Stella and Jim, who were both staring at the television. "Can we go somewhere private? I need to talk to you."

"We can talk here." Surely, nothing could be discussed that needed to be private, right? Jim and Stella were engrossed with the special *Zombie Shopping Hour* on the television and besides, Ron thought, I'm already a fucking zombie. What could possibly be more intense than that? My life–and post-life–can be discussed in public, because I've already been hit by a truck, eaten several people, taped my body back together, and moved to Las Vegas. And once you move to Las Vegas, Ron thought, nothing else can qualify as *We need to talk in private* worthy. Ha!

"OK. I'm pregnant."

Except maybe that. That, Ron thought, is private-conversation worthy. Dammit, I should have seen this coming. But wait–Bambi was a hooker, right?

"Wow. Do you know who the father is?" Ron quietly asked the obvious question. This couldn't possibly be about him, right?

"You." Damn, Ron thought, I'm wrong all over the place today. Can I go back to sleep, please?

"How do you know? You were a hooker." Ron saw Stella looking over at him. She must have been listening to the conversation from the beginning. I'm such a great fucking role model, Ron thought. No wonder Erika left me. I fuck hookers in Vegas.

"I was, Kenny– ur, Ron–but I only gave handjobs. It was Joaquin's business model. I haven't had intercourse with a man in a couple of years...until you came along. So to speak." Maria smiled and the dimples on her face smiled at the same time. It was truly beautiful, like a sunset over the Flatirons in his dream, Ron thought...and then, fuck, yep, Ron realized, his life was turning out just like his dream. He could only muster up a quickie, with a woman he really liked and really wanted to give the whole hog to, figuratively and literally speaking, and he got her pregnant. With a fucking quickie. Actually, given the fact that he liked Bambi/Maria quite a bit, he realized it could be worse. He looked over at Stella and reached over and hugged Bambi/Maria, and decided that his dream could go fuck itself. This real life was what he had, and he had to make it so that this real life was better than any dream. It was a lofty goal, but Ron was a lofty person, generally speaking. And to start towards his lofty goal, he decided to start calling Bambi by her non-Vegas name from now on. Maria. It truly was a more refined name, in the overall pantheon of female names. Waaaay ahead of Bambi.

"But Maria, I've only known you for a couple of days." Wait, wait, wait, this is all wrong. This is *all* wrong. He released Maria, sat back, and looked into her eyes. "Wait, wait, wait. How the hell do you know you're pregnant? It's only been a couple of fucking days!"

"I know, but I felt something kick inside me," she lifted up her tank top to reveal a slight bump where her flat belly used to be, "and I took five different pregnancy tests. Five. Different. Pregnancy. Tests."

"And?"

"All positive. You're going to be a daddy, Kenn–ur, Ron."

CHAPTER
-28-

When a woman gets pregnant, the first question the woman's friends, loved ones, and valuable business associates ask is, *what are you having*? And, really, the answer is more often than not one of three: boy, girl, or we're going to be surprised. Either you want to know what gender your child is going to be or you want to find out when it comes shooting out of its longtime uterine domicile, right? Nothing like looking down and seeing a huge pair of swollen testicles on a newborn and knowing you had a son, or vice-versa.

In this case, however, the surprise part wasn't limited to just female or swollen balls. No, Ron realized, if this really was his baby in Maria's swollen belly, was it possible that it was a zombie baby? Nothing else in his life made sense, so this nonsensical idea fit right in. He shuddered and his mind started to go down the path of darkness one's mind often takes when confronted with horrific possibilities...and this path had whole armies of zombie babies, rednecks with machine guns, and Ron's zombie baby eating its way out of its mother. Ron recognized this darkness happening and did what all good men do when under the duress of life altering events–he went to his bar.

CHAPTER

-29-

on had stumbled this stumble many times before–after a long day of drinking, trying to get to his hotel room, eyes blurry, legs wobbly, stumbling around Vegas looking for that hotel room. In any other city, it would be a Stumble of Shame...but in Vegas, everybody does it. The unique combination of sun, alcohol and unbridled human behavior in the great American desert makes the Stumble of Shame a Stumble of Normality. Kinda like how the Kardashians have made airing your dirty untalented laundry on network television a "show."

But while this stumble felt like the others, it wasn't. This had very little to do with alcohol, really. If Ron were pulled over right now by a policeman and forced to submit to a Breathalyzer Test, he'd probably eat the cop first and then blow a .00002 just for the fuck of it. No, this stumble was a direct result of Ron's dead brain filled with thought. Raging, angry, purple thought, kinda like Barney the Dinosaur playing Mel Gibson on a rampage. His girlfriend was pregnant. He was dead but wanted to be alive. There were men with guns. His 17-year-old daughter could drink, smoke, and shoot like...like, what, an 18-year-old? Ron wondered what the hell this world was coming to. And he knew he needed a drink. And he knew he was stumbling.

And he knew that he forgot his fucking sunglasses in the room where he had left his daughter, his best friend, and his pregnant girl...but as the automatic doors opened and he walked out of the Mirage into the fresh Vegas morning air–if air in Las Vegas is truly ever fresh–he didn't give a fuck. After the news he just received he needed a drink and there was no way a burning eyeball was going to stop him from that drink, even if the burning eyeball was his own. He had recently learned to deal with eyeballs, after all, and besides, he could always find a hooker to shield him from the sun if necessary. Ron was always surprised how many hookers hung around the Mirage in the morning. It was almost like they were preying on the lonely boys who were out all night and still didn't get any Vegas nookie. Either that or they were going after the businesspeople on their way to the morning's convention. Ron always wondered how anybody ever came to Las Vegas on business; he knew it solely as a place of pleasure. Until recently, of course.

Crossing Las Vegas Boulevard early on Halloween morning was a stumbling experience in itself. Half the people walking around were still up from last night and the other half were already getting started on their Halloween festivities. And, for many, that included dressing up like a zombie and Zombieing every chance they got–at the crosswalk, at the outdoor bar, and at the shitty gift shop at the end of the crosswalk...where, Ron could see as his gelatin legs meandered that way, you could buy a t-shirt with his picture on it. A picture of Ron Watson, covered in duct tape, Zombieing. With the singular word 'Brah' written in Blood Font above his head. Where the fuck do they get Blood Font?

Somebody stopped him in front of the gift shop. "Brah, picture?"

"Fuck you," Ron replied. Yeah, the first rule of fame is probably *don't blow off your fans*, but Ron really needed a drink, and this level of fame was bullshit. He'd been in Vegas what, five days? Surely somebody had saved a kitten in that time and deserved to be more famous than Ron, whose only claim to any kind of fame is that he was dead.

"C'mon, brah, picture!" A hand reached out of the early desert light to grab Ron's hand. He saw it out of the corner of his eye. Don't. Touch. Me. Mother. Fucker.

But the motherfucker didn't hear Ron's barely coherent thought and touched him. And grabbed his right hand. And pulled his right hand towards the gift shop. And pulled his right arm clean off his body at the shoulder.

"Whoah, brah." A small crowd had gathered by the gift shop window, presumably to get a picture with Ron, and now one of them was holding his arm by the hand and the others were noticing, as if a detached arm wasn't something you see in Las Vegas every day. Oh, fuck, Ron's suddenly coherent mind thought. A detached arm isn't something you see in Las Vegas every day, I'm sure of it. My cover has been blown and I'm gonna have to eat my way out of Las Vegas. Put my friends and my daughter and my unborn zombie baby somewhere safe and have a fucking human smörgåsbord. You do what you gotta do to survive, right?

Ron looked at the gathered throng and made a face–the kind of face you make at your mother when you're 12 years old and she discovers marijuana in the dresser drawer in your bedroom. The kind of face that says, *Whoops, silly me! It's not mine, I'm holding it for a friend!* The kind of face that says, *Wow, how did–wait, is this some kind of–wait, did I just turn into a zombie or something? I really should get that looked at. How's your sister doing? She still dating that asshole?*

"Yeeeah," Ron said, a little more seriously. He was hoping to scare the crowd into forgetting this little incident ever happened, as if that were possible. As if any of this had a happy ending.

The motherfucker holding Ron's arm looked down at Ron's arm, flesh dangling from where it had previously attached to his shoulder, the Stella tattoo clearly visible on his large dead bicep, a small amount of blood slowly dripping from the tendons that were previously connected. He looked up at Ron, as did the rest of the gathered crowd, at Ron's shoulder, where matching tendons hung delicately in the air. All right, Ron thought, they've collectively figured out what's going on, they've come to a group decision, and right now they're going to pull one of those bullshit citizen's arrests on me and three or five of them will try to hold me down while Motherfucker calls the cops on his cell phone with his free hand. All right, Motherfucker and your friends, let's do this. Ron crouched down, like a ninja tiger missing an arm, and prepared to battle. It wasn't going to end this way, no fucking way. Let's see what you motherfuckers got. Well, Motherfucker and friends. Whatever. Bring it.

"Brah," they all said at the same time. What the fuck was up with a crowd of people speaking as one? Was this some kind of doomed improv game?

"Nice costume," they said, in unison, nodding their heads.

Nice costume? That's it? Ron relaxed. His eyes cleared as the desert sun slowly rose into the sky and he realized that every single person in the crowd, including Motherfucker, was dressed like him. Like Ron Watson, Zombie. Ron Zombie. Zombie Brah.

Motherfucker brought Ron's arm back to him. "Here, brah." Uh, great, Ron thought, what the hell am I gonna do with this? Then another guy–Ron called him Asshole in his head, because, why not?–brought over a roll of Vegas duct tape. "Here, brah," said Asshole. Four girls from the crowd–Ron recognized them as bachelorettes from the other night and could see they had their bachelorette tank tops on underneath their zombie shirts–approached him. One took his dangling shirt sleeve and rolled it up so they could see what remained of his shoulder, another took his arm and held it in place, and the two remaining girls proceeded to reattach his arm by duct taping the shit out of the connection until it was reattached. How do you know when you've used enough duct tape for such an endeavor? When you can say you've duct taped the shit out of something. It's a technical term.

The girls finished duct taping the shit out of his arm/shoulder connection and, one by one, kissed Ron on the cheek and went back to the crowd.

Goddammit, Ron thought, now my arm doesn't work and I really need a drink, but at least it's reattached and, to top it all off, these people are being so nice to me. Sorta makes it hard to be a curmudgeonly zombie when humans are treating you like one of their own. Stupid humans.

The gathered crowd looked at Ron and said "Brah." Ron looked back and said, "Thanks. Brah. And Happy Halloween!"

"Happy Halloween, Brah," they said in unison and shuffled off, like zombies, towards wherever the fuck they were going. In Vegas, everybody ends up at the same place anyway.

Ron looked down at his right arm. It wasn't moving. No matter how much his black brain tried to talk it into doing something, anything, it was refusing, like a five-year-old refusing to eat vegetables. Well, Ron thought, I guess duct tape can't solve everything and I guess I'll have to masturbate with my left arm, like I do on kinky nights. Ha! Masturbate. Silly zombie. Still, at least he looked like he had all his limbs. He could deal with this. Maybe get a sling for his arm. Maybe make his arm detachable so he could truly scare people when he wanted to. Or, maybe, he could see a doctor. He figured between Stella and Maria, somebody knew a Vegas doctor who'd be willing to reattach a dead arm to a dead body. And, really, Ron thought, that would be the responsible thing to do, since he was going to be a father again. Fathers needed both arms, if possible. Fathers needed to be responsible, if possible...if that *were* possible.

Responsibility...shit, Ron's brain was a mess, literally, and he needed to see his bartenders. Sometimes a drink, early on Halloween morning in Las Vegas, can be your best friend.

CHAPTER

-30-

"Ron, what is up my brother? You look like shit!" Robert was tending bar. It was a good thing Carnaval Court was open 24 hours a day, Ron realized. That way they could service every kind of drunk: the afternoon frat boys, the evening club kids, the 3 am Bukowskis, and the 9 am zombies. Literally.

"Fuck you, Robert! And why the fuck are you dressed like a zombie?"

"Fuck you, Ron! Why the fuck are *you* dressed like a zombie?" Robert reached out to shake Ron's right hand, but Ron offered up his left. Yeah, Robbie, this other hand is hung over at the moment. Or something.

"Damn, I didn't realize you were a lefty."

"I'm not."

"Oh, well then–uh–how about a drink?!" Yeah, Ron thought, it was good to have a bartender by your side when everything was going to shit. And Robert was one of the best. No matter what sort of private hell you were going through, he always inspired you to smile...and have a drink. It was a trait of a very good bartender.

"Fuck yeah, Robman. The usual." The usual? Really, Ron thought? You're dead, your girlfriend is pregnant, and you lost a limb this morning. Was the usual going to cut it? "No, Robert, you better break out the whiskey."

"Damn, my buddy Ron is having a bad day. Whiskey for Halloween!" He reached over and grabbed the chord that led to whatever mechanism made the *A-ooooohga* sound and pulled it. Sure enough, the entire bar heard *A-ooooohga* as Robert pronounced in his loudest voice, "Whiskey on Halloween, everybody!"

Everybody, on a Thursday morning in Vegas, is a relative term. Normally "everybody" at this hour of the morning, at this particular bar, meant something close to nobody, but it was Halloween, and people appeared to be getting an early start on their Halloween traditions. If your traditions involved getting wasted before 10 am, that is. Damn, Ron thought as he looked around, there are some motherfucking people here, and they all look like they were up far too late last night at the blackjack tables.

"Here ya go, my man," Robert exclaimed as he brought Ron a glass of whiskey. "You want me to start a tab for you?"

"Fuck yeah, Robert, and keep 'em coming." Ron put the glass to his lips and drank the entire thing in one gulp.

"Bad night, huh?"

"You don't know the half of it."

"Looks like it was kind of kinky," Robert said, motioning towards Ron's arm as he poured another glass of whiskey. "Did you meet some chick who's into duct tape?"

"Something like that." Ron downed the second glass of whiskey.

"Damn, dude. You're pounding 'em today. Fuck yeah!" Robert sounded the *Ah-oooooga* horn again, stood up on the bar, and exclaimed to the bar patrons, "People getting drunk over here!" Fuck, Ron thought, I hate that horn. It's really the one thing about this bar I could do without. But, like everything, he thought, you take the good with the bad.

The good with the bad. Stella with zombieness. Maria with an unknown, unborn thing inside her. Robert with the stupid horn.

Robert refilled Ron's whiskey and poured one for himself. "What the hell, right man? I can drink on the job. Drinking is the job! Salud." He and Ron toasted each other and downed their whiskeys.

Ron was getting drunk. And drunker. And drunkest. He looked around. Surely he wasn't the dunkest–runkest–drunkest person here. This was a bar, dammit! Thisiswhatpeopledoatabar. Rink. I love you, man. No, I luuuuuuuuv you. You're the breast bartender on the whole fucking street. Teet. Beet. Give me a beat! I'm a fucking zombie! My girlfriend is pregnant with a zombie baby! Woo-hooooo! I'll never, ever, ever, ever be human again.

"Ron, buddy, I know what you need."

"Another drink?" The truth was, Ron wasn't really drunk at all. He'd down a few shots of whiskey, feel like acting like an idiot for a few minutes, and then be as sober as the day he was born. He wasn't sure how he felt about this. On one hand, he was assured that he'd never have to wake up somewhere after a day of drinking without knowing how he got there. On the other hand, why do people get drunk? To get into that delirious zone where nothing matters, everything is beautiful, and you have the charisma of a thousand Spanish conquistadors. And while Ron could get to that zone pretty fast, he also had to leave just as quickly. It felt a bit like a roller coaster. An undead roller coaster from hell.

Robert leaned over the bar and looked Ron straight in the eye. "I can help you."

"You always help me, Robert. That's why I come to you."

"No, Ron, I can *help you* help you." Robert winked as he said the second help. What the fuck was this, high school?

"What do you mean?" Ron was a little confused; what *did* he mean?

"I know about your condition," Robert said in a low tone, with a look that was all serious, like a meth dealer buying over-the-counter chemicals at his local pharmacy. His eyes might have burned holes through Ron's face it that were possible.

Ron looked around. The bar was filling up with Halloween revelers, most of them dressed like Ron himself. Surely Robert didn't know he was a zombie, right? Maybe he was talking about his new found fame or whatever the hell it was that made every-body want to look like him. That's a 'condition,' right? Fame sure seemed to be a 'condition' when celebrities couldn't handle it and went out and drove their BMW's off of cliffs after a night of doing blow off of each other's housecleaners' tits, right?

"I'm famous." Ron shrugged his shoulders, as if to say, *but I don't give a crap.*

"You're also held together by duct tape," Robert hit Ron's arm as he continued with his laser stare and his low tone, "field chalk and makeup, and you shuffle when you walk."

Oh, shit, Ron thought, he's figured it out.

"And you told me you're a fucking zombie when you were drunk this last time. And that your girlfriend is pregnant with your love zombie."

Oh. Well. There it is.

"Did I actually say love zombie?"

"Yep."

"Sorry, Robert. I mean, I don't want to trouble you with my own troubles, you hear people's troubles all the time. I don't mean to be a pain in the ass."

"Man, you sober up fast. And your troubles are my troubles, my man," Robert said as he grabbed Ron by the shoulders. "Look, I can tell this all bothers you."

"Very much," Ron said, and then he downed the whiskey in front of him.

"And you want it fixed." Ron nodded his head. Yeah, he wanted it fixed. Wait, *fixed*? What exactly were we talking about here? Robert glanced sideways, both ways, to make sure nobody could hear him. Then he whispered, "I have the antidote."

CHAPTER
-31-

All of a sudden, Ron felt like he weird kid in 6th grade who lived in a home with very protective, conservative parents who didn't believe in telling him anything, and all the kids at school were throwing around words like *penis* and *vagina* and the weird kid didn't know what the fuck they were talking about. *What's a penis? What's a vagina? There's really an antidote?*

"Um, what?" It was the first thing that came to Ron's mind and, truly, his mind was awash with enough crazy thought and zombie adrenaline that he couldn't have formed any bigger words anyway. You gotta play with what you have sometimes.

Robert looked him in the eye. "The antidote. I have it. You need it."

"There's really an antidote?"

"Yep."

"But how–what–you?"

"Dude, look at me. You know who I am?"

"Yeah, you're Robert. Best bartender in Vegas."

"And I know everything there is to know about this town. People tell me *everything*. Like you did. And people give me *everything*. You never know when gifts from customers might come in handy."

"I'm supposed to believe somebody walked in here one day and said, 'I'll have a vodka tonic and, oh, by the way, can you watch this zombie antidote for me?'"

"Believe what you want to believe."

"That is fucked up."

"Is it?"

"Is it?"

"Are you copying me?" Robert laughed and went to serve a drink to a customer a few chairs down, leaving Ron to contemplate this most recent turn of events. Really, there wasn't much to contemplate. If there was indeed an antidote, and if Robert indeed had access to it, then Ron did indeed want it. It was a no-brainer–kinda like a dead zombie. Ron laughed at his own joke. But was there really an antidote? Hell, Ron thought, Robert was his bartender, had been his bartender for years, and knew more about Ron and his Vegas indiscretions than anybody and had never given Ron a reason to doubt him. If Robert said there was an antidote, there was an antidote. There had to be.

A zombie antidote, in Las Vegas, where Ron had come to find himself. Surely the Gods of Irony were on the clock today. Would this antidote restore his arm and heal his deteriorating body? And did Ron even care? He imagined the answer to question #1 was maybe, and the answer to question #2 was fuck no. He was already falling apart. He knew he could live like this without too much difficulty. That's why they make wheelchairs, right? And those mobility scooters for old or lazy folks that they saw on the Shopping Channel the other night? And doctors? And marijuana? No, Ron decided, any physical healing he might get from such an antidote would be great, but even if he healed exactly 0%, he was still going to do it. Because mostly he needed to heal spiritually. Being a zombie was limiting him, in his relationship with his daughter, in his relationship with his girlfriend, and in his relationship with the world. If he were human again, he could come out of the shadows full time and embrace all three of those relationships...and that's truly what Ron wanted. No more eating at the kids' table; it was time to dine. Like a human being.

"So, whaddya think, old man?" Robert spoke at normal Robert volume–which is to say boisterous bartender loud–as he pushed another glass of whiskey towards Ron. "You want me to get you that special drink?"

"Is it good, Robert?"

"Oh, it's good, my man,"

"How do you know?"

"I've seen it in action. Everybody loves it around here."

"You mean people have *had* this special drink?"

Robert looked at the people a few seats away–tourists with button down Hawaiian shirts and zombie faces. They were obviously enjoying this overly animated discussion between Bartender and Customer. Vegas first timers, Ron thought. Most people would dismiss this conversation as nothing more than a marketing ploy, but here at Carnaval Court, animated conversations and Vegas Virgins went together like zombies and antidote.

"You trust me, right?"

"I think so."

"I'm your bartender, right?" Robert said boisterously, as he looked out over the bar.

"I *know* so!" Ron said this particularly loud, so as to join in the fun. He noticed that a crowd of people with his picture on their shirts had gathered just outside the bar, by the entrance.

Robert reached down under the bar and pulled out a small clear bottle, with a little bit of liquid in it. "You're in luck, Ronny boy, because this is the last of it," he said quietly. Then, at loud

Robert volume, he said to the bar, which had all of a sudden filled up with people, "Ladies and Gentlemen, my good friend Ron has ordered the World Famous, the Top Shelf, the Most Extreme Drink of Drinks, The Zombie Antidote!"

Wait, Ron thought, you're telling everybody? What the fuck? The crowd gathered around the bar erupted into a cheer and looked at Ron and smiled, all at once.

"Watch, ladies and germs, as I mix up the Zombie Antidote... blindfolded!"

Ron grabbed Robert by the arm and pulled him close. "You're going to mix it blindfolded? What if you fucking spill it? Isn't that the last of it?"

"Ron, I'm your bartender. Let me take care of you, my way."

Oh, fuck, Ron thought. My salvation, my path back to humanity, my forgiveness is right there in that little bottle, and he's going to blindfold himself and throw it up in the fucking air like it's a beach ball. If I believed in God I'd pray for that little bottle's safety right now...but instead, I'm going to trust my bartender. Ron figured trusting his bartender was about as close to organized religion as he was ever going to get.

Charlie appeared with a blindfold and put it around Robert's head and then disappeared again. Robert then started stacking empty tequila bottles atop his head: one, two, and three bottles balanced on his bald head precariously, like cheerleaders about to have a tragic accident that is going to make the national news. Robert grabbed an empty plastic cup and put it on top of the highest tequila bottle, then he grabbed the antidote, poured it into the cup, and threw the antidote bottle into the nearest trash can without even looking at it. The gathered throng of Halloween revelers cheers and gasped, often at the same time.

"I need some ice! Who wants to ice me?" Robert put a bucket of ice on the bar, and then he encouraged people to throw ice up and into the cup. Ron felt like he might throw up and thought, that's my life up there, you fuckers. If any of you knock that cup off I'll lick the antidote off of the concrete floor and then I'll eat you! Even if I do turn human!

People all around the bar threw ice at Robert's head. A few cubes made it into the cup, and Ron cringed the entire time. This–THIS–is how I get my humanity back?

Robert waved off the crowd, as he had enough ice in the cup to make the drink. Then, with a pogo-stick-like spring, he bounced up the in air as the cup went straight up and the tequila bottles went straight sideways, bouncing off the rubber mat below Robert's feet. The cup with the antidote came down and landed safely in Robert's hand, and he added tonic water to it and then bounced a lime off the overhead television into the cup, as the crowd at the bar burst into applause.

Yeah, okay, Ron thought, I guess I can trust my bartender. Hell, if you can't trust your bartender, who can you trust?

"Here you go, my man. Your Zombie Antidote. I'll put it on your tab."

That's it? Just like that? Ron was a little underwhelmed by it all. Sure, the presentation was fantastic, but just like that a bartender makes you a special drink and you turn back into a living, breathing thing again? Did other zombies know about this? If so, why were there any zombies left at all? Couldn't they all be rescued with a drink?

Ron looked at the drink in front of him. It looked like a gin and tonic. He smelled it. It smelled like a vodka tonic, which is to say it didn't really smell like anything at all. It was fizzy and it had a straw and a lime. And it contained Ron's humanity. That was fucked up.

But really, Ron realized, the vehicle for salvation delivery didn't matter. You wouldn't refuse to win the lottery just because the money came to you in a 1978 AMC Pacer, right? Right.

The Whipits launched into a superb cover version of 'Whip It,' by Devo. Ron reached over and cuddled the drink in his working hand, like it was a precious jewel. Well, here we go, he thought. Give the past a slip. A problem came along, and you whipped it, Ron, before the cream sat out too long. Something was going wrong, and you whipped it. Thinking about how he and Stella and Maria and their new baby would move to Colorado and buy a little place up against the foothills of the Rocky Mountains and live happily ever after without being zombies, Ron Watson brought the zombie antidote to his lips.

As the first fizz of the drink hit his nose, a gunshot rang out and the drink completely disappeared before Ron could get any of it into his mouth.

CHAPTER

-32-

Children all throughout the world are taught by their loving and optimistic parents that if you work hard, get an education, and treat people well, you will be rewarded with your hopes and dreams. Hopes and dreams are concrete things; once they are obtained, they cannot be taken away. Generally speaking.

Unless, of course, you've invested all your hopes and dreams money with Bernie Madoff, bought the Brooklyn Bridge from a guy on a New York street corner, or have a future brother-in-law like David Dickey, a name for which he was relentlessly teased growing up and that probably had a little something to do with the fucking asshole he was today.

Ron's hopes and dreams at the moment were manifested in the clear plastic cup Robert handed him, a cup that was now completely missing. And Ron's lap was wet. And Robert looked confused. Ron looked towards the direction of the gunshot. David Dickey was standing near the entrance of Carnaval Court. With a gun. And his sister Maria. And Stella. And a gun. Did I already mention the gun?

The gun, Ron noticed, was pointed at Ron for just a second, and then David pointed it at Stella's head. And then he pointed it at Maria's head. And then back to Stella's head. And then David made a face, a face that said, *Hey, look what I can do! Guns are fun!* And then he pointed the gun back to Maria's head again.

"No guns allowed in here," Robert said. "Especially if you're shooting up our product."

"Product?" David was not much for nuance.

"Our alcohol."

"Sorry, bartender. Collateral damage. I meant to shoot him in the head."

"Not much of a shot then, are you?"

David pointed the gun toward Robert. "Oh, you want me to shoot you?"

Robert chuckled. "You can try, but you'll probably hit this huge wall of tequila behind me. It's on special, ya know. Wanna drink?"

"Fuck you."

"Suit yourself."

The other customers at Carnaval Court didn't seem to be phased by any of this. They lifted their heads when they heard the gunshot and then went back to their drinks and conversations, and the Whipits went back to playing cover versions of songs made famous 30 years ago. Clearly, a little commotion was not going to ruin Halloween afternoon in Las Vegas. Priorities and all that. The bar patrons were obviously more interested in flying drinks than flying bullets.

"Jim's dead, Dad." Stella talked like she was having a lunchtime conversation with her father, not like she was being held hostage by a lunatic. Grace under pressure, Ron thought. Joan Jett under pressure, really. That's what she looked like. Ron half expected her to start singing about how she didn't give a damn about her reputation, or about how she loved rock n' roll and was looking for somebody to put another dime in the jukebox, baby.

Ron's cold black heart sank to new levels as the news registered in his cold black brain. Jim's dead. Motherfuckers.

"You?" Without turning towards him, Ron pointed at David, like he was trying to put a curse on him. "You. Killed. My. Best. Friend?"

"That's right, dickwad," David said as he pointed the gun towards Ron, and then at Stella's head, and then back to Ron. His agenda was clearly multifaceted, as multifaceted as a moron could muster. "I shot him in the head. Do you know why?"

Ron turned towards his daughter, his pregnant girlfriend, and the idiot who seemed to waving his gun around at random. I really should have eaten David when I had the chance, he thought. He felt like a diner at a fine restaurant who ordered the chicken and was having buyer's remorse because somebody else at the table ordered the rib eye, which was the house specialty, and, as it turns out, it was very, very good. This motherfucker, he thought, he shot up my Humanity-In-A-Cup, he killed my best friend, and he had a gun that he was pointing at my two favorite people in the world. Asshole dumbshits always have to make life miserable for everybody else. He stood up and took a step towards David. It was time to order the right meal and end this.

"No, asshole, I don't know why."

"Because he was a *zombie*. And so are you."

Ron's rage clouded his eyes and he began to shake, like a Polaroid picture, as he took another step towards David. "I. AM. NOT. A. ZOMBIE. I. AM. A. HUMAN!"

David stuck his gun right against Stella's temple, and Ron stopped walking towards him. Sometimes a gun to your daughter's head beats a Polaroid picture rage shake. Most times, really. "I can *prove* you're a motherfucking zombie," David said. "Girl, show him."

As Ron stood there shaking, a storm of furor, contemplating the wrath he would bestow on this motherfucking asshole who dared hold a gun against his only daughter's head and call him a zombie, Stella reached into her pocket and pulled out a piece of paper. "Sorry, Dad," she said quietly. "I've been carrying this around for a while. I didn't think it'd be used against you. I only had it to justify my infinite sadness. Fuckwad here," David glared at her, "ur, David, took it out of my purse. While he was holding a gun to my head. Like now." She pushed the gun away and walked over and handed Ron the piece of paper. "I wrote it, Dad." It was Ron's obituary.

CHAPTER

-33-

My daddy, Ronald James Watson, 40, of Longmont, CO, passed away on July 27 after a motorcycle accident on Colorado Highway 34. My name is Stella James Watson, age 13, and I miss my daddy very, very much.

Growing up he was my best friend and my favorite adult. He used to tell me, 'Stella, don't let the motherf*ckers get you down.' Yes, my daddy was a potty mouth, but most of you are. So don't you motherf*ckers get me down, even though my daddy's dead. He wouldn't have approved. And he wouldn't have apologized for his own language, either. You see, my daddy was the most straightforward, most honest person I ever knew, sorry, Mom.

Speaking of mom, my daddy was married to my mom for 9 years, but they split up for some reason. For a while I blamed myself, but then I realized these days most people have divorced parents. It's just easier to give up sometimes than to put the effort in, to be straightforward about it. It's my dad's obituary, so there's no room for bullsh*t.

During his short life, my daddy was a living contradiction—part small town boy, part larger than life adventurer who never stopped moving. My daddy loved going to Las Vegas with his friend Jim, kayaking down Colorado rivers, flying through the air on ziplines, riding his stupid motorcycle, and spending time with his family when he could. He wrote songs, painted pictures, and made me feel very, very special when he spent time with me. He told me I could be anything and do anything I wanted, because it was the Watson Way. I believed him, because that's how he f*cking lived his life. I wish he were still here. He would tell me this:

"Stella, you're a comet, and this life is your solar system. Blaze through it while you're here, but don't fly too close to the sun or you'll be extinct."

My daddy flew too close to the sun. He was never very good about taking his own advice.

Ronald Watson is survived by his daughter, Stella; his sister, Jonna Reynoso; his 2 brothers, Floyd K. Watson and Jack N. Watson; his nieces and nephews; and the rest of his family and friends.

Ronald is preceded in death by his parents, Aaron and Kim (Jacobs) Watson.

In lieu of flowers memorial donations may be given to the Big Brothers and Big Sisters of America, 494 West 1st Street, Longmont, CO 80111. The family of Ronald J. Watson wishes to thank St. John's United Church.

And with that, Ron became the first person or zombie in the history of time to ever read his or her own obituary.

Ron looked over at Stella, her eyes were as moist as his. I'm dead, he thought. Not the *I'm dead* you think when your mom walks in while you're masturbating to *Baywatch*, but literally *dead*.

I can never be human. I have an obituary. It's official; I'm dead. I flew too close to the sun, so this is my fate...it's the Watson Way. I can be anything I want, but really, I can't. I'm not a human, I'm not a living thing. I'm a dead mess of duct tape, tendons, and useless body parts. And this is why I'm here—not for the Watson Way, but for the Zombie Way. Not to go back to humanity, not to live life as it used to be, but to accept my end, my obituary, and to live life as a dead dude. To accept what's been given to me, not as a curse, but as a gift. I am a zombie. I will always be a zombie. No more bullshit dreaming of being a human. Here was proof that I am not. Ron collapsed on the Carnaval Court ground under the weight of his own impenetrable realization that he was what he was.

Maria came over and stood between Ron and David, who was pointing the gun directly down at Ron on the ground. David had a look in his eye like he'd just snorted enough meth to kill a moron.

"Oh, right, and you got my sister pregnant, you undead piece of shit," David said. "So now I have two reasons to kill you. Get out of the way, Maria."

"No, David. I'm not letting you do this." Ron realized he hadn't seen Maria in a few hours, but her belly sure looked more pregnant...and she sure looked hot. Ron wasn't much into pregnant women, but when the baby is yours the attractiveness equation completely changes.

The band started playing a Cheap Trick song. Ron saw that David was now pointing the gun at Maria and got up off the ground. Fuck this, he thought, and moved around Maria so now he was between her and David. "No, Maria. I'm not letting David do this. Shoot me, asshole. Let my daughter and your sister go and shoot me. I'm the one you really want." At this point, Ron didn't really have a plan, but did he need one? He was already dead. He was going to forever remain dead. He had his obituary. What's another bullet to a dead man? They wouldn't even need to write an obituary, because he already had one.

Speaking of bullets and serendipity, at that moment, just out-side Carnaval Court, a black 1968 Ford Econoline Van with no windows pulled up and out jumped half a dozen KILLZ Guys, all still dressed to kill–Ron wondered if they ever changed their clothes–and all sporting huge weapons, drawn and ready to shoot somebody. Shit, Ron thought, they've come back for me.

Maria, however, didn't see the KILLZ Guys and wasn't coop-erating with Ron's No-Plan Plan. She jumped between Ron and David. Fuck, Ron thought, make this easy. Get the fuck out of the way and go somewhere safe. I'm the one who's dead, not you. You have life ahead of you. I only have more death. I can live with that, so to speak. "No, David, my brother," Maria said, "you aren't doing this. Let Ron and his daughter go. Let's go find some other zombies to kill."

Ron could see, by the look on his face, that Maria's Meth-Mo-ron brother wasn't about to fall for her coercion. No, he look like he might shoot then and there. So he jumped back in front of Ma-ria. And David shot his gun.

Being that David wasn't a very good aim, the bullet went into Ron's chest instead of his head. And being that Ron was a zombie, the bullet went right through Ron's body...and into Maria, who was standing right behind him.

She crumpled to the ground of the Carnaval Court, clutch-ing her chest as everybody sitting at the bar finally noticed the KILLZ Guys. Fuck, Ron thought, I can't even take a bullet for my girlfriend. He kneeled down. She was bleeding from the wound in her chest. She looked at Ron for a moment and whispered, "Sorry."

"No, I'm sorry, honey," Ron said, and bent down and kissed her on the lips. When he pulled away, her eyes were closed.

Stella ran over and kneeled down next to her and checked her pulse. "Dad, she's out and her pulse is faint. We gotta get her to a hospital."

The KILLZ Guys started marching towards the stage.

Ron looked over at David, who was standing there in a daze, with a look that said, *Oh, shit, I just shot my sister.* It's a look that can only be matched by the *Oh, shit, I just fucked my secretary and my wife found out* look and the *Oh, shit, I just lost my life savings in a Ponzi scheme* look...on the Overall Scale of Looks, in the Order of Panics.

Everybody sitting at the bar noticed the KILLZ Guys at the same time. Ron looked down and saw Maria's face. It was as pale as the body of a Midwesterner at the beach for the very first time.

Stella grabbed Ron's arm. "Dad, she's fading fast. She's gonna die." She looked over at David. "She's going to die, you fucking idiot."

David, who seemed to finally understand the gravity of the situation, took his gun, put it in his mouth, aimed it up towards his brain, and pulled the trigger. Blood and bits of brain went skyward, landing harmlessly amongst the bar patrons, who had all stood up from their barstools at exactly the same time. The airborne brain-bits matched everybody's zombie costumes, so when they landed, it was like adding vanilla food coloring to vanilla frosting. Maybe a little bit tastier, but no less hard to see.

The KILLZ Guys stopped their march. One of them went over and turned off the power to the stage. The Whipits stopped playing and lifted up their hands as if to say, *What the Fuck?*

Stella was leaning over Maria, laying on the ground of Carnaval Court. She turned and said at Ron, "Dad, you have to save her, because she's going to die. You have to bite her."

"Stella, why did it get so fucking quiet in here?"

"Bite her, Dad!"

Ron was having a hard time believing what he thought he was hearing. Bite her? Maria? He realized he had saved Jim with a bite, but look where that led them all to. Jim was now permanently dead. This was almost like three strikes and you're out. First strike you turn into a zombie, second strike you're completely dead, third strike...okay, maybe two strikes and you're out. Sometimes Ron had trouble counting, particularly when he was under a lot of stress.

"Bite her, Dad. Save her. Save her and your baby."

The Lead KILLZ Guy was standing on the stage, forcefully speaking into a megaphone: "We've come for the zombies. All humans are safe and should leave the bar now."

Maria had stopped moving and Ron knew she was running out of time, so he swallowed hard, looked over at the KILLZ Guys and the bar patrons, who so far were not moving from their defiant stances at the bar, and pulled up Maria's shirt. Hello girls, he thought, as her beautiful breasts jumped up and greeted him warmly, like puppies who have just woken from a nap and can't wait to go for their daily walk. Damn, Ron thought, I have missed you. And I never want to live without you. He leaned down and bit, hard, into her chest as his face was cradled by the contained breasts of his girlfriend. His zombie girlfriend, hopefully. Assuming this still worked.

She was as delicious as he thought she would be, so to guard against the temptation of making her breakfast, lunch, and dinner, he quickly sat up and turned his attention to the bar. It was as good a diversion as thinking about baseball might have been, because at that very moment every patron at the bar reached into his backpack or her purse and pulled out a weapon of their own and aimed it at the KILLZ Guys.

CHAPTER
-34-

In America, everybody's armed. And, depending on what political circles you run in, if you're not armed, you're either a complete jackass moron who can't defend his own family when the illegal alien bad guys inevitably break down your door or you're a highly evolved human being. There is no middle ground, especially if you put any stock into the comments under Internet news stories.

Ron looked around. Yep, everybody here had a weapon, and everybody here was aiming it right at the KILLZ Guys, standing by the entrance to Carnaval Court. They, in turn, had their own weapons and were aiming them at the bar patrons. This could get ugly. This would get ugly. Ron didn't want it to get ugly. He knew ugly, and it wasn't very nice. In fact, Ron knew ugly from both sides of the equation. On the left side of the equation, the KILLZ side, the knowns were that they had their orders from their "superiors"–a concept Ron remembered quite clearly from his KILLZ days–and that their next bonus/review/raise would be less than they hoped if they didn't complete their orders–another concept Ron remembered quite clearly. The unknowns were that they were still government employees and, as such, couldn't be completely trusted to be A) fully trained for what their "superiors" had ordered them to do and B) fully engaged in their task with their heart and soul. Government employees quite often don't grow up wanting to be government employees; oftentimes they dreamed of being major league baseball players or doctors or rocket scientists or DJs. And, when an armed individual isn't fully engaged in his or her task with his or her heart and soul–especially when it involves what might soon be a bloody war–who knows what could happen.

On the right side of the equation, Ron thought, there were a bunch of drunks with guns. Yeah, ugly was about the only place this could go.

Stella looked around, and Maria moaned. Ron reached down and covered Maria's mouth to cover the sounds, as the Carnaval Court had become very quiet. He didn't really feel like attracting attention at this particular moment. Somehow, he knew this was about him.

"We only want zombies, the rest of you can go," the lead KILLZ Guy was saying through his megaphone.

The bar patrons looked at each other and laughed. Stella chuckled, too. Ron looked at her and wondered what the hell she knew.

"We. Only. Want. Zombies. The rest of you can GO," the lead KILLZ Guy said again. Clearly he was getting agitated. Sometimes you just wanna do your job and get your day over with, ya know? He was like a waiter in a restaurant that closed at 10 and a party of eight showed up at 9:50; do I really have to fucking do this?

Ron looked at his daughter. Her face was a combination of be-musement and inevitability, which, Ron realized, is not easy to do. Again, he wondered what she knew. Stella looked at Ron and said, "Dad, you need to help. This is going to get nasty. Go to the stage and talk to them. You're a celebrity now, see?" She lifted up her shirt to show off her Brah bra. Jesus, Ron thought, they've thought of everything. "Only you can prevent what's about to happen."

"Only zombies," the megaphone said.

One of the patrons, a man dressed as a zombie–hell, everybody in Vegas was dressed as a zombie for Halloween–yelled to the KILLZ Guys, "Only zombies?"

"Only Zombies," the main KILLZ Guy said, through his megaphone. "No humans."

The patron laughed and looked at the other people around the bar. A massive crowd of people had gathered outside the entrance to Carnaval Court, all of them with guns, all of them aimed at the KILLZ Guys. The entire bar and the gathered crowd faced the KILLZ Guys and, over their weapons said, in unison, "We're all zombies."

The place was dead quiet. Ron, for perhaps the first time in his life or post-life, decided to listen to his daughter, and he made his way quickly to stage. He climbed up onstage in front of the lead singer of the band, a beautiful blonde who was dressed like a sexy German fräulein, and the gathered crowd erupted in applause at the site of Ron on stage.

"Whoa, uh, yeah, thanks," Ron said, into the microphone. "Hey, yeah," he said, over the applause. As it died down, he spoke. "I'm Ron Wat–"

A shout came from the crowd. "You're Ron Zombie!"

"Whatever, I guess I'm Ron Zombie, then," Ron said, as the crowd, still pointing guns at the KILLZ Guys, started chanting.

"Zombie."

"Zombie."

"Zombie."

"Zombie."

"Hey, all right, calm down, everybody."

Another shout came from the crowd. "You're an American Badass!"

This time, Ron didn't have time to quibble with the peoples' assessment of him.

"Badass."

"Badass."

"Badass."

"Badass."

"Okay, I'm a badass, whatever. Look, friends, we don't need to do this. You KILLZ Guys–you guys dressed in black. I bet you don't even know who you're working for anymore, do you? You have a government job. You're just following orders. ‹Hey, Bob, go make me some coffee.› ‹Hey, Jimmy, go file these papers.› ‹Hey, Steve, go round up all the zombies in Las Vegas.'"

"Boo!" from the crowd.

"I'll tell you what, guys," Ron said. "Why don't you guys get back into your government-issued vehicles and go back home to your loving wives and children, while you still have them. Because if you stay here and get slaughtered by all of us, your loving wives and your children, especially, are going to miss you very much." He looked over and smiled at Stella, who smiled back at him. Really, it was the best father-daughter moment Ron thought he had ever had...outside of talking her out of watching him eat, that is.

"And you zombies," Ron said. Like his speech class final in college the morning after a particularly wild night at a sorority house, Ron was making all this shit up. And also like his speech class final, Ron felt like he was acing it. However, unlike his speech class final, Ron hoped this speech wasn't graded on a curve. How many speeches had ever been given to zombies, anyway? You can't grade on a curve when there's only person taking the final.

"You zombies, you might think that solving your problems with a gun is the human way. Well, I'm here–Ron Zombie is here–to tell you, it's not. That's the easy way out. You want to be human?"

"Yeah!" from the crowd.

"Brah?" Ron figured he had to throw that in. Sometimes, when the crowd is in the palm of your hand, you can stretch out a little bit.

"BRAH!"

Ron looked over at Robert and kept going, with one final flurry. "You want to be human? You want to be HUMAN?" Carnaval Court was, at that moment, as future generations would recite the story, the quietest it had ever been or would ever be. Ron took a deep breath, looked over the gathered throngs, and delivered his own personal zombie manifesto, in a deep, dark, zombie voice: "You have to party like a human."

Robert jumped up on the bar, sounded the *Ah-oooooga* horn, and yelled, "FREE SHOTS AT THE BAR," just as somebody turned the stage power back on and the Whipits kicked into a Berlin song. The previously brandished weapons disappeared, and all Ron could see were tops of heads, bobbing up and down, circling towards to the bar to get their free shots and then back again to the dance floor, where a zombieing line dance had broken out. Ron figured if anybody could invent a country line dance to a Berlin song, it was this crowd. He quickly named the dance The Zombie Slide.

Ron looked over, saw Stella holding Maria up by the loudspeaker, and knew what he had to do. He was no longer human, so he no longer belonged to the human race, but he surmised that maybe the human race wasn't the only race to belong to. And then he marveled at the fact that he could use a big word like surmise. He was a long way from 'brains' and the Denver International Airport, but he was *home*, with the people and the zombies he loved. He ripped off his right arm with his left, held it aloft in the air, and yelled into the microphone, at the top of his voice, "THEY CAN TAKE AWAY OUR BODIES BUT THEY CAN'T TAKE AWAY OUR FREEDOM!" The assemblage at Carnaval Court exploded at that moment, the ebullition unlike any other seen in Las Vegas before or since...as anybody who was there would tell you.

"Who has duct tape?" Ron asked through the microphone, although he was sure nobody could hear him over the music and the revelry. Still, rolls of duct tape shot up in the air, seemingly from every hand in the place, and moved with the music like the entire place was one organic being, composed entirely of zombies, humans, love and raw pleasure. If there was a way to bottle the vibe that Halloween afternoon, it would have produced enough zombie antidote to turn Ron, Maria, Jim and every other zombie in Las Vegas back into humans. Ron, however, was no longer concerned with becoming human. He had more significant things on his docket, namely his girlfriend, his daughter, and his unborn... uh...thing. He held his right arm aloft as he dove into the crowd on his back and crowd-surfed on raised duct tape all the way over to where Stella and Maria were. And then the three of them got the fuck out of Las Vegas.

EPILOGUE

O n a dusty highway leading from Las Vegas, a 1968 El Camino SS with chrome rims and a shell painted a different color than the car body drives silently through the fading light of day. In its driver seat, a 17-year-old girl, very much in love with her daddy, smokes a cigarette and ponders if maybe she should change her look from Joan Jett to something more modern. She changes her mind as her daddy pops Joan Jett's Greatest Hits into the muscle car's cassette tape deck and "Bad Reputation" blares from its speakers. Ah, fuck it, the girl thinks, Joan Jett is pretty cool. Even for an old chick.

In the El Camino's passenger seat, a man...ur, zombie sits. His right arm is duct taped to his shoulder with VEGAS duct tape. He went to Vegas to find himself, and now he's leaving. He thinks he found what he was truly looking for: his daughter, but more importantly, a comfortability with who or what he is. Isn't that truly what makes us all human?

In the El Camino's bed, a former woman, now zombie, pregnant with...with something, is pressed up against the open window between the bed and the cab of the El Camino, moaning, trying to rip a piece of flesh–any piece of flesh–off of the driver. The driver and her daddy laugh. This too shall pass, and they'll eventually stop off at some truck stop somewhere and find a pimp or meth dealer or lawyer and dine like civilized zombies.

On the shoulder of the highway, just outside of Clark County, they see a man hitchhiking. They stop. It's not a man at all...it's Jim. He's wearing white velour track pants, and a green fluorescent *Girls Direct To You* t-shirt. A spot of dried blood is caked on his chin...and on his shirt.

"We thought you were dead."

"He wasn't much of a shot."

"You look like shit."

"Fuck you."

"You wanna come with us?"

"Where are you going?"

"Brains."

"What?"

"We don't know."

"Yeah, all right. But where do I sit?"

"In the middle."

Jim climbs in the cab of the El Camino and sits in the middle. He pushes the 1968 cigarette lighter into its socket and waits as the highway miles slither away like snakes in fresh cut grass.

When the lighter pops out, each of them light up a cigarette, take a drag, blow the smoke out into the stale air of the cab of the El Camino, and say, in unison, "Vegas is one crazy fucking place."

Ron nods his head, slowly, repeatedly, and looks out onto the surrounding landscape. Nothing but desert, desert, and, to mix things up, desert. A thought comes to him. He turns to his best friend and his daughter and opens his mouth to speak.

"Wanna go back?"

FIN.

AUTHOR'S ACKNOWLEDGMENTS

I would first and foremost like to thank my writing group, without whose deadlines none of this would have happened. Your guidance and enthusiasm and willingness to slog through the story while it was still a nascent zombie was invaluable. Jonna, Jack, Floyd, Kim, Aaron...if Ron were here he'd say "BRAINS!" but I'll just say thanks. No, forget that, that's not fun. BRAINS.

A very special thanks to Anthony (Vegas Robin to my Vegas Batman) and the good people of Las Vegas: Rob, Charlie, Robyn, Flippy, the Whipits, and Crystal Meth, cocktail waitress extraordinaire. You all have made Vegas my second home and have become my friends. Sure, I pay for the privilege, but, like Ron says, if you can't trust organized religion you gotta trust your bartenders. BRAINS.

A warm appreciation to my laser-sharp copy editor Lindsay Ricketts. You mentioned the Oxford Comma and I mentioned "what?" so it's obvious you have BRAINS.

And a heartfelt admiration to cover designer extraordinaire Stewart Williams (www.stewartwilliamsdesign.com), who came up with five different amazing cover possibilities and ultimately captured the time, the place, and the soul of American Badass. You're brilliant. BRAINS.

I also want to thank my family for putting up with my schedule: Vegas trips, writing sessions, Vegas trips, revision sessions,

Vegas trips...I know not every husband/father get this kind of leeway, and I appreciate it very much. BRAINS.

Last but definitely not least, BRAINS to the people at Wooden Stake Press for taking a chance on me, *American Badass*, and Ron Watson. This is a dream come true...

BRAINS.

www.ronzombieamericanbadass.com

ABOUT THE AUTHOR

JEFF CHACON is the author of *American Badass*, a Vegas Zom-Com (a genre Jeff made up) novel and co-author of the cult comedy classic *E-Male: of mouse and men*. He has appeared on theater and rock and roll stages all over Colorado and California in several productions and bands you've never heard of. He lives with his wife and kids in Denver...and visits Las Vegas. A lot.

www.theejeffchacon.com

ABOUT THE PRESS

Wooden Stake Press LLC publishes zombie books (obviously), humor, fantasy, magical realism, and more. Visit us on the web at www.woodenstakepress.com.